3 1994 01331 3678

SANTA ANA PUBLIC LIBRARY

5/07

D0758305

BLACKOUT

A Selection of Recent Titles by Guy N Smith

NIGHT OF THE CRABS
THE SLIME BEAST
SNAKES
THE SUCKING PIT
WEREWOLF BY MIDNIGHT

BLACKOUT

Guy N. Smith

FICTION SMITH, G.
Smith, Guy N.
Blackout

                        $27.95
CENTRAL   31994013313678

This first world edition published in Great Britain 2006 by
SEVERN HOUSE PUBLISHERS LTD of
9–15 High Street, Sutton, Surrey SM1 1DF.
This first world edition published in the USA 2006 by
SEVERN HOUSE PUBLISHERS INC of
595 Madison Avenue, New York, N.Y. 10022.

Copyright © 2006 by Guy N Smith.

All rights reserved.
The moral right of the author has been asserted.

British Library Cataloguing in Publication Data

Smith, Guy N.
  Blackout
  1.   Storms - Middle West - Fiction
  2.   Horror tales
  I.   Title
  823.9'14 [F]

  ISBN-13: 978-0-7278-6432-1
  ISBN-10: 0-7278-6432-7

Except where actual historical events and characters are being
described for the storyline of this novel, all situations in this
publication are fictitious and any resemblance to living persons
is purely coincidental.

All Severn House titles are printed on acid-free paper.

Typeset by Palimpsest Book Production Ltd.,
Polmont, Stirlingshire, Scotland.
Printed and bound in Great Britain by
MPG Books Ltd., Bodmin, Cornwall.

To Carol and Dan Windley

PART ONE

The Great Storm

One

The crashing report shattered the spring tranquillity of the sheltered hollow, a noise that grew in magnitude as it rolled up the mountains behind, echoing and re-echoing, rumbling on like distant thunder until, finally, it died.

A gunshot.

Inside the cabin a slim, fair-haired woman froze in the action of slicing tomatoes. The knife fell from her slender fingers, clattered into the sink. She stared out of the dirt-stained windows, cringed from what she might see. Across the wide clearing a dove clattered out of the willow grove, disturbed from an early roost, sped for the safety of the lower mountain firs. A jay shrieked its protest.

Then the silence rolled softly back. It was as though the shot had never been fired. Except that it still reverberated inside her head.

'Mommy! Mommy!'

Adele heard a door opening, the patter of small feet coming from the cramped end bedroom.

'It's all right, darling.' No, it isn't.

'That was a shot, Mommy.' The young girl stood in the kitchen doorway, her freckled face pallid, her expression bordering on panic. Even at nine Nicola was small for her age, spindly legs protruding from beneath her blue-and-white flowered dress. But even in fear her features were pretty; her likeness to her mother was unmistakable. Her father had told her repeatedly that she would make a fine-looking woman when she grew up. She had a long way to go yet but already she was shaping up to his expectations.

'Was it?' Adele's voice quavered slightly, seemed to come from far away, a whispered question which she did not want answered.

'Didn't you hear it?' Incredulity verged on a reprimand.

3

Nicola saw her own terror mirrored in her mother. 'I was asleep and it woke me up. You *must* have heard it.'

'Maybe it was thunder, the atmosphere's gone sultry after this spring heatwave.'

'It was a *gunshot*.'

'Oh, I see, well that isn't altogether surprising, considering . . .'

'Ben told me that Daddy wanted to shoot himself.'

Oh, Jesus Christ! Ben was a big-mouth. You couldn't trust a twelve-year-old, Ben less than most. His hearing was acute, he must have been eavesdropping that night after Christmas, the time when Blair's depression was getting into full swing. They said that folks who threatened suicide never actually carried it out. Blair had come close, a doctor has access to a hundred different fatal drugs. Adele still did not trust her husband.

'Ben imagines things. What a terrible thing to say.'

'No, he didn't imagine it, he heard Daddy say it. On Boxing Night. I *know* he was telling the truth. I also know that Daddy meant it because he was ill. He still is.'

'Daddy was probably just speaking figuratively.'

'What's figur . . . figurey?'

Adele closed her eyes, sighed. How the hell did you explain that to a child? 'Daddy was . . . just sort of saying that because he was very low. Pressure of work had got him down. He didn't mean it. No way. It was a stupid thing to say but he couldn't help it.'

'Ben thinks he did mean it. He also said that you'd hidden the key to the gun cabinet so that—'

'*Nicola!*'

'It's true, isn't it, Mommy?' A piercing shriek.

'Not entirely. I was just taking precautions. I was over-reacting.'

'But you let Daddy go hunting with a gun today. And Ben's got a gun, too. They might've had an accident!'

Her words hit Adele like an electric shock, her fingers gripped the edge of the sink until her knuckles whitened. Suicide was one thing, gun accidents were another. Both ended in death, or injury if you were lucky with the latter. Ben was too young to carry a shotgun, even a twenty. Adele and Blair had argued about it. In the end she had weakened, let her husband have his way. As usual.

4

'That was a gunshot, Mommy.'

'All right, it was a gunshot.' Adele fought to bring her worst fears under control. 'But you expect to hear shots when somebody goes hunting with a gun, don't you?'

'I s'pose so.'

'Well, then.' Adele retrieved the knife, made a hash of cutting through a tomato, it squelched and oozed a morass of pips. 'It was probably just a jackrabbit they shot.'

'If it was, then I refuse to eat it. I hate killing.'

The ongoing argument was about to start up, the direct result of primary-school indoctrination by an animal-loving, obsessed vegetarian teacher. Adele wasn't going to fall for it this time. 'You don't have to eat it, darling. They probably missed it, anyway. Now, would you like to give me a hand with supper?'

'No.'

'All right, you don't have to, we're on vacation.'

Some vacation, Blair and Ben out hunting and fishing every day, all day, and herself stuck here in a backwoods cabin that had supposedly been converted into a holiday lodge! A timber structure with basic amenities that surely contravened every rule in the book. If it rained, the roof would leak; if the wind got up, there would be a draught from every direction. And a classic fire-trap to boot.

Blair had fixed up this stay, and she had gone along with it because she thought it might help get him back to normal. It might just do that, but in the meantime she would have to endure innumerable inconveniences.

'Ben says he and Daddy are going fishing in the river tomorrow, Mommy.'

'That will be nice for them.' At least it didn't involve firearms. They might drown in the deep water instead. 'Go and look out the door, see if there's any sign of them. Supper's nearly ready.'

Nicola sighed. 'There isn't. The veranda door's open, I can see from here.'

'They might approach from the back.'

'We had salad yesterday, Mommy, when we got here. I don't want salad again. Why can't we have fries? Or burgers?'

Nicola voiced her dislike of anything that was currently on the family menu, on principle. If Adele had been frying at the

woodstove she would, in all probability, have wanted salad.
'Because it's too hot for a fry-up. Now, please, go and have
a look out back and see if you can spot Daddy and Ben.'
Bare feet stamped the floor unwillingly. Adele heard the
click of the latch. The door thudded shut again almost immediately.
'They're not in sight, Mommy. Nowhere.'
Oh, God! Adele was fighting panic again. Maybe if she had
been on her own she would have rushed out to go and look
for her husband and her son, but for Nicola's sake she had to
appear calm.
'Well, salad doesn't go cold waiting, does it?' It was meant
to sound casual; it came out fully charged with tension.
'I don't like salad, I'm not eating any.' Nicola turned, walked
away. The door of the tiny bedroom slammed as if to enforce
her stubbornness.
That was when Adele began to sob uncontrollably.

Ben thrilled to the feel of the Brescia over-and-under-
lightweight twenty-gauge. It seemed to vibrate in his small
sweaty grasp. An object of power, a means of *killing*.
'Don't you load a shell until I tell you, and keep the barrels
pointing either at the ground or into the air. Don't shoot
anywhere you can't see, like bushes and undergrowth.'
Don't . . .
You forgot all of that once you were on your own. It was
magic, like a dream, and your only worry was that you
might wake up and find that the gun was still locked away
in the steel cabinet. Dad would position him somewhere,
tell him to stay put, and move on to find an ambush point
for himself.
Ben's cammos were a size too small, they had been a
Christmas present just before his tenth birthday and he had
grown some since then; they were too tight under the arms
and in the groin, the trouser bottom did not reach below his
ankles and the seam on his ass was threatening to split. A
matching cap hid his short-cropped fair hair, his blue eyes
were bright and alert. But all that didn't matter one jot. He
had the gun, for real.
He glanced sideways, furtively, at his father. Folks back
home would not have recognized Dr Blair Lund, that small,

insignificant white-coated medic with rimless glasses who sat in his consulting room, morning and evening, listening expressionlessly to his patients describe their ailments, true or imagined. Out here, he was changed beyond recognition; a short dark beard strengthened the weak jaw, the brown-and-green hunting attire adorned a fighting man, a guerrilla embarking upon jungle warfare. The Browning five-shot twelve-gauge slung on his shoulder completed the transformation.

He sucked on a half-smoked cigar. Out here it was macho, back home it would have been hypocritical, for the Surgeon General had determined that cigarette-smoking was dangerous to your health. The guy had forgotten to mention cigars but he probably would not have approved.

'Where are we headed, Dad?' It was obvious that they were going into the willow grove but Ben needed confirmation.

'To the grove.' Blair pointed ahead. 'Maybe we'll get a pigeon flying in to roost or find a jackrabbit grazing on the edge. We'll surely find you a shot, Ben. But you'll have to stop talking or they'll hear you and take off.'

Dad was somehow different out there, Ben thought. At home he was quiet, withdrawn, like he had things on his mind. He was reminded again of that awful night when he had listened in on a conversation between his parents. They had been upset; Mom was crying, he thought his father was, too. Then Dad had threatened to . . .

Ben went cold, his guts balled and he began to shake. He'd told Nicola because he had to tell somebody. They had clung to each other and sobbed.

But Dad was OK now. He'd been ill, Ben wasn't sure exactly what; Mom had spoken of 'pressure of work' and 'deep depression'. Dad worked long hours, often he was called out in the night if there was a traffic accident or somebody was suddenly taken ill. Weekends, too, more often than not. They did not see much of him at home.

Which was why they were having an early break this year, a couple of weeks away from New York. Mom wasn't too keen on a cabin back of beyond, and neither was Nicola, but Dad had promised that they would all be going to Fort Lauderdale in the summer like they usually did. Mom and Nicola would spend most of their time on the beach, Dad said he might take Ben sea-fishing, try to catch a shark. Just a small one, nothing like Jaws. Worse luck! Still, they might catch a glimpse of a great white.

'Stand right here, keep your eyes peeled for pigeons flying or a jackrabbit sneaking out to graze. Take your time, pick your shot, squeeze the trigger, don't snatch.'

Ben jerked out of his reverie, this was no time to dwell on depressing thoughts. Dad was fine and the only things he'd be shooting at from now on were fur and feather.

'I'll be farther down this track,' Blair began to move away, 'so don't shoot low in this direction. I'll come back to collect you towards dusk.'

Ben trembled with excitement. His father wasn't going to stand over him, tell him when to hold his fire, when to shoot. Suddenly the boy had become a man, a hunter. Like the mountain men.

Ben had a book at home all about those early explorers and trappers; it fascinated him. S. E. Hollister had killed a grizzly bear with a hunting knife, he'd been badly mauled and bitten but he'd lived; John Colter had been captured by five hundred Blackfoot and tortured. But he'd escaped, outrun them on foot, killed a brave with his own lance, swum across a river and then run another two hundred miles in seven days before he'd finally made it to safety at Lisa's Fort on the Bighorn River.

Other heroes sprang to mind: Daniel Boone, Davy Crockett. Ben had a video of the Alamo.

Ben tugged his bearskin cap tight down on his head, the Hawken long rifle in his hands had grown an awful lot heavier but he had the strength to match it. The .54-calibre was accurate up to two hundred yards and was capable of dropping a buffalo stone dead.

He stood with his back to a tree trunk, that way no marauding redskin could shoot an arrow into his back. Ben would deal with any foe who showed himself, red or white.

A sudden flap made him start, look up. A bird had soared overhead, closed its wings momentarily to slow its pace; gliding now, preparing to land in the topmost branches of a tall willow.

The long gun came up with ease of practice. Ben swung with the slowing bird, blotted it out with the barrel and squeezed the trigger like he'd done a thousand times before.

The deafening explosion and the recoil were simultaneous, the Hawken belched its villainous black smoke.

It was as though the bird had hit an invisible barrier; its wings closed, it was thrown back by the impact, somersaulted twice in a puff of feathers. Then it plummeted downwards to bounce on the springy grass. It lay there, still and dead, blood seeping from a wound in its grey head.

I got it!

Ben ran forward, heady with the smell of black powder smoke, grasped the pigeon by the neck, held it aloft. John Colter couldn't have bettered that shot and *he* was one helluva marksman.

'You open that breech at once, Ben, your second barrel's still loaded. The way you're waving that gun around it could still go off any second and shoot you or me!'

Reality destroyed fantasy. John Colter stepped back into the mists of time, left behind a boy who had just made his first kill with a fancy breech-loading scattergun. The breech clicked open, a bright green spent shell ejected.

'That's better.' Blair stepped forward, nodded and smiled. 'That was a tolerable good shot, Ben. But don't forget, safety is a priority. Now, we'd better be getting back for supper and you can show Mom what you've shot. I'm not sure whether pigeons are still in season out here but, no matter, it'll taste real good for dinner tomorrow. The best pigeon you'll ever've eaten, I'll warrant.'

Mom looked real bad, Ben thought as they walked back into the cabin. She was white-faced and red-eyed as though she'd been crying. His father did not appear to notice.

'Supper's on the table.' She turned back to the sink.

'Ben shot a pigeon.' Blair leaned the shotguns in a corner of the room. 'A flier.'

'I heard the shot.' Adele winced at the memory.

'*I'm* not eating any of it!' Nicola yelled from her bedroom. 'It's cruel to kill animals.'

'We'll go fishing tomorrow.' Blair spooned salad on to his plate. 'The river's running low after this dry week or two, there should be some trout for the taking if we go about it the right way.'

Nicola shouted again but the closed door muffled her words. Adele sighed softly, wondered how she was going to pass the two weeks that lay ahead. But at least Blair was beginning to look more relaxed.

Killing, it seemed, was the answer to her husband's problems. And young Ben was fast taking after his father.

She shuddered.

Two

'There's been a storm warning on the radio.' There was no mistaking the anxiety in Adele's expression. She ignored the two trout which Ben slapped proudly on the sinktop. 'There's a hurricane headed this way. They say it'll reach Wyoming by midnight.'

'It'll most likely have spent itself by the time it reaches here, just a few strong gales.' Blair began gutting their catches. Trout should be eaten fresh in order to enjoy them at their best.

'The wind's starting to get up already.' Adele's prediction about draughts through the walls was fast coming true. 'That last one, two years ago, wreaked havoc in the Yellowstone National Park.'

'We're protected here by the mountains.' Blair scooped a pile of slime into a plastic bag; there did not appear to be a waste bin handy. 'We'll be OK, this cabin in its original state must've stood for more'n a century, maybe a hundred and fifty years. It's taken everything the storms could throw at it and it's still standing.'

'I'll grant you that, and it hasn't changed much since, no matter how that guy told you it'd been renovated for leasing.'

'You want me to cook these?'

'Please. Nicola won't be joining us. She won't eat trout any more than she'll eat jackrabbit.'

A muffled shriek from behind the end bedroom door protested at the killing of animals and fish. A sudden gust of wind drowned it, shook the cabin.

'That one sure found its way down here from the mountains, Blair.' Adele was tense.

'We'll be OK, I tell you. Weather forecasters always exaggerate bad conditions, err on the safe side. I read about a guy once who played down severe gales and a twister cut

11

a swathe through half a state. Folks sued him for negligence, some even sent death threats. Never did hear the outcome.'

'I hope you're right, Blair.' She put some plates on the scrubbed table. 'Hurricane can be as bad as earthquakes. At least with earthquakes you've a rough idea where they'll occur, give those places a wide berth.'

The trout sizzled in the pan. Outside it was getting dusk an hour before its time. Storms always made Adele tense, just the same now as when she was a child. Worse, if anything, because her unease scared Nicola, and there was no way she could hide it. Back in the city it wasn't quite so bad, there were people all round, everybody sharing power failures and ripping winds; company, even if nobody gave a shit about you. Out here you were on your own, three miles down a rutted track before you reached a highway and then another mile to the nearest habitation.

'I hope to God the power doesn't fail.' She spoke her thoughts aloud, immediately wished that she hadn't because, out of the corner of her eye, she noticed Nicola standing in the doorway, watching and listening.

When Adele turned round, Nicola had gone back to her bedroom. Doubtless she would reappear before long.

'The power shouldn't be any problem.' Blair turned a fish in the pan. 'The electricity works off a generator out back, runs on kerosene. No lines to come down. If it gets chilly, all you have to do is stoke up the fire. We got it made here, it's folks in the cities who'll suffer, blacked out and debris all over the place.' It was the first time for a long time that Adele had heard her husband sound optimistic to the point of euphoria. If it took a cabin in the wilderness and a hurricane to return him to his former self, then that was fine by her, she'd put up with the rest.

'It's just how the trappers used to be.' There was awe in Ben's words. 'They used to hole up for the winter in a cabin like this one, lamps run on animal fat, or candles, wood to make a fire, plenty of food, coffee. Some of them used to read a lot, too. Real cosy.'

'I'm glad you think so, Ben,' Adele snapped. 'Personally I think you would've found it a lot different from the books and films if you'd lived in those days. They were like animals, they had to be just to survive. They were dirty and smelly, mostly they died of disease if some misfortune didn't befall them first.'

'No, Mom, they were *real* men. They outwitted, out-fought the Indians . . .'

'*Native Americans!*' Nicola was back in the room, she glared angrily at her brother. 'If Mrs Klein heard you say that, you'd get a detention.'

'Let's not start that all over again.' Blair turned from the stove, pointed a fork threateningly. 'In the days we're talking about they were "Indians" because Columbus thought he'd landed in India. Whatever you choose to call them today, we're talking about history and we should be proud of our heritage. Nowadays your Native Americans run the Little Bighorn as a tourist attraction, they're proud of it because they massacred the white soldiers there. We don't hate them for it. You have to keep things in perspective, you can't change history.'

'Is the storm going to get worse, Mommy?' Nicola looked fearfully at the outer door, rattling its latch.

'Probably, but Daddy says we're well sheltered in this valley.'

'I'm going to bolt the door.' Nicola ran back down the hallway, struggled to shoot the rusty bolt. 'That's better, nobody can get in now. I've already locked the back door.'

'I don't think anybody's likely to bother us,' Adele smiled, a forced reassurance that was belied by a trembling lower lip, 'because there's nobody within several miles of here. And, anyway, nobody would be out and about on a night like this.' Somehow her words lacked conviction.

'What's that?' The child stiffened, stared wide-eyed, the last vestige of colour draining from her features. 'I heard something out there.'

'Probably a tree coming down on the edge of the forest.' Blair speared a fish, transferred it to a plate. 'Don't worry, there's none growing near enough to fall on the cabin. In big forests there's trees blown down every time there's a big wind. Now, supper's ready.'

'Ugh!' Nicola grimaced. 'I wouldn't eat that if I was starving.'

'I'll do some fries,' Adele managed to smile without a quaver this time, 'and you and I'll eat after the ravenous hunters have finished. How's that?'

'All right, I s'pose.' She leaned up against a doorpost. 'The storm's getting worse, just listen to it.'

Another strong gust shook the building. Adele's hands shook as she took over from Blair at the stove. The wind down the chimney had fanned the fire to a roaring blaze, she'd have to be careful not to burn the fries.

Hopefully, the storm would have blown itself out by morning. In the meantime it looked like being one helluva night.

'I hate guns.' Adele stared fixedly, almost hypnotically, at the fire through the open stove door; if you looked long enough the flames made pictures, changed just as you recognized them. Eerie, they reminded you of long-forgotten things, some of which you didn't want to remember, landscapes that revived sad memories. The churchyard where her parents were buried; the hills behind the homestead where she'd been brought up as a child. A log fell, showered sparks, destroyed it.

'A gun is like a fire,' Blair answered, 'a good servant but a bad master.'

She lowered her voice, glanced towards the closed kitchen door. 'Ben's got an obsession with them.' Ben and Nicola should be sound asleep in their beds. *If* anybody could sleep through this terrible gale. Rain spots were starting to splatter on the windows, the wild night was only just beginning.

'Most kids are fascinated by guns.' Blair's hand found hers, squeezed it gently. 'For some it's just a phase, they grow out of it. Others get firearms into perspective, go hunting when they're old enough. Ben's different, though, he's interested in the historical aspect, most boys his age are into *Terminator* and the like. I think it's better that he understands how and why our ancestors grew up with a gun by their side, used them to survive.'

'I suppose you're right, in a funny sort of way,' she admitted grudgingly. 'I'm always worried about . . . about the consequences of guns.'

'I'm OK now, really I am. Me, I could live like this for the rest of my life but it wouldn't be fair on you and Nicola. And Ben has to finish his education. Maybe I shouldn't have brought you here.'

14

'I don't mind if it helps.' He sensed the tension in her hand.
'I guess it's the storm that's making me edgy. That and . . .'

'Yes?'

'Well, I can't explain this, but if it was somewhere else, another valley, another cabin, I'd maybe feel easier.'

'Whatever do you mean?'

'I don't know. It's just that there's something creepy about this cabin and its surroundings, nothing that I can put a finger on, Blair. Maybe it's because it hasn't changed much since pioneering days, like you said. Those primitive men wintering in here, maybe with a native woman they'd traded for a horse or whatever. Who knows what these walls have witnessed, they're the very same timbers, I'll warrant, just the odd beam replaced here and there. Just like it was in those days. Oh, I guess it's the storm that's got me feeling this way. I'm sorry.'

The overhead light flickered, dimmed and brightened again.

'See, Blair, the storm can affect the power supply.'

'No way, there's no cables, pylons, nothing for the wind to buffet. Probably just a change in voltage. I don't understand generators except in principle. A kerosene-driven engine provides the power, turns it into electricity. The electric current flows into loops of wire, which rotate on a shaft between electromagnets which create magnetic fields when the current passes through them. Carbon brushes collect the current that's generated in the rotating coils and press against copper rings at the end of the shaft. Simple, if you don't go into it too deeply.'

'And where did you learn all that?' She laughed.

'I studied physics at college.'

'We had a generator at home when I was a kid. It worked off a windmill. I never enquired beyond that.'

'Same principle, you just need some form of energy, kerosene or wind, to drive the engine to make the electricity. Some folks use car batteries.'

'It's all too technical for me.' She found herself staring back into the fire. The way the logs had burned and fallen reminded her of this same valley, the mountains towering above, the tiny cabin below. Then everything collapsed in a shower of sparks, transformed it into a burning wasteland, destroyed it forever. Adele shuddered in spite of the heat. The wind outside howled and mocked her. It, too, could devastate a landscape. The light dimmed, came back on. It was not as bright as it had been.

Adele caught her breath, braced herself at the prospect of being plunged into darkness. Here it would be a thousand times worse than in the city, trapped in a wooden shack at the mercy of the elements.

'The storm obviously does affect generators, Blair.' Please prove me wrong, give me some more technical spiel and make it convincing even if it's a load of bullshit.

'It can't.' He was puzzled.

'What, then?'

'A problem with the generator that has nothing to do with the storm, it would happen just the same on a still summer day.'

'Like what?'

'A fault with the wiring. Or maybe just something real simple like running out of kerosene.'

'That's all we need.'

'I'll check it first thing in the morning. I can't go outside tonight in this.'

She nodded. The cabin shuddered as a squall hit it, the curtains billowed. Surely it would never withstand this coming night.

God, the place was a dump! Her eyes roved around the kitchen. An existing wooden framework had been strengthened, new timbers added where necessary. Any modern conveniences were the most basic and cheapest available. As Ben had pointed out, it was much the same as it had been a century and a half ago when the early trappers had holed up here for the winter. Those scars and gouges on the uprights had probably been made by them.

A smell assailed her nostrils, lingered for a moment and then was gone, brought with it a prickling of her skin. Even in that short time she recognized the mingled odours: unwashed clothes, stale sweat, a leathery smell like saddles and horse trappings, one of cooking and coffee that was strong and aromatic in its primitive way. Then just wood smoke from the stove as the downdraught caused it to billow outwards.

16

'Blair!'

'What?' He sensed the fear in her voice.

'Nothing. I . . .'

At that moment Nicola began to scream hysterically in her bedroom.

Three

Nicola stood white-faced in the open doorway of her bedroom. Her eyes were wide, seemed to have filmed over, stared unseeing. Her hair was straggling around and matted with sweat. Her mouth was still open but the piercing screams had subsided to inarticulate gurgles. She pointed behind her into the room, was clearly too frightened to turn and look.

'My darling, whatever's the matter?' Adele rushed to her, held her close.

The girl tried to speak but the words refused to come.

Ben appeared outside his room, clad in green-and-white pyjamas, the nearest he could find to cammos, rubbing the sleep out of his eyes. 'Nick's had another nightmare, Mom, like—'

'Be quiet, please, Ben!'

Blair looked into the small bedroom. At a glance it seemed much as it had been since their arrival, the single bed with sheets thrown into a rumple, a bedside table and an old cupboard improvised to serve as a wardrobe. The door was flush against the wall; there was nowhere anybody or anything could have hidden. But that was a ridiculous notion, anyway.

'It was probably a rat seeking refuge from the storm.' Blair felt obliged to offer some logical explanation for his daughter's fright. There had once been a rat in the playhouse on the lawn when Nicola was very young and she had become hysterical.

'Come through and sit with us by the fire.' Adele lifted her up, carried her through the hallway. 'Then, if you feel like it, you can tell us all about it.'

She made no move to stop Ben following them: on a night like tonight it was better if they all huddled together.

'I'll make some drinks.' Blair reached down some mugs, the blackened kettle on the stove was already boiling. He felt

18

an urge for a cigar, decided against it; Nicola was anti-smoking, this was no time to provoke another outburst of indoctrinated idealism.

'Chocolate for Nick, strong and sweet.'

'Coffee for me.' Ben had developed a taste for the beverage at an early age because his heroes almost always drank it. Blair didn't accept that there was any real harm in caffeine but he had warned his son about the dangers involved in drinking from streams. Identifying with mountain men had to have limits imposed.

'Was it a rat, Nick?'

The girl clung tightly to her mother, shook her head, glanced fearfully in the direction of the doorway then jerked her head away in case she might glimpse again whatever had scared her.

'You've had a nightmare, darling.' Adele spoke soothingly, kissed Nicola tenderly. 'I can tell by the way you've been sweating. You're hot, maybe starting a fever. Blair, perhaps we should drive into town tomorrow and get some medicine.' *Or go home and leave this dreadful place forever.*

Blair pursed his lips thoughtfully. There was no way anybody would be driving anywhere for a while after tonight, all the roads would be blocked by fallen trees. He smoothed his fingers across Nicola's forehead, felt for her pulse. 'There's no fever there, I'm certain. I guess it's a combination of factors: the storm, strange surroundings, culminating in a bad dream. Unless, of course, it was just a rat or a mouse in the room.'

'*No!*' The shriek was the result of a build-up of vocal pressure, the sound suddenly released from a stricken throat. Harsh and shrill like the screaming before it.

'It doesn't really matter what scared you.' Adele held her close. 'Because it wasn't anything that can harm you and anyway it's gone now, whatever it was. Let's all have a drink and maybe you can sleep in with Daddy and me tonight.'

'It was . . . it was . . .' Nicola was straining to form the words, her voice constricted as if she was afflicted with an impediment of speech.

'What . . . what was it?' Blair dropped to a crouch, every muscle in his body taut. Somehow he sensed that there was something wrong that went deeper than a child's nightmarish fantasies.

19

A dead branch, snapped and whirled aloft by the hurricane, banged on the roof, clattered across it, made them all jump. The gently swinging unshaded light bulb dimmed on reduced voltage, created shadows in the corners of the room, shapes that moved in time with the wafting curtain.

'A . . . a . . . *man!*' Nicola yelled, dug her fingers deep into Adele's flesh, closed her eyes tightly.

'A *man?*' Blair was angry with himself because the nape of his neck prickled. That was ridiculous, impossible. The doors were bolted and locked, nobody could have got inside. And even if they had found a way, there was nowhere for them to hide. He had looked.

'Yes.'

'All right, you saw a man.' To have ridiculed the distressed child at this stage would have been both pointless and potentially harmful. Nicola was close to hysteria. 'Perhaps it was me you saw in the light from the open door when I looked in to check that you were OK.'

Blair had not checked but he had to try to convince his daughter of logical reasons for her fear.

'No, it wasn't you, Daddy. He wasn't like you at all.'

Again Blair's flesh goosebumped, an icy trickle started up his spine. 'People can look different in the half dark, even somebody you know well.'

'*It wasn't you!*'

'OK, it wasn't me.' Humour her without appearing to do so. 'Maybe if you tell us what he looked like, we might have some idea as to who it might have been.'

This was getting crazier by the second.

Nicola shied as if the ogre of her darkened bedroom had suddenly reappeared before her. 'He was tall and big.'

'I see.'

'Not like an ordinary man. At least, he didn't dress like anybody I've ever seen.'

'What did he dress like?'

'He had clothes that were like those in Ben's book, a floppy cap. And a beard. And he smelled awful, like he didn't ever change his clothes and didn't wash, either. He stank of cooking and coffee and he must've left the door open when he came in because it was terribly cold. *That's what woke me up.*'

Adele closed her eyes, it was all she could do to stop herself screaming like Nicola had done. *Because she had smelled that same man herself only a short time ago.*

'This whole cabin stinks,' was all that she could find to say on the spur of the moment, turning her head away in case her daughter glimpsed the fear in her eyes. 'Whoever stayed here before us were as dirty as pigs and the owners didn't bother to clean it out. I'll maybe have a go at cleaning it in the morning.'

'*I tell you, there was a man in my bedroom!*' Nicola screamed in anger this time because her parents refused to believe her.

'All right, all right.' Blair tried to defuse the situation, the last thing they needed right now was a screaming match. 'There was some guy in here, probably Becker, the owner, checking if we were OK. But he's gone now and I guess he won't be coming back. Certainly not if he's overheard what your mother's got to say about the place. Now, let's drink our drinks and then we'll turn in, do our best to get some sleep. This lot will probably have blown itself out by morning, hurricanes travel fast. By daybreak it'll maybe've spent itself, just a few strong gales sweeping up the garbage in New York streets.'

An uneasy silence settled on them, even the storm appeared to have calmed momentarily.

'I hope it was a mountain man.' Ben slurped his black coffee. 'A real one like John Colter or S. E. Hollister.'

'Don't be silly, Ben,' Adele snapped. 'Your mountain men died out before the turn of the century.'

'I'll bet there's still a few left.' Ben's enthusiasm was undeterred. 'There has to be, they had kids, kids who don't want to live in populated places, still live in places like this, hunt for a living.'

'I doubt it, especially these days.' Adele glanced at Blair, blamed him for all this. He encouraged their son to hunt, and it had become an obsession.

The hurricane had used the brief lull to gather its strength; the cabin rocked, something crashed against the wall outside.

'What's that?' Adele stiffened, looked towards the door as though it might hurtle open at any second.

'Another branch, probably.' Blair was aware of his own uneasiness but he must not let it show.

The lights flickered, almost went out.

'They won't last, Blair.' Adele clasped Nicola to her.

21

'They're still burning.'

'The hold's filling up but the ship's still afloat,' she answered curtly. 'Your optimism knows no limits.'

'Power cuts aren't a disaster, just an inconvenience. We've had plenty back home in the past. You light a few candles, use torches to move around the house, and make the best of an early night.' He smiled but he knew there was no chance of anything happening between himself and Adele tonight. She was far too tense and besides, they would in all probability have Nicola in the bed between them.

'And I suppose you anticipated this and brought a pack of candles along?'

'Of course.' He moved across to the cupboard, fumbled on a shelf until he found what he was searching for. 'See, "twelve long-lasting candles", so the packaging says. All part of a hunter's backpack in case he has to camp away from base.' He ripped at the paper wrapping. 'They'll be more than adequate. *If* we need them.'

'Good.' Her relief was evident. 'I'll set a few ready.' Maybe Blair was planning a longer hunting trip with Ben, leaving her and Nicola all alone in the cabin. No way were they stopping here on their own.

'Dad?'

'Yes, Ben.'

'How far is Bent's Fort from here?'

'Way south of here, don't rightly know for sure, Colorado, New Mexico way. Why?'

'Mountain men used to meet up there once a year, long after the Santa Fe Trail had been opened. A kind of reunion. I'd like to go there.'

'For Christ's sake!' Adele muttered beneath her breath.

'Not this trip, son, too far. Another time, perhaps.'

'Just wondered.' Ben lapsed back into silence.

The storm was gathering even greater force, lashing the shack with renewed anger; this man-made edifice had defied it for too long, tonight it must be dashed to matchwood.

Nicola was crying softly, her face buried against Adele's bosom. Blair finished positioning his candles, leaned up against one of the uprights. He was restless, bored by this enforced confinement; not that they would have hunted after dark, simply that he was prevented from doing so had the whim

22

taken him. Sheltering from a storm was one thing, being imprisoned by it was quite another.

They might not get out of here for days. Relief forces would be too busy clearing the highways of fallen trees and debris to worry about a track that led off into the wilderness. He would maybe have to walk to the road, hitch a lift into town and hire a chainsaw, clear the track himself before they could get away from here, waste the rest of the vacation cutting up blown timber.

Right now he needed a smoke. He pulled a pack of cigars out of his pocket.

'Blair, don't smoke in here, please.'

'We'll all die from passive smoking,' Nicola protested.

'All right.' Reluctantly he returned the pack to his pocket. 'Maybe we should all turn in, then.'

'I don't wanna go to bed yet.' Nicola was overtired, the memory of her nightmare still haunted her. 'Let's stop here.'

'For a while longer, then. But if the power goes off we'll have to go to bed.'

They were having to shout to make themselves heard above the wind. Conversation died.

Then the lights failed. They did not even flicker an advance warning this time, just plunged everywhere into stygian darkness.

Nicola screamed, a piercing shriek of terror. Adele was holding her close, trying to comfort her. Blair groped his way along the table to where the chain of waiting candles began.

It was in those few moments of total blackness that Adele detected that awful stench again; just a whiff at first that might have been a reminder of what she had smelled before. Unwashed flesh and stale clothes that stank of urine and worse. Rancid grease and worn leather, a nauseating odour that might have been rotting meat like the time when a steak had fallen unnoticed behind the cooler and slowly decomposed. Ugh, it was getting stronger by the second.

'Mommy, I can smell him again!'

Oh, God, Nicola had picked it up too! 'It's all right, darling, it isn't anything,' Adele shouted, wanted them all to hear her reassurance, her lie.

'That man's here again, Mommy, the one who came into my bedroom!'

23

'Nobody's here!' Blair shouted in an attempt to make himself heard above the roaring of the wind. *Where the fuck had his lighter gone?* 'I'll have the candles lit in a minute if you'll just be patient.'

Something brushed against him, he grabbed and his fingers closed over an arm. 'Who the—'

'Dad, you're hurting me!'

'Where the hell are you going, Ben?'

'There's some matches over on the shelf.' Ben's voice was shaking; he was scared too.

It was suddenly very cold, as if the wind had come straight from the snowy peaks of the highest Rockies, an icy blast that found every crack in this crude dwelling. Adele's flesh was pimpling, she knew that her teeth chattered even though she could not hear them. And Nicola was shaking against her, sobbing.

This was no ordinary cold, even the depths of winter could not have produced that iciness that froze you. And the stench was stronger, nauseating so that you wanted to throw up.

Blair felt it too, smelled it, almost panicked in his haste to locate the missing lighter in his pockets. His trembling fingers closed over something flat and hard. Thank God!

The flint sparked, the wick didn't catch. He thumbed it frantically. It fired; a tiny flame that was horizontal in the draughts, might extinguish at any second. Just enough light to make out the off-white of a wax candle standing in an empty preserve jar. He jabbed at it, shielded it with a cupped hand.

The flame caught, grew, showed him three frightened faces watching him. The fire burned up, added its own weird glow. He stumbled across to the next candle, it burned easier than the first. Six in all, they might all extinguish, the flames were going crazy in all directions.

Then came the shadows, a multitude of shapes that were both man and beast, leaping for you, darting back as the wan light increased. A black huddle in every corner, writhing, changing before your imagination could dwell upon it.

Blair leaned against the cupboard. This place stank, the draughts must have stirred up a lot of smells that had lain hidden, dust and filth in the corners. He wished that he'd lit that cigar, it would have masked a lot of them. He still might.

'See, there's nobody here!' he shouted almost hysterically. 'Nobody at all.'

Those shadows could have hidden anybody, anything, the way the candles were playing with them.

The gale calmed suddenly. In a way, that was worse, like a rampaging bull drawing back to make its final charge. You tensed, braced yourself.

That was when they heard the howl, long and drawn out, a wild animal of some kind baying its wrath at the storm, maybe scenting human prey. Wild and fierce, not far away, maybe twenty yards outside the building.

Nobody spoke, everybody stared towards the door, prayed that the rusted bolts were strong enough. Blair thought about lying that it was the wind funnelling down from the mountains but right now the wind wasn't blowing. He was fast running out of lame excuses for everything.

The hurricane renewed its assault on the cabin, blew out two of the candles, the rest would probably follow. Ben had joined his mother and Nicola over by the stove. He was scared, real scared. His eyes asked questions which he was afraid to put into words because he didn't want to hear the answers.

Rain was lashing the windows, the wind might blow the panes in. Blair found himself mentally measuring the frames, wondering how big an animal might be able to squeeze in through them.

He wondered to himself if that creature was still howling out there or whether it was slinking round the building trying to find a way in. He moved over to where the five-shot was propped in the corner, reached a box of buckshot off the shelf.

They had to sit out this night of terror, wait for daylight.

Four

The only light in the cabin was from two surviving candles and the glow of the wood stove. The shadows had deepened, encroached. You sensed them creeping up on you but when you turned around they darted back. Lurked, waited.

Nicola was sucking her thumb, her eyes were closed but she did not sleep. Adele stared fixedly into the embers of the dying fire. The last log had burned quickly; there was a ready-cut stack under a tin sheet out back. But nobody was going outside to fetch them.

The room was deathly cold.

Ben glanced across at the darkened corner where the twenty stood. At least, he thought it was still there. Dad had the Browning, sat with it across his knees, some shells clutched in his hand. You didn't load a gun indoors, that was an elementary rule that had been instilled into the boy. Ben didn't dare ask if he could have the weapon because he knew what the answer would be. If there was any shooting to be done, his father would do it.

'What time is it?' Adele broke the long silence.

Blair bent forward, squinted at his wristwatch in the half-light. 'Two fifteen, another four hours till it gets light.'

'Jesus!'

'Storm's eased a bit, I reckon the worst has passed. I'd say the eye passed this way but the valley sheltered us.'

That smell had gone. Well, nearly, just a lingering whiff now and then. Adele took a deep breath. There was a different kind of aroma now; musty, as if this place had been shut up for years. Stale. Well, she supposed, that wasn't altogether surprising. She had an idea that the cabin wasn't rented out much at all. If ever. Nobody in their right mind would want to holiday in a hovel like this. Blair was number-one sucker.

All he thought about was the hunting and fishing, accommodation came bottom of his list of priorities.

He had his faults, but if she had to start all over again she wouldn't change him. She managed a half-smile to herself even in the icy near-darkness of a backwoods cabin, where the wind was doing its damnedest to blow it down, and there were wild animals outside baying for the blood of humans trapped inside.

He was a good father to the kids, he bought expensive Christmas presents, took them on holidays. During the close season for hunting. Maybe bringing them along on a trip like this was a mistake. He worked hard, too hard. That had made him like he was. It had been touch and go after Christmas so maybe this break was a saviour and it was her duty to go along with it. Blair would protect them with his life, if necessary.

Adele had done her duty as a wife, there was nothing she could blame herself for. She had brought Nicola and Ben up to the best of her ability. Sex was the hardest part where Blair was concerned. In the early days it had been pleasurable, it was only after Nicola was born that it had gone a bit over the top. Even then she had gone along with it because it pleased her husband.

Oral wasn't as dirty as she had supposed, according to a recent survey. Something like sixty per cent of couples did it; she would rather have been in the remaining forty, but if it made for a successful marriage then she'd join the majority.

If dressing up in black stockings and suspenders turned her husband on, so be it. It didn't do anything for her. Then, one night, he'd tied her up, used some old neckties and belts, fastened her to the bed real tight. It had been quite scary, like rape. He hadn't hurt her, though. The part that concerned her was when he'd left her bound, gone downtown for a drink, come back and pretended to be a complete stranger.

Bondage had become routine, a ritual, an integral part of their sex life. Logically, there wasn't any harm in it, it was just that she would rather have screwed him the way they used to. She became worried about him.

But there was no chance of anything kinky here, the cabin was far too small, the kids were only a yard away on the other side of a flimsy partition wall. Sure, you can sleep between us tonight, Nick. What's left of the night, anyway.

The wind had dropped, there was scarcely a rustle of breeze outside. It was so still, so eerie. So damnably cold.

'I wouldn't like to be here in winter.' Adele tried to break the uncanny silence. 'You'd be snowed in for months.'

'The mountain men were.' Ben jerked his gaze away from the far corner. 'They holed up in a place just like this . . .'

'Just shaddup about your damned dirty, stinking mountain men!' Adele was close to breaking point. 'I wish you'd start living in the present instead of burying yourself in the past.'

'What's that?' Nicola sat up on her mother's knee, head to one side. 'I heard something outside. Listen!'

They were all listening, holding their breath. A metallic sound as Blair instinctively slid the magazine on the Browning; if necessary he would load five shells. Just to be sure.

A faint gust of wind soughed through the willows in the grove as if sadly reflecting upon the damage done by the hurricane. Then silence again.

Then a muffled, dragging sound like footfalls. One . . . two . . . They stopped just outside the window.

'*There's . . . there's somebody out there!*' Nicola whispered, hugged her mother.

'Nonsense.' Blair slid shells into the magazine, clamping it home. 'I'll go take a peek.'

The darkness hid his shaking fingers as he tugged at the curtain. It ripped, shredded into a strip, hung down almost to the floor. Shit, it was rotten!

The pane was dusty on the inside, opaque with raindrops on the outside; Blair wiped at it with his free hand. Without warning the frame crumbled, fell outwards with a crash. He heard the glass break, shards tinkling.

'What's the matter?' Adele half rose, Nicola still clung to her.

'The bloody window was rotten.' He spoke in a low voice, steeled himself to look outside.

His first thought was that day had broken, the valley right down to the willow grove was bathed in a silvery glow. Trees showed in a grotesque outline, a mass of black shadow where the gale had ripped through them. It took him several seconds to realize that it was bright moonlight, that the heavy clouds had been driven westward by the storm and the skies had cleared.

'Is there . . . *anything* out there?' Adele bit on a fingernail.

He didn't answer, instead eased his head slowly through the small gap, looked left, then right.

There was nothing in sight. At least, not in the patches of ethereal light. The deep shadow could have concealed an army of bestial horrors.

Daddy, there was a man in my bedroom.

Blair poked the gun barrel over the sill. Nicola had had a nightmare, nobody could possibly have got inside the cabin. He stared, but still nothing moved. Yet those had definitely been footfalls they'd heard, it had to be some forest beast disturbed by the storm.

Maybe a grizzly bear. He gripped the barrel tighter. There were bears up there in the mountains but mostly they kept out of the sight of humans. The wardens warned hunters to take care; mostly the authorities were afraid of the bears being shot rather than the animals hurting anybody.

The forests were a haven of wildlife – big cats, deer, raccoons, caribou. It could have been any one of those prowling around the shack.

A sudden howl rent the nocturnal stillness had Blair bringing the gun up to his shoulder. A sound that chilled the blood, if it was not already frozen by the inexplicable coldness of the atmosphere.

The sound hung in the air, prickled the back of his neck.

'Blair, what is it?'

'I don't know.' And he wasn't too keen on finding out. Noises are magnified on still nights, it might be something as innocuous as . . . what?

He felt the others crowding him, Ben jostling for a look outside, Adele at his other shoulder, still holding Nicola.

'Dad,' Ben breathed excitedly, tried to point but there wasn't room. 'Something's moving on the edge of the grove!'

Blair would never have admitted, even to himself, that his son's eyesight was sharper than his own; the boy was imagining things just as his sister had done. The doctor screwed up his eyes, they began to water in the cold, blurred his vision.

But there was something moving on the fringe of the willows.

He pawed at his eyes, made out an indistinct shape, bigger than a dog. Maybe twice as big. It moved with an arrogance, emerged from the shadows. Its colour was almost a camouflage against the moonlit background. Pointed erect ears, there was a powerful purposefulness about its every movement.

Blair heard the others gasp, felt them pressing up against him. Damn them, they were cramping him, made a shot impossible.

'Dad . . . there's more of 'em!'

Jesus in heaven! Even as he watched, Blair saw more of those huge animals, they seemed to be following the other in single file as if it was their leader and even they were in awe of it. Huge shaggy beasts, but none of them matched the first one for size.

The Lunds watched, transfixed, almost hypnotized. It was like a scene from some widescreen wildlife movie, a family of wild animals being filmed by a hidden camera with telephoto lens. Ben was counting beneath his breath, 'Five, six . . . eight . . . eleven . . .'

A massive pack, there must have been twenty or more, and now the column was separating in opposite directions, fanning out. Circling. It was like some unbelievable bestial training in discipline and tactical formation; the nearest stopped, the others continued in a circle, dropping off at intervals of fifteen or twenty yards, standing still. The moonlight glinted evilly on eyes that were fixed unwaveringly on the cabin.

As if they knew there were humans inside.

The big one, the leader, squatted on its haunches in the centre. Its head went back, it howled, a sound that was terrible to human ears.

'Oh, my God!' Adele shielded Nicola's eyes, would have stepped back except her legs seemed incapable of movement.

The animals had ringed the cabin, undoubtedly they were at the rear as well. Watching and waiting, occasionally glancing at their leader, perhaps awaiting a signal to attack.

'What . . . what are they?' Adele asked in a whispered, shaking voice.

'Coyotes, I guess.' Ben was standing on the balls of his feet, trying to see past the end of the cabin.

'Coyotes!' Blair half turned. 'Those out there are not coyotes, I can assure you of that, coyotes are about two sizes smaller. *They're grey timber wolves!*'

'*Wolves!*' Adele stifled a terrified shriek, hoped that Nicola had not heard. 'If they get at us, they'll tear us to pieces!'

'They won't get in here,' Blair answered grimly, worked a shell into the chamber of the automatic. But all the same, a pack of hungry wolves was a daunting prospect. The wardens warned you about grizzlies, they seldom mentioned wolves. Because a human hadn't been killed by a wolf since before the turn of the century. You seldom saw them, they were nocturnal hunters, preyed mostly on deer. They slunk away at your approach. A hundred years ago they had presented a threat to Man because they were numerous, hunted in packs. Like now.

'Blair, what are we going to do?' Adele's tone was loaded with panic and desperation. 'If they get indoors . . .'

'They can't.' He tried to sound confident. 'The storm's probably made them pack, they're scared.' They don't look scared to me. 'I'm gonna teach 'em a lesson.'

He aligned the barrel on the big feller. The beast sat there and openly mocked with wide, slavering jaws. 'Let's see how he likes fifty grams of nickel-plated shot right in the chops!'

The watchers clasped their hands to their ears in anticipation of the deafening noise; they didn't want to look but there was no way they could drag their gaze away from that nightmarish scene.

'Sixty yards, no more,' Blair was muttering to himself as if he needed to boost his confidence. 'A good distance but buckshot should splatter 'em. Take that, you bastard!'

He squeezed the trigger, held it. The heavy automatic bucked against his shoulder, the long barrel spat vicious flame. An ear-busting report, the following four were continuous, the valley erupted to the crashing reports and their echoes.

The cold air was heavy with gun smoke, spent shells bounced back into the room.

'Well, I'll be fucked!' Blair stared in disbelief.

The circle of wolves did not move. No rolling, kicking wounded, no corpses stretched out on the soaking grass. They just sat there unconcernedly, still looking towards the cabin. It was as if they were not even aware that a magazine of 00 goose-shot had been loosed in their direction.

'You . . . missed!' It was the only explanation the bemused and frightened Ben could offer.

'Missed, be buggered!' Blair was angry and confused, scared too, because he had faith in his own marksmanship.

31

Last season he had dropped a bounding buck in thick cover at roughly the same distance as those wolves sat and that had been an instinctive snap shot. These were sitters, he had blasted the big one twice, picked three more after that.

The wolves had survived. Worse, they didn't even appear to notice.

Blair was white-faced. There were more shells in the cupboard but he didn't bother fetching them. His mouth was dry, his arms were trembling and not from the weight of the heavy twelve-gauge. He did not try to offer an explanation because there was none.

Nicola was sobbing softly; Adele closed her eyes and opened them again but those awful beasts were still sitting out there. It seemed even colder than before but that was probably because the window was broken.

Wolves are scared of fire, Adele had read somewhere, *Ben's beloved mountain men used to light huge fires at night to keep them at bay.* But the Lunds' stove had died and all the kindling was outside. *Please God, let us get away from here. Blair, you gotta think of something. Fast.*

'Dad, *look*!'

Blair shook himself, tried to focus out to where Ben was pointing. Once again he stared in disbelief.

The wolves were moving; they stood up, stretched, turned away unconcernedly. And set off back whence they had come at a steady, leisurely lope.

Nobody spoke because there was nothing to be said. Yet this pack was a thousand times more frightening than one which might have attacked the cabin, maddened with rage, ravenous for human flesh. Worse was the prospect that they might return, just sit out there, invincible to gunshots, just waiting and watching.

'Well, they're gone.' Blair stepped back from the window, the warmth of the Browning's barrel comforting to his frozen hands. 'At least they've bloody gone.'

'That window . . .' Adele was scarcely coherent.

'I'll find a board somewhere, block it up.' Blair went round the candles, relit them. He had difficulty in holding the lighter steady.

'What time is it, Blair?'

'It's . . . two fifteen . . . Christ, my bloody watch must've

32

stopped.' Except that digital watches rarely stopped suddenly, they lost time gradually when the batteries were running out. 'Anyway, let's get to bed. When we wake up it'll be daylight and everything'll be different.'

Adele's nostrils flared; she felt suddenly dizzy as if with a fit of vertigo, had to clutch at the table to steady herself.

That stench was back, the stale body odours and everything that went with it. And it was much stronger than before.

Five

'Blair, it's light. Wake up.' Adele shook her husband gently, tried not to wake Nicola, their daughter needed all the sleep she could get after last night.

'Uh-huh.' He stirred, rubbed his eyes. He had gone to bed fully clothed like the rest of them. He felt stiff and cold, was aware that he had a slight headache, one of those which would get progressively worse as the day wore on.

'What time is it, Blair?'

Christ, if you ask me once more I'll go fucking mad. He looked at his watch, saw with a start that it still showed two fifteen. 'My watch has gone wrong. Remember?' He tried to sound casual.

'I'd forgotten.' She hadn't, but it was easier to say that. 'Anyway, the sun looks to be shining.' She stared, the single curtain was in tatters, it was probably because of the storm blowing and raining in through the ill-fitting window. 'I can't hear a breath of wind.'

'I'll make some coffee.' He eased himself off the bed. 'Then I'll go and see what the damage is.'

'Blair . . . be careful.' She tensed as the memory of those awful wolves flooded back.

'I'll be right back with the coffee.' He let himself out into the hallway. God, it stank foul out here, maybe the septic tank needed emptying, the rain had flooded it, lifted the cover. Like everything else in and around this place, that chore had been neglected, too.

He stared aghast at the kitchen. *Jesus, what a fucking shithole!* The board he'd found and wedged in the window was still in place, as were most other things. The Browning lay on the table surrounded by unwashed mugs. *But it was as if the entire cabin had deteriorated overnight, fallen into a state of dilapidation.*

The upright timbers had warped, sagged beneath the weight of the roof, which bowed and looked like it might cave in at any second. A section of wall had cracked, split right open so that daylight peeped through. Where cupboards had been added, the paintwork was flaking. The floorboards were covered with dried mud, giving the impression of never having been swept. Except that Blair had watched Adele sweep it on their arrival.

'Christ, what a bloody stink!' He spoke aloud, retching with nausea as the foulness came at him like a waft direct from the Augean stables.

It hadn't been as bad as this when they had retired to bed, even in the flickering light of the candles, he was certain of that.

He hastened to check on Ben; the boy was sleeping soundly but his bedcovers were sprinkled with soil. A slight movement attracted Blair's attention, he looked up. From between the twisted rafters a tiny trickle of soil filtered down. As if somebody had shovelled earth on to the flat roof and it had found a gap in the ageing pine trunks.

Something had happened during the Great Storm, cloaked by darkness, gales and driving rain. *Everything here was different, a sudden inexplicable ageing process that had brought with it decay and rotted everything that was perishable.*

There would not be any coffee until he boiled the kettle, and that wouldn't happen until he lit the stove. He had to go outside, fetch some kindling.

Instinctively, he reached the gun off the table. He knew by the roughness of the barrels, before he even looked at it, that a coating of rust covered it. Metal sometimes rusted within a few hours if it was left exposed in a damp atmosphere. That was possible, even if it was improbable.

He had to exert force to draw the bolt on the door; it was as if it had been shut for years.

He loaded the magazine, pumped a shell into the chamber, and stepped outside.

The bright sunlight dazzled him for a moment, he shaded his eyes. A spring-like morning, he guessed it had to be around eight, no later. A dove flapped out of the willows, otherwise nothing moved. So still, so sunny. But cold enough to have been a January day.

Something was dreadfully wrong.

Then his eyes alighted on the station wagon parked where there had once been a track leading down from the highway. Its windshield was smashed where an airborne branch had struck it, the nearside wing was dented. That was only to be expected after last night.

But the metallic bodywork could not possibly have corroded to that extent in a few hours. The tyres might have punctured in the storm but they wouldn't have perished.

They had. The Lunds certainly would not be going anywhere in their new Ford.

His priority was to get a fire going. They all needed a hot drink, some food. Then they'd walk right outa here and they wouldn't be coming back.

The logs crumbled, powdered to his touch. He scooped handfuls of rotten wood-dust into a galvanized bucket; the metal bottom collapsed when he lifted the handle. His neck was prickling. He looked all around him but there wasn't a living thing in sight.

The stove roared fiercely after he had fetched some of the dry wood pulp in a plastic salad bowl. He returned to the bedroom carrying the two steaming mugs of coffee. Nicola was still sleeping the sleep of the exhausted.

'You took your time.' Adele did her best to smile, then she saw his expression. 'Blair, is something wrong? Oh, God, what have we woken up to?'

'I don't rightly know.' The curtain had finished its rotting process overnight like most other things. He thought that the bed sheets would probably rip into fragments too, if you pulled them hard.

'Whatever do you mean?'

'Seems like moths and dust hath corrupted.' He tried to make a joke of it for her sake but it sent chills all over him. 'I guess the place was in a pretty shit shape before the storm, the hurricane just finished it off. The timbers in the cabin are rotten, the station wagon's rusted and the tyres have perished. You name it, it's aged years.'

She closed her eyes. 'We'd better get outa here right away.'

'Which is what I'm thinking, too.' He nodded. 'Let's eat first, pack what we can carry and we'll walk right on up that track.'

There wasn't any track, no trace of where it had been, either.

He stared from the window, the valley was just like it once was, grass and ancient trees. Saplings had blown down, it was as if only the established timber had survived. Just like it had once been, a century or more ago.

Adele swung her feet to the floor, gently shook Nicola. 'Time to get up, darling.'

The girl's eyelids flickered. Her expression began with confusion, changed to fear, darting glances around the room. 'Mommy, is everything all right now?'

'Everything's fine, Nick. The storm's moved on and the sun's shining. We've decided we're going back to New York. Only problem is the car's broken down so we're going to walk to the highway and hitch a lift, hire another. Come and give me a hand fixing breakfast.'

'What's the matter with the car?'

Kids asked the most awkward questions at the worst possible time. 'The hurricane hit it.' It was only a part lie. 'Smashed it up, punctured the tyres.'

'It stinks awful in here, Mommy. Just like last night when that man came into my room.'

Adele's stomach knotted, her mouth was dry and sour. *Yes, Nick, you've hit the nail right on the head. It smells just like last night, only worse.* 'Maybe the storm has flooded the drain.'

'Why's the room in such a mess, Mommy? It's like some-body's been walking all over the floor with muddy boots and the mud's dried.'

'It's always like that after Daddy and Ben have come in from hunting or fishing.'

'But you swept the floor after them, I saw you do it.'

'I must have missed some. Now, get a few plates out of the cupboard and set the table. Daddy's lit the stove so I'll fry up some bacon and eggs.'

'Why're we going home?' Ben stood in the doorway, his features clouded with disappointment. 'Dad, you said we were going up into the mountains today to try for a buck.'

'Storm's put paid to that, I'm afraid.' Blair was tight-lipped. 'There'll be that many trees down you won't be able to walk the forests. Best go home, maybe try somewhere else next week.'

'Aw, Jeez!' Ben kicked a lump of dried mud; it powdered, gave off a cloud of dust.

'*Ugh!*' There was no mistaking Adele's cry of revulsion, something dropped from her hand, smacked on the floor. She leaned against the open cooler door, came close to throwing up. 'That bacon's rotten. I only bought it the day we came and it's been in the cooler since.'

They all stared at the morass of decomposing black meat on the floor.

'That's what has been stinking the cabin out.' Blair tore off a sheet of kitchen towel, gathered up the mulch and threw it into the fire. 'Bad bacon. At least we know what's caused that smell now.'

Adele's eyes met her husband's, said, *Liar! But I know you're doing it for the kids' sake.* 'Well, we'll have to make do with fried bread and tomatoes. I'll open a can of beans, too.'

She turned back to the cooler, held her breath as she pulled open the fruit tray. And recoiled.

'I don't believe it, the tomatoes have gone bad too, along with the cucumber and lettuce!'

'I guess it's because the generator failed, the cooler temperature rose,' Blair lied again.

'You never checked the generator out, Blair.'

'There's no point now that we're leaving. I'll write to Becker as soon as we get home, demand a complete refund.'

'Just look at this loaf!' Adele held out the bread bin at full stretch.

The other three looked. The object of their attention had once been a freshly wrapped loaf of bread, according to the label; now it was solid and green with mould. Adele replaced the lid, put the bin back on the working surface.

'Well, I guess all that's left to us is beans and coffee. And, please, Ben, let's not have any comments about mountain men. They're more than welcome to this hovel if they care to move in after we've gone. In fact, I'll leave them the rest of the canned stuff, we're certainly not going to haul that with us on foot.'

Ben spooned his beans hungrily, slurped his black coffee. Just when their temporary lifestyle was becoming idyllic, Mom and Dad had decided to up and leave. It was Mom's idea, for sure, probably because Nicola didn't like it here. Women! One bit of a storm and they were up and running for cover. 'Why

38

can't Dad and I come back after we've gotten you transport home?' he asked with his mouth full.

'Because this place has become uninhabitable.' It was Blair who answered him, eyes averted.

'Uninhabitable!' Ben looked around the room. 'Trappers have stayed all winter in places a lot worse'n this.'

'That'll do, Ben!' Adele was edgy. 'Now, put your dirty crocks in the sink, and we'll pack as much as we can carry.'

Within twenty minutes they were loaded up. They all had backpacks containing their clothing, Blair had the Browning slung on his shoulder, Ben carried the twenty.

'Don't you load that gun, Ben!' A stern hypocritical warning because the magazine in the automatic was full. 'Now, we should be at the highway before midday.'

'How'll you know it's midday, Daddy?' Nicola held on to her mother's arm. 'You're the only one with a watch and it doesn't work. Mummy's and mine are back home and Ben lost his.'

'When the sun's right overhead it'll be midday.' He hoped she wasn't going to ask questions all the way, there were a lot he either couldn't answer or didn't want to. 'Now, we just head down the track . . .'

The track wasn't there any more; he'd seen from the cabin that it was overgrown but there surely should have been signs of its original route. There weren't, it was as though it had never been.

'There's no track any longer, Dad.'

'No, but it followed a line past the willow grove and up along those . . . tall . . . pines . . .'

The grove was still standing, much of it, anyway. But the firs were nowhere to be seen on the brow of hillock before it fell away out of sight.

'Which firs, Dad?'

'They probably blew down in the wind. We'll find them lying, then we'll know we're right.'

There was no sign of the wind-blown conifers. Just rough grass, still brown from the winter frosts. And beyond the rise where the land had levelled out gnarled oaks twisted like resurrected prehistoric creatures.

'I don't recall seeing those oaks, Dad.'

'Maybe you just didn't notice them.' An uncertainty had

39

crept into Blair's voice. 'I guess we'd better head that way, the highway has to be over there somewhere.'

The oaks were thicker than they had at first thought, an age-old forest that smelled sickly sweet with rotting vegetation. A track led into it; Blair decided to follow it.

Even in bright spring sunshine the wood was a forbidding place. The boughs of the trees were leafless but they entwined, in places almost obscuring the sunlight.

'It's creepy.' Nicola voiced what the rest of them were thinking, gripped Adele's arm more tightly.

'We'll soon be out of it, Nick, the wood surely can't be that big.'

Apparently it was. Some time later the path they were following divided, forked in opposite directions. Blair hesitated, peered ahead. There was no sign of open ground, just trees and more trees. Right or left? He thought about tossing a coin but it might have alarmed the others. He made a decision, turned left.

The path narrowed, the trees were thicker now, it wound around the massive boles; again he had to make a decision on which fork to take. He led them to the right this time.

'I think we're coming to the end of the wood now!'

Ben was close on his father's heels. 'Look, the trees end up ahead, I can see grass beyond. We can't be far from the highway now.'

The wood was thinning. Blair looked up, saw that the sun was beginning to dip in the sky. Which meant that it was well past noon, they had wandered in this forest for longer than he'd thought. But once they hit the highway it didn't really matter. They'd thumb the first vehicle that came along, climb aboard and in no time at all they'd be . . .

There was no sign of the highway. They stood looking out across a landscape that somehow looked chillingly familiar. The silence was the worst part; they'd expected to hear the hum of traffic, the drone of heavy trucks.

There wasn't a sound to be heard.

'Where are we, Mommy?' Nicola addressed Adele, somehow she didn't want her worst fears confirmed by her father. Because he was their protector and an admission from him that he'd headed in the wrong direction would have been frightening.

40

'Some place where we didn't intend to be,' Adele muttered beneath her breath. 'But at least we've found a way out of the forest,' she added by way of consolation.

Blair visibly shied from the landscape that confronted them. The tall mountains in the background, you saw them from everywhere in these parts; a willow grove, they were plentiful, one looked much the same as another.

But there was no other cabin quite like the one they stared down upon, a shambles of rotting timbers and a sagging roof, a wreck of a rusty Ford station wagon with perished tyres and a smashed windshield standing out front.

Nicola let out a hiss of realization, half hid behind Adele. Ben tightened his grip on the twenty-gauge, instinctively checked that he had shells in his pocket. Blair did not speak because there was nothing to say that wasn't already obvious to everybody else.

'We must've gone round in a circle, Dad,' Ben said it for his father.

'I guess so.' Blair spoke in a whisper, as much to himself as to his companions. 'I forked wrong somewhere.'

'We gonna turn back, Dad?'

'No.' Blair did not look at the others, stared straight ahead. 'That forest's a lot bigger'n we thought, we'd probably get lost worse still. Best thing is to follow it along the outside, all the way until we come to the end. Then maybe we'll be able to see the highway.'

The wood stretched on, the valley appeared to be much larger than Blair had thought. Steep banks, deep hollows, at times they were hidden from the valley.

The sun was low in the west now, soon it would be below the mountain peaks and shadows would stretch across the valley. Then dusk. Then night again.

Blair resisted the temptation to hurry. Adele had Nicola on her shoulders, bent double. Ben was tiring, too. Surely to God they must emerge on to open ground soon, see the highway in the distance, hear the murmur of traffic.

The oaks petered out above a deep hollow, deformed branches silhouetted against a sky that was already turning saffron. The slope was steep, slippery after the rain. Hopefully, after they reached the top, it would be downhill all the way to . . .

41

The willow grove below them was unmistakable, a kind of triangle that struggled to a point. The mountains above were already in shadow but the battered, rusted Ford was only too recognizable. The watchers shied from the sight of the tumble-down cabin; had she not been breathless after the climb, Adele might have screamed.

They looked in silence, eventually accepted what they saw below them.

'It'll be full dark in less than an hour.' Blair unslung the Browning, transferred it to the crook of his arm.

'What . . . what are we going to do?' There was despair in Adele's voice.

'We got a choice.' Blair licked his sips. 'We can either camp out here and it's gonna be damned cold after dark.'

'No!' Adele breathed. 'Those wolves. . .'

'Or,' he turned back to where the cabin was fast becoming just a dark shape in the hastening dusk, 'we can go back and light the stove, heat some beans and make some coffee.'

Nicola's fingers gouged Adele's flesh. She smelled the foul-ness again, it had lingered in her nostrils. She, too, whispered, '*No!*'

Furtively, his back towards his father, Ben slipped two cartridges into the twenty. Whatever his parents decided, he might have need of a gun.

Six

The rotten kindling gave off such heat that they had to move their chairs back from the stove. The candles burned evenly with no draught to flicker them.

They had eaten well, there was ample supply of canned foodstuffs in the cupboard. Spaghetti had made a change from beans, the strong coffee was welcome. Any other time, any other place, they might have felt drowsy, relaxed and succumbed to sleep.

But not here in this filthy cabin where that cloying stench still lingered and decay had taken its toll.

'I don't wanna go to bed.' Nicola sat on Blair's lap, gripped him tightly.

'I don't think any of us will go to bed tonight.' He did his best to speak reassuringly. 'We'll stay right here and keep the fire burning. Then, in the morning . . .'

God in heaven, what would they do tomorrow that would be any different from today?

'There have to be other folks in the area, maybe three, four miles away,' Blair mused. 'If we can find 'em, they'll show us the way back to the highway.'

'They're probably in the same fix as us.' Adele's confidence had drained to a low ebb. 'Blair, what do you think has happened here? The car's rusted to a twenty-year wreck, the cabin's about ready to collapse and we can't find our way back to the highway.'

'Maybe the highway doesn't exist any more.' He spoke pensively.

'That's crazy, it can't just disappear overnight.'

'Well, we don't seem able to find it. It's like this isn't the same place that we arrived at three days ago. The hurricane's responsible in some way, I'm sure of that, but how or why I don't know and maybe we'll never find out.'

43

'I saw a movie once about a guy who woke up one morning and—'

'That'll do, Ben!' Adele snapped. 'I don't want to hear another word about mountain men or . . .'

'It wasn't a mountain man, Mom, it was—'

'Well, we don't want to know.' She glanced at Nicola. The child was sucking her thumb, that was a sign that she might drop off to sleep soon. They all needed to sleep but you were scared to close your eyes. Perhaps they should take turns keeping a lookout.

'I've been thinking.' Tiredness was taking its toll now, Blair knew he had to talk to keep awake. 'Those wolves, they were probably a lot further away than I thought. You can misjudge range in the moonlight. I remember once, some years back, I was hunting ducks in Oregon's high desert country. We were out under the moon. A skein of honkers came right over me. I pulled five times, never lifted a feather. Jeez, I was wishing a hole would open up and swallow me! Joe Warner, a guy I was hunting with, he'd shot the desert for years, went out by moonlight regularly, he said what the hell was I thinking of, firing at birds that must've been eighty, ninety yards up. The moon makes things look bigger, nearer. Those wolves looked big for that reason, they were maybe three hundred feet away. They could even've been coyotes.'

'They weren't coyotes, they were timber wolves. I looked 'em up in my *Pocket Guide to Wild Animals of the Western States*. They should've run, anyhow,' Ben stirred. 'Any animal would with lead pinging at it. The noise would've scared 'em, anyway.'

Damn you, Ben, why don't you keep your bloody mouth shut! 'They'd probably never heard gunfire before, didn't relate it to danger.'

'There's always hunters in the mountains, shooting deer. Those wolves'd know what gunfire was, for sure.'

'You'd best get some sleep, Ben, we don't know how far we might have to trek in the morning.'

Nicola straightened up, her thumb came out of her mouth, she was wide awake instantly. 'What's that, Daddy?' There was fear in her whisper.

'What's what, Nick?'

'I heard something outside.'

They were all tense, listening. Not so much as a rustle of the breeze blowing the dead leaves that the storm had piled in a corner by the log stack. 'You must've *thought* you heard something, Nick.'

'I heard something. There, now. Listen!'

A movement, something crunched softly. *A footfall.*

'There's somebody outside!' Adele's whisper was barely audible.

Blair rose to his feet, slid Nicola to the floor. She clung to her mother. He slid a shell into the breech of the Browning, it chunked almost deafeningly.

Adele sensed the smell again, faint at first, growing stronger by the second. Human flesh that had not stepped outside the clothes encasing it for months, impregnating them with its staleness.

The footsteps had stopped. Blair thought about going to the window but the board covering it could not have been removed quickly or quietly. He shivered, it had gone damnably cold, like the room was going to freeze in spite of the heat from the fire.

No sound came from beyond the walls. They must have been mistaken. Or whoever, whatever, it was had crept quietly away.

A knocking came from the outside door, heavy decisive thumps.

Adele almost screamed, somehow she managed to check it. 'Who is it?' She asked the others in a quavering voice. Which was the most bloody silly question she'd asked in many a year.

'I'd better go find out,' Blair gripped the gun. 'Won't know until I do. Like we said, there has to be other folks roundabouts somewhere, maybe one of 'em's got lost like ourselves and just happened to find us. Which can be no bad thing right now.' He didn't manage to convince himself and he knew the others didn't believe him. All the same, he had to go see.

In her mind Adele was screaming at him not to go, not to open that door because there were things out there it was better not to see. Nicola was shaking. And Ben, defying everything that had been instilled into him regarding gun safety, gripped the loaded over-and-under with both hands.

The stench was stronger than any of them had ever known it.

The door was knocked again, a heavy banging that shook it; a screw fell out of one of the hinges, rolled on the floor. Whoever was outside was becoming impatient.

'Who's there?' Blair tried to sound authoritative.

There was silence, he heard the sound of laboured breathing. A deep voice growled something but the words were incomprehensible.

'I said . . . who is it?'

'Sage.' A single meaningless reply that was more of a growl. It sounded as if their unknown caller was scuffing the veranda with his boots in his impatience.

Blair hesitated. There was no way he could view the stranger from safety. It was dark outside and their only torch had corroded during the previous night. The acid from the batteries had seeped out and eaten away most of the casing.

'You gonna open this door?'

'*Don't*, Blair!' Adele whispered from over by the stove.

Blair shifted the weight of the gun, it was comforting. Nothing could withstand a charge of 00 at this range; five rounds of rapid would annihilate them. But on the other hand, the stranger was human, it was no prowling wolf out there. There was no reason to suppose that his call was menacing, there were still backwoodsmen of sorts, mostly guides who took out the hunters from the cities, or wardens who patrolled the forests. Or bandits preying on rich sportsmen. Or killers and convicts on the run. Psychopaths.

'Listen,' Blair called, 'I don't know who you are, I have to be careful. I'm going to open the door but I've got a gun. Understand?'

A grunt, it sounded impatient.

'All right, step back from the door, stand where the light will fall on you and I can see you. Don't come any closer. Got it?'

Another grunt, the tone of it sounded like the other had agreed to the proviso. Blair stretched out, drew the bolt one-handed, scraped the door inwards. Another screw popped out of the bottom T-hinge, the door sagged and he had to force it right back. Then, Browning half raised, he waited for his eyesight to adjust to the half-darkness of the rickety porch.

udes up in a cave, hope they'll be safe, pushed on. Mebbe
'll go back for 'em, bring 'em here. This is as good a place
s any to stand off Kiotes if it comes to it.'

'Coyotes?' Ben echoed. 'Coyotes don't attack you, they're
cavengers, but we saw wolves last night.'

The man looked puzzled. 'Allus wolves in the mountains,
ey're no trouble 'cept when food's scarce. Me, I'd sooner
ngle with a pack o' wolves any day than run in with Kiotes.
hey're worse'n the Blackfoot and the Gros Ventres, got the
d blood o' both tribes in 'em and more besides. And when
ou got the likes o' Koot stringin' along, you make sure they
on't ketch you.'

'Coyotes?' Ben was still confused.

'Cauites!' Sage threw back his head, bellowed coarse
ughter. 'Boy, you ain't bin in these parts long, I kin see.
amn my luck to find another lot o' dudes just when things're
ttin' too hot fer comfort. Cauites aren't Kiotes, and don't
k me to spell it 'cause I never see'd it writ down. Kiotes
e Injuns, least folks here around thinks they are but I reckon
nows better. Injuns they might've bin once but they come
m the fires o' hell and if they ketch you . . . don't let 'em!
rn that gun o' yourn on yersel' fust. And there's Kiotes and
ot out there in them woods right now, so the less light you
w, the better. Now, how about some o' that cawfee?'

Blair walked over to the stove, poured boiling water on
ne instant coffee. The man called Sage looked on in aston-
ment.

Wal, I never did! Don't you know how to boil up cawfee
ns? What's that 'un there you got, looks like sand to me.'

Blair ignored the question, pushed a steaming mug across
table. 'Where are you from, Mr . . . Sage?'

est call me Sage. Never did find out ma other name,
be never had one. Me, I'm from Virginia but that was
time ago, scarcely remember it. I've travelled just 'bout
y trail hereaparts, some that folks know, lots they don't
prob'ly never will. Started out ketchin' beaver. Good
ey if'n you kin ketch enough 'cause they don't pay a lot
furs. The more you trap, the more you earn. Done toler-
well but the furrin's gettin' harder, too many at it since
ikes o' me opened up the trails. Don't do much now, more
ey in guidin' folks west, wagon trains mostly. There's

It was a man, all right, six feet tall, perhaps more, muscular
inside the loose-fitting clothes he wore. The garments were
made from some kind of animal skin, fringed at the shoulders and fastened with thongs. From beneath the low-crowned
wool hat, coarse and bushy hair, flecked with grey, spilled
down to his shoulders. A thick beard hid most of his lined
and weathered features, and when he grinned Blair saw that
a couple of front teeth were missing; the rest were yellow,
either he didn't clean them or he was a heavy smoker. A pair
of soft calf-length boots was made from the same hide as the
rest of his clothing.

It was everything that either hung from their nocturnal visitor,
or was affixed to him, that had Blair staring in astonishment.
The leather belt encircling his waist had two flintlock pistols
shoved behind it, there were at least four knives of varying
sizes in sheaths. A leather pouch was suspended from his thick
neck, doubtless containing bullets; a powder horn was hanging
from his shoulder along with a ball-screw, wiper, awl, cleaning
rod and an obviously home-made ramrod. Blair recognized
them all, one by one, for they were depicted and accurately
described in that book which held such fascination for Ben.

The other watched him with obvious amusement, leaned
on the longest rifle that Blair had seen outside a museum.

'You done, mister?'

A horse stood patiently beyond the veranda, a big black,
its flanks flecked with sweat like it had been ridden hard. It
was heavily loaded, boxes and sacks strapped on to it, probably its role was as a pack horse, it was accustomed to being
led rather than ridden.

'I smelled your cawfee afore I saw your lights. Damn
dangerous showin' lights at night.'

'We don't have any power. The storm took it. Just candles.'

'Nothin' wrong with candles, lamps're brighter. Kin use a
fire, though, too risky to light one out thar.'

He's crazy, Blair thought, some old coot who's lived out
here all his life, doing what Ben would do if we gave him
the chance. Or else he's one of those freaks who play at it
and this guy's really gone to town on the part. There's ranches
for dudes, no reason why they shouldn't have a centre for
would-be mountain men. Easy money for somebody, give 'em
a bundle of hides to dress up in, let 'em loose in the moun-

tains. Eat what they kill, that way you don't even have to feed 'em. Probably they sleep rough, too.

'You gonna stop pointin' that musket at ma belly? Cain't say I've seen one like that afore.' The head was thrust forward, the dark eyes were wide with amazement. 'Where'd you get that? Never see'd one in the tradin' post – mostly Hawkens, everybody shoots Hawkens. Accurate at two hundred yards, drop a buffalo so's he don't even twitch.'

'You'd better come inside.' Blair moved back into the hallway, lowered the Browning. 'Go through into the living room, there's coffee on the stove. My wife will pour you some.'

'Keep that door shut.' The stranger dragged it closed behind him. 'Best not show too many lights, not tonight, nohow. Outside ain't no place to be right now but my hoss'll warn us if there's danger.'

Blair's spine prickled right the way up into his scalp.

Ben stared open-mouthed, his gun forgotten. This guy was just like a picture out of his book, one that had suddenly come to life and stepped right out of the pages.

Adele was on her feet, she had backed away, Nicola went with her. The stench was almost suffocating.

'Can you fix some coffee for our visitor?' Blair stood in the doorway.

Nicola's expression was one of sheer terror as the candle-light fell full upon the stranger. Disbelief at first, then her mouth shaped up for a scream but it was some seconds before she managed to get it out.

'*Daddy, that's the man who was in my bedroom!*'

48

Seven

'I think you've got some explaining to do, mis you are,' Blair stood in the kitchen doorway, the Browning swung up to centre on the strang ening buckskin-clad figure.

Ben had moved back, there was an ominou safety catch on the twenty was pushed forward. sion his father surely would not be angry about i indoors.

Adele pulled Nicola behind her, the child was ically. Even the shadows appeared to have b nocturnal visitor. It was deathly cold in the ro

'I kin use some cawfee, bin ridin' since nigh it's safe to move out there. Allus travel after

'*What's your name?*' Blair yelled, he had d antries, there was something decidedly sinister

'Told you once. You forgotten already? *Sage* it, too, if'n you're hard of hearin'. I'm a re tapped a pocket that bulged square and solid Sometimes I read the Bible. Depends. When up for a long winter he has to do somethin plumb crazy. Me, I read. Many's the winter I' afore Christmas till the thaw comes in spring out with ma snowshoes to try get some fresh

'You've been here before, then?' Blair's

'More times'n I kin remember. Allus hea late fall.'

'It's *spring* now!' Blair's tone was challen are gone.'

'S'right. I was headin' down towards Yello with some dudes from back east, when a bu on ma scent. Kiotes alone are bad news b his gang're ridin' with 'em, that's double tr

49

people headin' west all the while, without a good guide they'd never make it. Lots die, fever and Injuns.'

Adele clasped Nicola to her, even Ben was looking scared. Mountain men and wild tribes were fascinating in books, in real life they were scary. Blair thought, this guy's some kind of over-the-top Wild West enthusiast; there was probably a centre somewhere not too far away that took in these nutters, let 'em play out their fantasies. This was all going a bit far, but for the moment, he'd humour the man who called himself Sage.

Sage pulled a wry face, spat on the floor. 'Jesus, you drink beaver piss? This ain't cawfee!'

'It's instant.'

'Whassat?'

'Never mind. You'd better go and check that your dudes are all right. With Blackfoot and renegades at large you never know what might have happened to them.'

'You're right,' Sage took another swallow of Jenco. 'Fact is, I'm gonna bring 'em here. Best we're all together.'

'I . . . er . . . I don't think there's room,' Adele spoke falteringly. 'There's nowhere to sleep, we don't have enough food and . . .'

'Lady,' he regarded her almost piously, 'what that lot've bin through this past week, this ol' cabin'll be like paradise. They bin sleepin' rough, eatin' whatever I could ketch, mostly snared rabbits. Mighty tasty. Once I got a buck with an arrow, daren't risk gunfire. Fires had to be small and hidden, put out when the cookin' was done so it was cold nights. All they drank was water outa streams and they complained like glory! They'll love it here, you see if they don't. You come on one of the trains that got attacked by Injuns?'

'No-oo, we came by automobile.'

'Automobile? You mean trains? But the railroad ain't got nowhere near these parts yet.'

God, this guy really played the trapper game!

'I reckon you come on one o' them wagon trains guided by Koot, cain't be no other explanation. Or one of his men, don't matter which. In which case I'm awful sorry for you but I don't understand how you're still alive. Your scalps should be drying round a brave's waist and the wolves oughta be gnawin' the flesh off'n your purty bones. You bin lucky but, me knowin' what's out there in them woods, your luck cain't last much longer. Still, you're sure born lucky 'cause old Sage turned up just when you needed him most and them Injuns is scared o' Sage, he's scalped one or two o' them in his time.' He laughed, a hollow sound that seemed to add to the icy atmosphere.

'Mommy?' Nicola's whisper seemed louder than if she'd shouted.

'It's all right, darling. There isn't anybody else out in the woods, it's all a game of make-believe.'

'Mommy . . . *that is the man who was in my bedroom.*'

Blair found himself believing his daughter. Somehow you'd believe anything right now. Maybe it was all a nightmare, they'd wake up soon.

'It's Koot what's slaughtering the wagon trains, with the help o' the Kiotes.' Sage appeared not to have heard Nicola's accusation. 'Guess you don't know about the Kiotes, p'raps I'd better tell you, not that it'll make any difference. Wal, there was a Blackfoot medicine man, Black Bear, who discovered that the evil powers were greater'n the good ones. The Evil One'd help him whereas Manitou wouldn't. So Black Bear got some of the Blackfoot and Gros Ventres braves together, convinced 'em he'd make 'em invincible, immortal. So they broke away from their tribes, called themselves the Kiotes. They did some real terrible things to their prisoners, mebbe I'd best not go into that with the young girl here. Story goes that one day they captured this army scout, Koot, did things to him which I'd best not tell you, neither. Koot died under the torture but Black Bear reckoned he could raise him up from the dead. And he did just that, had him walkin' and talkin', and killin'. Made him a deal in return for his new life, Koot would hang around the forts, wait for wagons to roll in lookin' for a guide to take them on the last and most dangerous stage of their journey. These fancy folk from back east fell over theirselves to hire Koot, he was the real genuine article.'

He's crazy, Blair decided, stark raving mad! He's no play actor from a centre, he's probably escaped from some prison for the mentally insane. Probably a psychopath on the run. He'd shoot Sage if he had to, the guy probably had the strength of three men, there might be no other way.

'Koot led the wagons into a Kiote ambush. He made hisself

real rich lootin' money, the Kiotes took valuables, horses and guns. And prisoners.' Sage grinned. 'Koot was gettin' too well known around the outposts, so he gathered together other whites – drunks from the bars, outlaws on the run. Together, the Injuns and the renegades are an army, maybe fifty of 'em. And the only thing they squabble over is the wimmin!'

Adele paled in the shadows which had crept out of the corners now that the fire was dying down. She didn't like the way Sage's dark eyes ran up and down her.

'Take a tip from me, lady.' Sage wasn't smiling now. 'If'n it gets to it, and Koot or Black Bear looks like gettin' their hands on you, turn a pistol on yourself or put a knife into your heart. That way it'll be quick, and whatever they does to you after won't matter, 'cause you won't know nothin' 'bout it!'

'This is all nonsense!' Adele spoke as forcibly as she could but there was no hiding the tremor in her voice.

'T'ain't!' Sage snapped. 'You don't believe me but you'll see for yoursel'.' He belched loudly. 'The sooner I get them folks back here, the better. Black Bear and Koot'll pick up ma trail as easy as I'd read the Bible.'

He half turned towards the door, checked when he found himself staring down the barrel of the Browning. 'Now, that's a right unfriendly way to treat a guest, mister.'

'Maybe,' Blair was tight-lipped, 'but when somebody walks out of the night, starts talking about Injuns and renegades, a man can't be too careful.'

'Yep, s'right.' Sage relaxed; the others had the impression that beneath those animal-skin clothes he was like a coiled spring, ready to unleash himself without warning. 'I like a man who's alert, have to be that way myself. Now, if you'll take a tip from me, you'll bar the door after me, douse those lights and be ready to let us back in when we return. And if the Kiotes show up, keep on shootin' but save enough for yerselves. Don't let 'em take yuh alive.'

Blair's skin was prickling all over. Once this guy was outside, there was no way he was getting back in again. Maybe he'd just wander off into the forest, get sidetracked by some other fantasy.

'Nice to have met you . . . Sage.'

'I'll be back shortly, and don't ferget what I telled yuh.'

53

Blair stood in the open doorway, watched the other go. A tall man of indeterminable age; easy, loping steps as he headed to where the pack horse stood heavily laden in a patch of moonlight.

The moon was just about full, a silver ball in a velvet sky, flooding the landscape with its sinister, ethereal light.

Blair shivered, he was cold but for some reason he was compelled to watch. There was something not quite right out there. Not just the rusted station wagon with its perished tyres, not the forest with its huge age-old trees that hadn't been there yesterday.

Something else . . .

Sage reached his horse, swung up into the saddle with the ease of a practised rider, kicked his mount's flanks. It moved forward, picked out a trail that was invisible to the human eye.

A silhouette, man and beast. That was when a cry escaped the medic's lips, realization of what it was that had troubled him. Now it made him rigid with a terror that defied disbelief of everything that the mountain man had told him.

For neither horse nor rider threw a shadow on the brightly moonlit ground.

Eight

'It's all a load of garbage.' Blair hoped that he looked composed by the time he returned to the kitchen. 'He's crazy as a . . .'

'Koot?' Adele tried to make a joke out of it for Nicola's sake.

'The whole thing's a fantasy, a fabrication.' He did his best to make it sound convincing. And failed. 'The local hobo, probably lives in a cave in the forest, scares the shit out of all the tourists and gets a buzz from it. But apart from that, he's quite harmless.'

'He came into my bedroom last night,' Nicola insisted. 'I know it was him because he looked the same. And he *smelled* the same.'

'Unwashed people smell much of a muchness.' At all costs Blair had to allay the child's fears. 'He's just making a tolerably good job of it.'

'Looked real enough to me.' Ben slipped the shells out of the twenty and hoped his father didn't notice.

'Some folks get their kicks out of modern war-gaming.' Blair glared angrily at his son in the candlelight. 'They dress up as soldiers, fight battles, relive Vietnam. Their guns fire different-coloured dyes. A splot in the face with red and you're dead and out of the game, blue on the arm or leg and you're wounded, deduct two points. Or whatever. Overgrown kids. We used water pistols when I was a kid. Sage is doing his own war-gaming, living out his own fantasies. We just have to ignore him.'

'Wolves, and now Injuns and renegades. It's all just too real to dismiss, Blair.' Adele almost gave way to her despair.

'Whatever's happened, the storm triggered it off.' He sank down into a chair, propped the shotgun between his knees. 'I can't explain how or why, just that it did. If everything hadn't aged so, I'd say Sage's shelter had been blown down and forced him to look for alternative accommodation.' But that didn't explain the deterioration and the wolves.

'It was a real Hawken.' Ben's fear was temporarily forgotten. 'Real pistols, too. Fifty-calibres. They weren't replicas.'

Trust Ben to notice.

'We gotta find a way outa here tomorrow, Blair.'

'We'll find one.' Again he attempted to sound more confident than he felt. 'We'll make an early start, soon after daylight. Christ, if we just keep walking we've *gotta* come out someplace.' *Unless we get lost and go round in circles again like we did today. The Yellowstone is real big country.* 'But we have to stay here for the rest of tonight, try to get some sleep. I'll keep watch if it makes you feel any easier.'

'Sage'll be back, I just know it,' Adele muttered, 'and, like as not, he'll bring those folks with him he talked about.'

They lapsed into silence. Nicola fell asleep against Adele, she was too exhausted to remain awake any longer. Ben's head fell slowly forward, jerked back up suddenly. He was fighting drowsiness but it would beat him in the end. Adele might risk a catnap, she promised herself that it wouldn't be any more than a doze.

Something hit the outside of the board that Blair had fixed over the broken window.

An impact that splintered the rotting woodwork, cracked it; a force that tore it from its temporary fitting, sent it crashing into the room.

Adele was instantly awake, pulled Nicola to her. Ben shied, flung up an arm to shield his face. Blair came up out of his chair, swung the Browning up to cover the open, jagged square of bright moonlight. His finger hooked around the trigger, he was only a half-squeeze away from loosing off a round.

'What's that?' It was a stupid question to ask but Adele didn't feel stupid, just scared to hell.

'The board fell in.' Blair eyed it warily, there was something protruding from the shattered square of chipboard. 'Maybe it was too warped to stand the pressure where I'd jammed it in the frame. Or perhaps the wind's got up again.'

Outside it was still and silent.

A moonbeam slanted in through the open space, fell on the

board. The upright shaft was still quivering, trimmed feathers shimmered in the half-light, bright colours scintillating.

'It's . . . it's an . . . *arrow*!'

They all stared at it, transfixed, a length of willow, tipped with instant death, flighted by feathers dyed red and yellow. There was no mistaking the force with which it had hit and demolished the window covering.

Blair was the first to move. Three paces took him to the opening in the wall; he flattened himself to one side, peered out cautiously. The open ground between the cabin and the grove was bathed in bright silver. The station wagon seemed to have sunk even lower on its corroded chassis. Elsewhere there was no cover until the shadows of the willows began. Nothing moved.

'Injuns, Dad?' Ben's tone was a mixture of fear and fascination. 'It has to be.'

'Don't be bloody stupid!' Blair spoke angrily in a low voice. 'The only natives in these parts are those who run the Little Bighorn and they don't go round shooting arrows. They're civilized. Anyway, they're too far from here. You can take it from me, that was Mr Sage up to his crazy tricks again, trying to make out there's non-existent Kiotes howling for our blood. Damned fool, he could've injured one of us. If he shows his face round here again . . .'

A shadow parted from the dark silhouette of the automobile, took shape. A human, bent double as it sprinted across open ground in the direction of the tree in long bounds; it wore some kind of close-fitting headgear that was woven into thick curled spikes like a deformed steer.

'Jesus alive!' Blair pushed the gun barrel through the opening, worked a shell into the breech. The man was closer than the wolves had been, an easy target for a sportsman who could drop a bounding buck. His finger rested on the trigger but he did not take a pressure. Because it would have been first-degree murder.

'There he goes, Dad!' Ben had squeezed up alongside his father, he was just able to see over the broken sill. 'Look, he's got a bow! Shoot 'im!'

'Crazy as Sage is, I'd be in mighty trouble with the law if I blasted him in the back.' Blair lowered his gun.

'That wasn't Sage, Dad. No way!'

Jesus, that boy contradicted everything you said! 'It was him, 'cause there isn't anybody else around. He's tried to scare us with his stories, now he's taken to firing arrows at the cabin. Maybe, though, I should've put a shot over him, just to warn him.'

But it was too late now, the running figure had made it to the edge of the grove, the shadows had swallowed him up as if he'd never existed.

'It looked like an Injun to me.' Ben turned back into the room. Adele was cowering over by the dead stove with Nicola.

'Blair, we can't take much more.'

'I should've shot him.' Blair closed his eyes momentarily. 'Maybe in the legs with small birdshot, except that I was loaded up with heavies.'

'It wasn't Sage, Dad, I swear it. That guy was much younger, smaller, he could run like a buck. He was—'

'*Shaddup, for Christ's sake!*' The doctor's nerve was close to cracking, back where it had been before they had come out here. He took a deep breath. 'I'm sorry, Ben, but I wish you wouldn't keep on, you're frightening your mother and Nicola.' And me.

Ben fell silent. Blair thought about boarding up the window again but the piece of wood was smashed, he'd have to go outside and hunt for another. He decided to leave it for now but they'd better sit clear of the opening in case another arrow came hurtling through. That madman was capable of anything.

Except that he knew full well it had not been Sage. Ben was right, Blair had known from the moment he first set eyes on the running figure, he'd tried in vain to convince himself otherwise. It was as if they were all going mad.

'Well, we're out of kindling and nobody's going outside. Let's wrap ourselves up in some blankets and sit it out till dawn.'

Daylight seemed as far off as ever, sometimes Blair thought that the sky was lightening but it was only the moonlight. He'd got out of the habit of checking with his watch, two fifteen was having a demoralizing effect upon him.

He could have used some coffee but he'd have to wait for the dawn. Then he'd get a fire going, make a quick brew, and they'd head right out of this place. Whatever happened, they would not be returning.

'Dad, I can hear somebody coming!'

Blair stiffened, listened. Ben's hearing was sharp, he'd picked up a distant sound. *Horses' hooves, muffled as if they'd been covered to deaden the noise.* More of a vibration than a sound.

'I guess Sage has come back.' Blair sighed loudly. 'Well, he can stay out there, sleep in the automobile. Or what's left of it. Don't go near the window, Ben.' *Because I'm scared to hell of what we might see outside.*

There were four silhouettes against the silvery background. The man in front, leading the overladen horse, was undoubtedly Sage. Another, much smaller figure, led a second mount upon which two figures sat side-saddle, holding grimly on to the reins. They were unmistakably female, crinkly long dresses swayed in time to the animals' movements.

'He's brought his party back, like he said he would,' Blair whispered.

'I'm not having them in here!' Adele rose stiffly, defiantly. 'I don't care who they are, their misfortunes are no different from ours. There's . . . something *wrong* with Sage, and I don't mean just plumb crazy.' She shuddered. 'And I don't expect the others will be any different.'

The party was closer now, past the station wagon; they did not appear to notice it. You had to listen hard to pick up the slight noise made by the horses' hooves.

'Hold it right there!' Blair poked the barrel out of the window. 'Not a step closer, Sage. You could've killed one of us with that damned arrow.'

'Arrer?' Sage stood full in the moonbeam, every detail of his bearded features visible. His eyes seemed to glow for a second, it was probably a reflection. 'What arrer?'

'The one you fired at the window. You're not coming inside again, not after that.'

Sage gave the impression of uncoiling, a tenseness that brought every muscle to full stretch. He half turned, scanned the open space behind him. His companions huddled, one of the women gave an audible gasp of terror.

'Damn Kiotes've found us and Koot won't be fur behind.' The long rifle swung in an arc towards the darkness of the distant willows. 'They'll be watchin' us. Git that door open, mister, we're bringing the hosses in, too, all our supplies are loaded on 'em.'

'You're staying right where you are.' Blair elevated the barrel, prepared to let off a warning shot if the others advanced any further. 'We don't want you in here any more than we want your fictitious Indians.'

Sage appeared not to have heard. His grip tightened on the reins, the horse was tired but it responded. And that was when Blair Lund squeezed the trigger.

The night erupted with the shattering explosion, magnified inside the cabin so that Adele's and Nicola's scream went unheard. Outside, the second horse shied, spilling its burden in a heap of fluttering dresses, bolting even as it shed its load. The small man was helping the women to their feet, urging them to hurry.

Sage had whirled, his back towards the cabin, a cougar at bay, rifle at the ready. 'Git in the cabin, bust the door down if'n they won't open up!'

The far shadows moved, smaller ones detaching themselves from the huge black mass; figures that darted, crouched.

'*Kiotes!*' Sage had dropped to one knee, the long rifle belched vivid flame and villainous black smoke, a mighty report that trembled the walls of the shack.

One of the darting figures straightened up to its full height, Blair had a glimpse of a horned head thrown back, an upstretched arm loosing its grip on a long lance. The shape folded, crumpled, and sank from view.

The night air was filled with wild cries even before the echoes of the Hawken had died away, screams of rage that might have come from the fiery depths of hell itself. Shadows moved forward, were lost from sight.

Something whacked against the outer timbers, the occupants sensed its force, listened to it quivering and humming. Adele pulled Nicola to the floor, crouched over her. Ben was trying to load the twenty, a shell slipped from his fingers, bounced and rolled. He found another, there was a metallic click as the breech closed.

Blair had the stock of the Browning to his shoulder; he sighted an advancing shape; it vanished before he could squeeze the trigger.

Somehow Sage had forced the door, maybe the strength of

the pack horse. The other three were crowding in behind him, the man struggled to force the door closed. The rusted bolt was shot home loudly.

'You gett'n away from that winder.' Sage pushed Blair to one side. 'If you cain't shoot with that pretty gun o' yours, help Jameson and the wimmin to load.' He had a heavy pistol in either hand, the hammers cocked loudly.

Over by the table the man called Jameson was struggling to reload the flintlock rifle. Blair saw that the other wore dark, tight-fitting clothes and a soiled white collar that identified him as a preacher. A wide-brimmed hat kept his features in shadow.

That stench was back even amidst the pungent aroma of burned powder, the interior of the cabin might have been the lair of some wild creature that habitually fouled its own quarters.

Sage's pistol bucked in his hand, the watchers heard his wild shriek of exultation, the killing cry of the hunter. 'Got the bastard!' A second shot thundered. 'Nother 'un, gimme the rifle.'

There was an open space of square moonlight as Sage turned to take the rifle from his companion. Blair spotted an advancing shape, a skin-clad figure approaching the veranda at a crouching run. He swung the shotgun, held the trigger back.

Four 00s crashed simultaneously, he was aiming for a chest shot. He saw the features for a moment, a painted wooden totem mask whose malevolence had given it life. A crazed expression of evil that never faltered even after the last shell had ejected.

Sage rested the long barrel on the sill, fired. The savage was thrown back, obscured from Blair's view by the ensuing smoke pall.

'Leave the shootin' to me, git loadin'!' the mountain man grunted. 'Didn't nobody ever teach yer to shoot? Too late to learn now.'

'The Lord will preserve us as He has done on several occasions lately.' The man at the table addressed his two female companions, handed the reloaded pistols to Sage, took the Hawken by the barrel. 'May He forgive me for aiding in the taking of human lives.'

'You learned well, preacher,' Sage cocked his weapons, turned back to the window, ''ceptin' that time when you rammed a double charge in ma rifle. Ma shoulder's still sore!' He gave a laugh.

Adele was regarding the newcomers with no small amount of curiosity. Their dresses were made from expensive cloth, the kind that only the wealthy could afford, though the fashion was a century or more out of date. The hems were mud-stained, snagged and torn. Fashionable or not, it was not the kind of attire to wear outside such places as New York or New Orleans.

She regarded their features, there was a similarity in the pertness of the noses, the shape of their mouths. They might have been sisters. The man was frail of stature, there was a pallidity about his complexion which bespoke a lifetime spent indoors.

'I'm Victoria.' The smaller one, with chestnut hair done up in a bun beneath her wide-brimmed hat, smiled nervously, nodded towards her companion, a taller woman with flaming red hair that was matted and straggled. 'This is Prudence. My cousin. James is my brother.'

'Pleased to meet you.'

'Rather it had been under different circumstances. Fleeing from savages and bad men seems to have become an occupational hazard. The wagon train was attacked, we were lucky to survive. We wouldn't have had it not been for Sage.'

'Like I said, one o' Koot's men guided 'em straight into an ambush,' Sage glanced back into the room, 'sixteen killed, tortured, scalped an'—' He checked himself as he noticed Nicola's horrified expression. 'Got these'n out, bin runnin' since. Takin' 'em to Fort Peck where they kin join up with another train but Koot's outguessed me on that. You think o' somethin', he's already thought of it. Mebbe we'll head south. If'n we get outa here, that is!' He laughed, the sound had Adele's stomach contracting.

This was madness. Blair reloaded the Browning. There weren't any tribes on the rampage these days, hadn't been since the turn of the century. And yet . . . he stared at the arrow embedded in that piece of wood, there was no denying the evidence.

'They've drawed back.' There was a hint of triumph,

boasting, in Sage's announcement from the window. 'Thought they'd mebbe surprise us with a rush, pulled off after a couple bit the dust. Back in the ol' days, Injuns never attacked at night, feared that if they got kilt their souls would get lost in the dark an' they'd never get to the happy huntin' grounds. That don't worry the Kiotes, they'd get kicked outa there anyway, probably have been. Their god, if'n you kin call him that, looks after his own!'

Adele shuddered. These people that Sage had brought back with him were as weird as he was. Like they'd been cut off from modern times, lived in the past. A sudden thought, one that was almost comforting. Maybe they belonged to some strange sect, she had read about such religious groups, folks who hid themselves away and worshipped in their own manner, had nothing to do with the outside world. Like Branch Davidians.

In which case she was going to keep her children as far away from them as possible, which would not be easy in the cramped confines of this ramshackle backwoods cabin.

'It's startin' to git light,' Sage grunted. 'If'n the Kiotes are goin' to attack, they'll do it soon before we kin see 'em too plain. There's a number o' tricks they might try. Or mebbe they'll just wait and starve us out. No tellin', they ain't like ordinary Injuns.'

Nine

'You from one of the wagon trains, too?' There was much more than a casualness about the way the woman called Victoria asked the question. Her expression, her narrowed eyes, were loaded with suspicion.

'Er . . . no.' Adele jerked out of her uneasy doze, saw that full daylight was streaming in through the window. She could see the others plainly now. 'We came by . . .' She hesitated, they must have seen the station wagon outside and they clearly did not know what it was. 'We came by our own transport.'

'Foolish and dangerous!' An admonishment. The other was staring at her fixedly, made Adele shudder. 'I never saw clothes like yours before, even back east. They're *men's* clothes! A woman should dress with dignity, know her place, even out here.'

'Oh, I see. I'm sorry.' Jesus, she hadn't meant to apologize, it just spilled out. 'We didn't bring anything else to wear.'

'Your children attend Sunday School?'

'Yes.' The lie came easy, it saved a lot of explanations.

'Good. The Lord is our only hope. James is travelling to convert the savages to Christianity. Once they turn to God, the looting and murdering will cease.'

'Ne'er a chance.' Sage chuckled, spat on the floor.

'A godless man,' Victoria's eyes blazed angrily, 'even though he does profess to read the Bible. I sometimes doubt it.'

'Saved ma life once.' The trapper turned around, tapped the square shape that bulged in the breast pocket of his hide jacket. 'Arrer got me right here. Woulda kilt me fer sure if I hadna had ma Bible. Tore through some o' the pages so's I cain't read 'em no more but it never so much as scratched ma skin.'

'The Lord saved your life in spite of your incessant profanities.' James spoke in a flat, expressionless voice. 'Thank Him for His great mercy each time you pray.'

'Mebbe I'll try this here prayin' one o' the days.' Sage's smoke-blackened features grinned.

'We shall all pray together shortly.' The preacher dusted at his clothes with thin white hands. 'If you choose not to join us, Mr Sage, then kindly desist from distracting us.'

'Better get that fire goin' so's we kin boil up some cawfee.' Sage stood up, stretched. 'I'll go fetch some kindling.'

A sudden neighing and stamping of hooves from the hallway reminded Adele that the horses were inside. There had not been so much as a snicker from them during the shooting. The stench of fresh dung filled the room as Sage went through into the hallway.

'Better graze and water 'em.' He began leading them outside. 'After we've had some cawfee I'm gonna slip out, do a recce. Mebbe when it gets dark agin we'll try and find a way through. Gotta see what's goin' on out there fust, though.'

They heard him out back gathering some dead branches which the storm had strewn across the open ground. Blair looked out through the window; it seemed as peaceful and as sunny a morning as any he'd ever seen. Almost normal, if you didn't know otherwise.

'Now, that's real cawfee, not like that puma piss o' yours.' Sage slurped his drink, broke wind loudly.

'Mr Sage!' James wagged a disapproving finger, pouted his thin lips. 'I shall be much obliged if you will kindly refrain from using crudities and obscenities. Especially as we have children in our midst.'

'I wuz brought up to cuss, never did nothin' different, preacher. Still, mebbe I'll try and say it nice 'n' quiet. Mebbe.'

'It would be appreciated if you'd try.' James seated himself on a chair in the corner, obviously with no wish to join in the conversation.

'We were planning on leaving as soon after daybreak as possible.' Blair saw that the first rays of morning sunshine were slanting in through the window. 'We need an early start. Yesterday we went round in a circle, ended up back here. Today we're planning to follow the outside of the forest in a westerly direction until we come to . . .'

'You'll end up at the foot of the mountain.' Sage threw back his head, laughed throatily. 'An' unless you're plannin' on a steep climb, mebbe three, four days, you won't get nowhere. 'Sides, you wouldn't get as fur as the mountains, Kiotes'd get yuh if Koot didn't beat 'em to it. Koot'd travel from here 'cross the Nevada desert an' back to get his paws on a purty white woman, that's one thing the Kiotes won't hand over after a raid. They got a dozen and one uses for wimmin afore they're through with 'em!'

Blair went cold and his guts knotted at the other's words. 'Maybe we could tag along with you now, Sage? You could see us clear of danger, set us on the right track.'

'Christ on a mule, no! Sorry, preacher, I cussed afore I could stop it, slipped out just the way it allus does. Nope, I cain't have nobody tagging along with me, the Kiotes'd smell us afore we got clear. If'n we travel together, we go after dark. All of us. Me, I'm gonna take a look-see, maybe work out a trail we'll take tonight, hev to play it the way it comes. A man cain't make plans where Kiotes and Koot is concerned.'

'How long will you be gone, Sage?'

'Agin, can't rightly say. Might be a coupla hours, might be till dark afore I can git back. Git a bunch o' Injuns between me and here, with no way round or through 'em, and yuh have to stay put till they move. Expect me when you see me, and don't cry no tears if'n you don't, 'cause that'll mean ol' Sage weren't clever enough for 'em.'

Adele's mouth was dry. She took a long swig of strong black coffee. Ugh! It might rot your guts but it'd sure keep you awake! Suddenly the prospect of not having Sage around was disconcerting, you found yourself relying on him in spite of . . . everything.

'I'll be leavin' now.' Sage stood up, looked at each of them in turn, settled on Blair. 'Guess you're in charge, Blair, whilst I'm gone. Damned if I kin work out that gun o' your'n, it don't have no powder nor shot, just them things you feed it. It ain't ever likely to do no harm to a Kiote nor any other Injun. Still, it makes a bang, it'll sure skeer 'em, keep 'em from rushin' yuh.' He moved towards the door. 'I'll go on foot, travel faster 'n' quieter that way. When the sun gets low in the sky, bring the hosses back inside. With luck, I could be back by then. Pray for me, reverend, 'long with everybody else.'

James put his fingertips together, closed his eyes. When he opened them again there was no sign of the man called Sage. 'May the Lord go with him.'

66

'I doubt very much whether the Lord would want to!'

Victoria pulled a wry face. 'He smells, he takes the Lord's name in vain and . . .'

'We are all His children. If we repent, our sins will be forgiven us.'

'Sage shows no signs of repenting, James, and I doubt he ever will.'

'Give him time.' The preacher was an inveterate optimist. 'He will join the fold. But we must be patient, we cannot manage without him, our lives depend upon him. God moves in a mysterious way, it is Him who has sent Sage to save us, we must not spurn His servant.'

'Huh!' Victoria turned away, piqued.

'They're weird,' Nicola whispered, her ear up against Adele's. 'They frighten me.'

'We'll be leaving soon.' Adele kissed the girl's forehead. 'Tonight, maybe sooner.'

'I'm going to have a look at the generator.' Blair scraped his chair back, the prospect of spending the whole day cooped up with these strangers was not a pleasant thought. They would probably bicker all day.

'Don't, Blair. It's dangerous out there. Anyway, if we're leaving, it doesn't matter whether the generator's working or not.'

'I'm just curious to know why it failed. Ben, you can stand by the window, watch the front. I'll keep an eye on the back whilst I'm out there.'

Ben scrambled up, grabbed the twenty. Even in the midst of a crisis his fantasies were becoming reality; he had a gun, he was posted as lookout.

'And don't load that gun. Keep some shells in your hand, just in case.'

'Sure, Dad.'

The sunshine had a spring warmth to it but in the shadow of the cabin it was icy cold. Blair turned up the collar of his hunting jacket, glanced around. The horses were grazing peacefully enough. He stared across at the grove. Nothing moved, no doves perched on the leafless branches, no cawing crows circled. He shrugged his shoulders, they were probably out feeding. All the same, he was uneasy.

The generator was housed in a ramshackle lean-to, a motor

layered with thick dust, a jumble of wires patched up with insulating tape that was furling. It had a dead look about it.

The tank was half full, so it hadn't run out of kerosene. Maybe the wiring had shorted through lack of maintenance, but Blair abandoned the idea of investigating further, the contraption would need an engineer to get it going again. The fault probably had nothing to do with the storm, it was just a coincidence.

He started, whirled round, knew instinctively that somebody stood behind him.

'I'm sorry if I startled you.' The younger of the two women stood there, her attractive features flushed with embarrassment. Her hat was gone, her fiery red hair glinted in a stray sunbeam that had encroached on the shadows. Yet in spite of her nervousness there was something about her that had Blair's heartbeat stepping up a gear, his pulses racing. Dishevelled and trail-worn from weeks spent trekking through the wilderness, she radiated a loveliness that no man could have failed to notice; alluring in a strange way.

'You made me jump.' He smiled. 'I guess I was too busy trying to work out what's wrong with this contraption.'

'I must apologize for my companions.' She moved a step closer. 'All James and Victoria think about is spreading the Word. I wish I hadn't allowed myself to be persuaded to accompany them. I wish I could go back home. Without them.'

'We should be leaving before long.' He was aware that she had moved closer, her eyes were gazing up into his own. 'Sage'll be back before long.'

'I'd like to go with you . . . Blair.'

He swallowed. 'We have to get away from here first.'

'Will that *ever* be possible?' It was the way she said it, the hopelessness, like she had some sort of premonition, that started a shiver in his spine.

'I reckon so. This is the craziest situation I've ever been in, I don't understand what's happened but there has to be an explanation. There aren't any wild natives left, haven't been for a century at least.'

'The country's crawling with them, from Boston to here and beyond.' Her eyes were wide with incredulity. 'You must know that, you've trekked here like us. Every trail is fraught with danger, Indians and bandits.'

'Oh, sure. I'd forgotten.' She was crazy like the others. They must've escaped from some institution. But it didn't explain what had happened in this small valley.

'My parents deprived me of the thing I want most in life.' She was right up against him now. 'A man. And children. I should have left but I didn't have the courage. My parents died of smallpox when I was fifteen, I went to live with Father's brother and his wife. They were obsessed with religion, indoctrinated James and Victoria. I almost got like them. Not quite. It isn't too late but there's not much time left. Oh, Blair!'

Suddenly her arms were around him, her full lips were seeking his, finding them, crushing them, her slender body trembling and heaving with an emotion that had been denied her.

He sensed a pleasant, familiar sensation. Then, suddenly, he recoiling, fighting to extricate himself from her embrace.

Oh, God, her body, her full lips, were as cold as January ice. And her breath was foul, as if something inside her was in the final stages of decomposition.

'Blair, what's the matter?' She clutched at him, her eyes blazed the anger of rejection.

'Nothing.' It was all he could do not to push her away.

'Am I so repulsive to the opposite sex that you cannot bear my body against yours?'

'It's not that, not that at all,' he lied, his instinct to flee from her.

'What, then?'

'I have a wife, a family. I'm happily married.'

'A slovenly bitch and a couple of brats!' She spat. 'At least give me what I want, Blair. Put me in child!'

'There's only a wall between us and your cousins.'

'I don't care, I've done with them and their bigotry. I want to go back in there and scream at them that I'm no longer pure, that I'm pregnant with a bastard child. I want to pay them back for what they've done to me!'

There was something terrifying about her, more so than ever Sage had been. An evil that festered, spawned. 'Look, this is neither the time nor the place. Let's get outa here first, then—'

'Get . . . *out* . . . of . . . here?' She repeated his words slowly, threw back her head and gave a hysterical laugh. 'Are you mad? Don't you understand? None of us will ever leave here. We are destined to remain in this place for ever!'

Her words hit him like a physical blow, reeled him back against the ageing wall. The shriek of a maniac but he believed her. She told the truth. None of them would ever leave here.

'Maybe we can talk about this another time, Prudence.' His lower lip trembled.

'There will be no other time!' She was beside herself with a terrible fury, tore at the front of her dress. He shied at the sight of full breasts that were shaped with youth, yet the flesh wrinkled with age, nipples that had dulled from pink to brown but were erect with the arousal that trembled her body. 'Put me in child now, there will not be another opportunity!'

No, I don't want to see you naked! She stank of an exhumed corpse.

'Prudence!'

She started, wrapped her torn dress around her as a figure darkened the entrance to the generator shed, white features that were near skeletal beneath the wide brim of the black hat. A clerical collar glowed luminously.

'I was . . . talking to . . . Dr Lund, James.' Prudence's voice quavered, the fury was replaced by fear of the one who ruled over her very existence.

'*I . . . heard . . . you!*' The preacher was shaking, holding on to an upright to support himself. 'Whore, you have shamed your family; the merciful Lord will cast you into hell so that the flames will destroy your vile body! Get thee hence from this refuge, darken not our threshold again!'

Blair heard a sob, Prudence turned, pushed her way past James and then she was fleeing out across the open ground, her torn dress billowing in her wake.

'Stop her!' Blair found his way barred by the preacher, a grim figure in black with folded arms, fury clouding his pallid expression. 'For God's sake, man, there's savages out there who'll—'

'Take not the name of the Lord thy God in vain.' The reply was rhetoric.

'Get out of the fucking way!' Blair pushed him, the other staggered back. Tottered and clutched at a frail support.

'How dare you, sir!'

But Blair wasn't listening. He pushed past James, ran out.

Into the open. Prudence was perhaps a hundred yards away and running across the rough ground with an amazing fleetness of foot, her skirt lifted in case it should entwine around her feet.

'Stop! Prudence, come back!'

If she heard him, she gave no sign. Blair paused only to pick up the Browning, then he was running in pursuit. He thought he heard the missionary calling after him but he ignored the shouts. Damn it, once she reached the forest there was no telling what might happen to her. At the very best she would get lost, at worst . . .

He was gaining on her, he had maybe closed the gap to fifty yards. He was breathless, he was accustomed to walking and climbing but it was a long time since he had last sprinted. His chest felt as if it would burst, his lungs hurt.

Then, all around the fleeing woman, the scrub bushes came to life. They moved, rose up, were cast to one side to reveal bronzed human shapes, dressed in crudely-fashioned hide clothes. Jet-black hair had been pleated, twisted and waxed, so that it resembled horns sprouting from their heads.

Kiotes!

Blair pulled up instinctively. The Kiotes, their faces painted hideously, snarling like wild animals, closed in on Prudence. Blair heard her screams as she was dragged, lifted. Then they were jogging, carrying her as they might have transported a canoe over dry land from one watercourse to another.

The twelve-gauge automatic came up to his shoulder, the sight moved along them, kept pace with the leading brave. Blair could have squeezed, mown them down, they were ideally lined up for a burst of five buckshot loads. But he held his fire because of Prudence, he would undoubtedly have injured her.

Fuck it. They were getting further and further away. From somewhere he called upon a hidden reserve of energy, started after them. Maybe if they set her down he might be able to pick off one standing furthest from her, and the rest might scatter.

They did not lower her, never once did they pause in that steady mile-eating trot, even when they reached the outskirts of the big forest. She appeared to be lying limply across their joined hands; she had probably fainted with terror.

It's your fault, Blair Lund. If you'd given her what she wanted, she wouldn't have run off. The thought almost had him feeling guilty. It also made him want to throw up.

He glanced down, looked up again, and then there was no sign of Prudence and her kidnappers. That dark, forbidding forest had swallowed them up. Blair increased his pace, reached the place where they had disappeared.

A narrow track, thickly carpeted with decades of rotting leaf mould, led through the mighty trees; twisting, winding, sometimes turning back upon itself. Blair followed it cautiously, gun at the ready. At the first sign of a Kiote, he would shoot. And keep shooting.

But there was no sign, no sound. It was as though captors and captive no longer existed, had merely been a figment of his distraught imagination. And he almost counted that as a possibility.

The trail veered sharply to the right, beyond the bend was screened from him. He stopped, cursed beneath his breath; the path divided, forked in separate directions. Here the ground was spongy, a multitude of animal tracks where deer and rabbits followed it to their favourite watering hole. The Kiotes' passage would be clear enough, their footprints would indicate plainly in which direction they had gone.

Even as Blair knelt down, a thought crossed his mind: the tribesmen had seemed totally unaware of pursuit, they had not even appeared to notice him out there on the open ground. Maybe they were too preoccupied with their capture. All the same, his skin prickled.

He stared, examined the churned mud and decomposing leaves. Only too well he recognized deer slots, he had tracked them often enough before; rabbits, too, how they hopped instead of running when they were undisturbed. Claw marks where crows had alighted to peck the ground in search of insects.

But there was not a human footprint to be seen.

Ten

'There wasn't a sign of her,' Blair told the others. He felt guilty as if he was making excuses for his own failure to find Prudence. 'No tracks, nothing. I daren't risk going any further into the forest and I couldn't be away from here any longer.' *She's gone and we won't see her again.*

Adele's look was one of profound relief at her husband's safe return. Blair was sitting over by the window, the barrels of the twenty resting on the remains of the sill. Nicola was cross-legged on a folded blanket, looking numbed with shock. There was no way of telling what the long-term effects on her might be.

James and Victoria were seated on chairs in the far corner, stoic looks on their faces, not so much as glancing at their companions, like sulking children who had been refused a request. They did not speak, pretended that they had not heard. They had no further interest in their cousin's fate.

The horses had been brought into the hallway, stood quietly, maybe sensed what was expected of them. Blair was relieved that there had been no hysteria within the cabin. Prudence was gone, and that was that. He preferred not to think what the Kiotes might do to her.

'Sage isn't back yet.' Ben stated the obvious, a sentry whose duty was to report to his commanding officer immediately upon the other's return.

'It isn't dusk yet.' Optimism was an important ingredient of their predicament, morale must be boosted. Dusk was barely a half-hour away, already the shadow of the mountains was beginning to creep across the floor of the valley. 'There's still time. He said he might have to wait until after dark.'

'I know he won't come back.' Adele spoke her thoughts aloud. 'We'd best leave on our own.'

'Not at this time of day!' Blair snapped forcefully. 'And

73

not without Sage to guide us. We got lost in the daylight the last time, we wouldn't stand a chance in the dark.'

'I can't stand another night here!' Adele wrung her hands despairingly. 'It's always tomorrow, and tomorrow never comes.' She stole a glance at the preacher and his sister; they had not moved, showed no sign that they had even heard, were just staring blankly at the wall. *'For God's sake, Blair, what's going to happen tonight? I can't stand it here a minute longer, I'm going out of my mind!'*

She was at breaking point; he knew that she couldn't hold on to her sanity much longer, she might have flipped by morning.

'Adele.' He walked across to her, spoke soothingly as he crouched down, took her hand in his own. 'I promise you that we'll go tomorrow, right after daybreak, no matter what. I give you my word. OK?'

'All right,' she nodded, fighting back her tears. She was only managing to hold on for the children's sake.

'Vengeance is mine, saith the Lord.' James spoke suddenly in a booming voice. 'The Lord hath given and the Lord hath taken away. Prudence has been punished for her sins. It is God's will.'

'I thought you preached forgiveness.' Blair was tight-lipped, angry. 'It was *you* who drove her from here, preacher. Her blood will be on your conscience for ever. I just hope you can live with it.'

'My conscience is clear. The Lord hath punished the evil-doer.'

Adele glanced at her husband questioningly. Perhaps later, if ever they found themselves alone again, he would tell her why Prudence had fled the cabin. They had all crowded to the window and witnessed the awful scene, Adele had screamed for Blair to come back but he probably had not even heard her.

After that James had returned indoors, conversed in whispered tones with his sister; they had shown no remorse for Prudence. It was almost as if they were party to a plot to murder her.

'Neither Victoria nor I will have any regrets if Sage does not return,' James announced in that same cold, expressionless tone. 'The Lord will not allow Sage's blasphemies to go unpunished.'

'Now, just you listen to me.' Blair whirled on them. 'I'm getting sick and tired of you two. *I* hired this cabin for a hunting vacation, you're here as my guests. Either you stop carping or you can leave this very minute. In other words, shut up! My family and I are leaving first thing in the morning. If you choose to accompany us, feel free. I can't say you'll be welcome.'

'*Nobody will leave this valley, ever!*' James turned away, stamped on the floorboards.

Nicola was doing her best not to cry. Nobody spoke because there was nothing left to say.

'Somebody's coming!' Ben's shout broke the uneasy silence, had Blair rushing for the window. '*It's Sage!*'

It was the mountain man all right, there was no mistaking his long stride, the way he carried the heavy Hawken and all its accessories without any obvious effort. He never seemed to tire.

'Woods is crawlin' with Kiotes.' Sage leaned his rifle up against the wall, slurped the coffee Blair handed him. 'Koot's lot are camped about a mile north o' here; either he's leavin' it to the Injuns to face our gunfire or else he's plannin' to come and take the wimmin on his own. Cain't tell, but none o' them seems in no hurry. Mebbe they're jest waitin', gonna starve us out. Whichever, tain't gonna be no campfire knees-up gettin' outa here. I'll hev to try and think o' something. Bin thinkin' all the way back but so far I ain't come up with nothin'. On ma own, it'd be no problem, damn Injuns and renegades'd never know I'd bin and gone, but with a party o'—'

'We have to go!' Adele almost screamed at him. 'Blair promised me that we'd leave at daylight at the latest.'

'Up to him, ma'am. Me, I'll go when I think we stand the best chance. Changed ma mind 'bout 'em rushin' us, they'd've done it by now if they was goin' to. So long as we've got food and water, powder and shot, they ain't gonna risk it. We could hole up here for months if we had enough supplies, and they ain't in no hurry, neither.'

'*No!*'

Sage shrugged his huge shoulders and Blair told him about Prudence.

'Whatever they planned on doin' to her, they'll've done it

by now.' The trapper showed no emotion. 'Thet's one woman that Koot won't git, fer sure.'

'That's a horrible thing to say.' Adele clenched her fists.

'Jest the truth, ma'am. Now, it's getting' dark, the moon'll be an hour or so later tonight so I'll take the fust watch. Ol' Sage has got eyesight like a huntin' owl, the dark don't worry him none.' He laughed. 'Don't need to see 'em, I kin smell 'em a hundred yards off, more if'n the wind's blowin' right.'

James and Victoria had not moved, had not even shifted their positions. Adele thought that perhaps they were praying.

'What's that hanging from your belt, Mr Sage?' Ben had been eyeing the object curiously ever since the mountain man had returned. It looked like the skin of some kind of animal, perhaps one that Sage had caught and killed out in the forest. Kind of hairy, it didn't look much like a beaver skin, it was too small, anyway. Maybe some other species.

'Oh, *thet*!' Sage lifted it with his hand, the underside of the thing released a droplet of blood; it was clearly freshly killed. 'Thet's a young Kiote brave, son, one that wuz learnin' his woodcraft, and not learnin' too fast, neither. Set with his back towards me, never heered me a-coming downwind of him. Never heered me at all, in fact. Allus takes the scalp, there's sometimes skin buyers from back east that'll give you as much as a beaver fur for 'em. Guess they sell 'em as souvenirs to the city folks.'

Adele retched, she was glad that she had not eaten all day. She wouldn't want to now. Most of all, she was grateful that Nicola had fallen asleep again.

Sage finished his coffee, moved across to the window. Outside it was almost full dark.

They sat in silence – nobody felt like talking even had there been anything left to discuss. Adele was close to tears, it was as if Sage was content to hole up here for as long as their supplies lasted. James and Victoria seemed to have resigned themselves to a lengthy siege. *It was as though the others did not want to go. As if, for some reason, they were prevented from doing so, that some inexplicable force trapped them here.*

But Blair had promised faithfully that they would leave first thing in the morning and she would hold him to his word. They would be moving on tomorrow, that was a certainty. She found some consolation and comfort in her own determination.

Something scraped, rasped, over by the window. In the light from the tiny flame Adele saw Sage's hairy features, his cheeks hollowed as he sucked on a blackened pipe until he got it drawing to his satisfaction. A strong pungent aroma filled the enclosed space, wafted by the draught from the open window.

'I hate smoking.' Nicola exaggerated a cough. 'It's bad for you, bad for people who breathe other folks' smoke, too.'

'Cain't do without terbaccer.' Sage smiled across at her. 'Even the Injuns smoke it. A lonely man's friend, a cold man's fire, a hungry man's food. Read thet in a book once. It's true. Allus had my pipe, ever since I wuz a boy. Never did me no harm. In fact, it's done me a lotta good. Never heered o' anybody complainin' 'bout terbaccer smoke before. 'Ceptin' him and her.' He jerked a thumb in the direction of the missionary and his sister. 'They've gotten the idea it's sinful, reckon that if'n the Lord'd intended you to smoke, he'd've growed you a chimney outa your head!' He laughed. 'Me, I like it as it is, nothin' to beat a good pipe o' terbaccer and to hell with anybody who objects!' He blew out a cloud of smoke in protest.

'It stinks!' Nicola was in one of her petulant moods.

'Smells real good,' Sage humoured her, 'specially on a frosty morning when you're downwind of it. Mighty good to chew, too, s'long as you knows how to spit.'

'It's disgusting!' Nicola turned her head away. 'It's worse than Daddy's cigars.'

'Ceegars is gentlemen's smokes.' The mountain man puffed hard on his pipe. 'I sometimes gets one given me at the tradin' post when I'm sellin' furs. They thinks that mebbe they'll get 'em cheaper if they gives me a ceegar. Sooner have ma pipe but I takes 'em just the same and I don't come down none on the price.'

'I hate killing, too. It's cruel.'

'It isn't.' Ben frequently argued the issue with his sister. 'You kill pests or else you kill for meat.'

'You don't *need* meat, Ben. When I grow up I'm going to be a vegetarian.'

'What's one o' them?' Sage was puzzled. ''Nother kind o' Bible-puncher?'

'Let's not argue over controversial issues.' Adele knew how

77

persistent her daughter was, it might end in a screaming row. 'We have to learn to tolerate other people even if we don't agree with them, Nick. And as we're leaving first thing in the morning, it really doesn't make a lot of difference.'

'Except that that stinking smoke is making my throat sore.' Nicola affected another spasm of coughing, waved her hands in an attempt to divert the smoke clouds. 'I'll be suffocated before morning what with that and the *other* smell.'

'Yes, well, we'll just have to put up with it.' Adele wrinkled her nose, the stench was exceptionally strong tonight, like rotting meat mixed with horse dung. And it was so cold in here that you huddled over the fire. She told herself that that was because there was no covering over the window, even if she didn't believe it. It was a different kind of cold, damp and icy, ate right into your bones, goosebumped your skin.

The room smelled like a crypt that had been opened up, the latest corpses not quite skeletal. Putrefaction and mustiness combining to produce a smell that was evil.

Sage removed his pipe from his mouth in order to drink from a flask which he produced from one of his many pockets. The aroma was so strong, Adele's eyes watered as it caught the back of her throat.

'Whisky.' He wiped his lips with the back of a gnarled hand. 'It was on the wagon train these folks were travellin'. No good leavin' it for the Injuns, gets 'em steamed up wuss than they already are. Mebbe it belonged to the Bible-puncher and he was keepin' it hidden in his wagon.'

'Indeed it was not!' James came out of his sulky reverie with seething indignation. 'Alcohol is the devil's brew, it is responsible for violence and killing. No drop has ever touched my lips, nor will.'

'Which is prob'ly why you're like you are,' he grunted. 'When Kiotes get their hands on yuh, don't make no difference whether you drink whisky or not. Better if you do, p'raps.'

'I shall bring the Word of God to the Kiotes.' James' eyes filmed like he had gone into some kind of trance. 'They are as other men, as ourselves, simply they have not had the opportunity to turn to the Lord.'

'I'll remind you o' that, preacher, when you're tied to a stake and the flames are startin' to scorch your privates. Or you're staked out on the ground and there's a buzzard standin' on your head peckin' your eyes out. Try tellin' 'em about God then, what they're a-doin' to you is much more fun. They prob'ly done all that to Prudence by now. And more, 'cause she's a woman.'

'She sinned,' James whispered, stared past Adele into the fire. 'I pray that she asked forgiveness at the end, that the Lord will see his way to—'

A sudden cry came from outside, one that embodied pain and despair, an anguished soul screaming in the fires of eternal torment.

'What the hell!' Blair pushed past Adele and Nicola but Sage was already blocking the window, the Hawken barrel thrust outside. The boom of the detonation reverberated the ageing woodwork, the flash from the muzzle lit up the room momentarily. Then sulphurous smoke was billowing every-where.

'Got one!' Sage's grunt was one of brief exultation as he turned, thrust the smoking rifle at the bemused missionary. 'Stoke 'er fast, preacher.'

The trapper's flintlock pistols were in his hands as he endeavoured to see through the cloud of swirling powder smoke.

'Kiotes?' Blair was at the other's shoulder. Somehow that scream had not sounded like the war cry of an attacking brave.

'See, they're runnin' skeered!' Sage made no attempt to shoot, the fleeting shapes beyond the smoke were already out of pistol range; he did not have powder and shot to waste. 'Snicked up whilst I was a-yakkin', mebbe thought they'd leave what they'd brung and git clear. Mebbe thought she was already dead.'

Blair stared, the smoke was dispersing, he could just make out a shape on the ground about twenty yards away. A huddled thing that writhed, groaned, and when it tried to crawl he knew it was human.

'What on earth is it, Sage?' Even now he was scared to ask *who* it was, praying that it might be some animal of the forest, its shape distorted so that it appeared almost human in the first rays of the rising moon. A wolf, maybe.

'No prizes for guessin'.' Sage shoved his pistols back into his belt. 'Guess them Injuns won't be back for a while. We'd best get 'un whilst we can. Jest as well left there for the wolves, for all the use it'll be, but we better act kinda civilized. C'mon.'

Blair followed the other through the hallway, where the horses were still restless at the suddenness of the gunshot, and out into the near-darkness of another night. The air was heavy with burned powder, in the willows beyond an owl hooted twice.

The creature was definitely human, and Blair found himself standing back. Well, it had once been human. Naked, its flesh was blackened as though it had stood too close to a smoking fire, he could see that the legs were broken which was why it could not crawl. It was trying to pull itself along by clutching at clumps of tough grass but it did not have the strength.

He sensed that the injured was female by the hips and buttocks, the breasts were hidden beneath the prone body. The head was hairless, dull and sticky with some substance. It groaned weakly.

'Telled you what they'd do to her.' Sage dropped to one knee, looked up.

'Who?' Because Blair needed his worst suspicions confirmed before he dared believe.

'Prudence, o' course, ain't no other white woman runnin' around these parts. Who'd yuh think it was?'

'Oh, my God!' Blair felt physically sick. Back home he'd treated traffic victims that were far worse than the pathetic figure on the ground, you hardened yourself to it after a while. Out here in the wilderness it was too awful to contemplate. You had to switch off, become a functioning robotical medic that analysed injuries and treatment in a cold calculated way or else you'd lose your sanity.

Blair switched off. The features that somehow uplifted themselves were unrecognizable and that made it easier. It wasn't anybody he knew.

'What happened to her?' His probing fingers discovered that the skull oozed blood, a deep cut encircled her head.

'Skelped. They do that right at the start.'

'Jeez, I don't believe it!'

'You're lookin' at it.'

He slid a hand beneath her, almost snatched it away. 'Her breasts are gone.'

'They dry 'em, use 'em to keep terbaccer in.'

Blair tasted bile, it scorched his throat.

'Don't look no further, Doc, there's every buck out there will've taken her. After they fire-dried her skin, made sure that she didn't cheat by dyin'. They give 'er back to us when they'd done finished with her and she weren't no more use to 'em.'

'We'd better get her inside, Sage, and I'll see what I can do, at least give her painkillers. I've got my bag with me.'

'Ain't no use, she won't last more'n an hour, two at the most.'

'I *have* to do something. You know, I campaigned for euthanasia at a debate when I was at college.'

'Never even heered o' that place, Doc, and I've travelled pretty wide from east to west, north to south, even bin up into the Rockies.'

'It's mercy-killing.' Blair looked away across to the forest. 'Sometimes, when somebody's suffering and there's no hope for them, it's kindest, sooner rather than later.'

'Allus said that, done it a time or two. Like when Toon, a trapper from Wyoming, had his horse throw him. Broke his neck but he still lived. No point in lettin' 'im suffer.' Sage drew a pistol, looked at it. 'I buried him after, read from ma Bible, couldn't've had a more Christian burial if that there preacher had been around.'

'I think you did the right thing, Sage.'

'Yuh want fer me to do it this time, Doc?' Sage straightened up, his hand rested on his belted pistol.

Blair's stomach churned. Suddenly he was being asked to play God. A life was ebbing away, Prudence might be dead within the hour; on the other hand she could linger on until tomorrow. We'll be gone by then, Sage will have to make the decision himself. Coward!

Blair scuffed the ground with his foot, he knew that the others were crowding the window, watching. That made it a damned sight worse. There was no telling the extent of Prudence's suffering; too weak even to scream now, just nerves and muscles twitching with unspeakable agony. Death was the only humane release from her agony.

Euthanasia was a criminal offence. His career would be finished, he might face a jury.

'Wal, Blair, what we gonna do? We leave her to suffer, go

81

when she's ready? Or do we do the decent thing? You or me?'

Head bowed, Blair turned, walked unsteadily back towards the cabin. Only when he reached the veranda did his hands go up to cover his ears in the futile hope that he might be spared the sound of the shot.

Eleven

'We must at least give her a Christian burial.' James's voice was flat; if he felt any emotion at the death of his cousin, it did not show. He did not mention her by name, as if it was taboo. Victoria sat dry-eyed beside him. She had not moved throughout the nocturnal hours. Not once had she spoken.

'Guess so.' Sage glanced out of the window, the body lay covered by a blanket by the veranda steps. 'I'll git diggin'. Blair, you 'n' the boy'll hev to give me some cover, jest in case. Them Kiotes are watchin' from the trees even though we haven't seen one since daybreak. They's still there, all right. I kin smell 'em.' He sniffed the air just in case any of the others doubted him.

Blair nodded. He stole a furtive glance at Adele, saw how she sat stony-faced over by the stove, angry and frustrated. Despair was beginning to set in; he wondered how close she was to giving up. Because by now they should have been a mile or more from here like he'd promised. It didn't look like they would be leaving in the foreseeable future. If at all.

They had made ready just before dawn, loaded the back-packs with enough food for two or three days. And waited in the hallway for day to break.

The horses were unusually restless, a sure sign that they sensed something that the humans didn't. Blair eased the door open, watched towards the east. The stars had lost their bright-ness, the sky began to pale. Adele held Nicola's hand, Ben had the breech of the twenty open, impatient to load the gun. Sage still watched from the window, he had not even bidden them farewell. Like he knew that they would not be going.

'We'll wait another ten minutes, let it get properly light.' Blair moved outside, he had a shell in the chamber of the Browning, four more in the magazine. Heavy 00 loads.

83

They waited, saw the grey early morning light filter across the valley; silhouettes became detailed objects.

That was when they saw the Kiotes, a dozen, perhaps twenty of them, ringing the cabin at a distance of two hundred yards, like statues with folded arms. Just watching.

Blair tensed, the gun in his hands came up, the stock touched his shoulder. Then he lowered it; the shot charges probably would not even reach the tribesmen from here. He heard Adele's intake of breath followed by a groan of despair.

'Sage,' he called out, edged back into the doorway.

'I seed 'em.' The trapper gave a low laugh. 'Didn't I tell yuh I could smell 'em? I know'd they wuz there, them woods 'n' mountains are full o' them and prob'ly by now Koot and his gang've joined 'em. There ain't no way outa here, Blair. You seen for yersel what happened to the woman, any o' us trying to get past 'em'll suffer the same. Or worse. We just gotta sit it out. They won't rush us. Not yet, anyhow.'

'Shoot 'em!' Blair almost screamed his frustration. 'You said that rifle of yours would drop a buffalo stone dead at two hundred yards.'

'No point.' The mountain man had his Hawken leaned up against the wall. 'Drop one an' another takes his place. I could sit here all day pickin' 'em off, if'n they didn't run, which they wouldn't. In the end there'd still be plenty left and I'd be outa powder 'n' shot. And that there gun o' yours wouldn't be a lotta use when they came pilin' in on us. Like I said, we sit tight, they ain't goin' nowhere. And neither are we, come to that.'

Adele sank back into her chair. Nicola was on her lap, face buried against her mother, sobbing quietly. Ben had unloaded the small shotgun. Blair ejected the shell out of the automatic's chamber. It was all back to yesterday and the day before. Today and tomorrow, and the days that followed, would be no different.

'I'd better get diggin' that grave.' Sage moved towards the door. 'Take me some time. You 'n' the boy stay on the veranda, keep your eyes peeled. Jest in case.'

The sun was high in the sky by the time Sage had finished, a dirt-grimed figure whose features showed no shine of sweat, whose limbs moved as easily as when he had begun. He dug down deep, was standing up to his shoulders in the oblong hole before he was satisfied.

'You hev to go down deep else the wolves'll dig her up. All we gotta do now is bury her.'

James clutched a Bible and prayer book, his sister followed him out into the sunlight. They stood by the graveside, waited.

'I'll need a hand,' Sage indicated the blanketed body on the ground, 'if we're to do it with dignity, that is. You take the feet, Blair, and we'll lower her as gently as we can. Not that it'll make much difference to her, might upset the Bible-puncher an' his sister if'n we jest chucked her in.' He smiled grimly through his beard.

It was warm in the sunlight, a noticeable contrast to the shadows and indoors. Blair had never known it this cold in spring before except perhaps at nights. The others had followed them out; it would have been churlish of them to have shunned the burial.

Sage had nailed together two lengths of wood in the form of a crude cross; it lay by the side of the open grave. With Blair's help he lowered the body, still wrapped in its blanket, down into the depths. Then they all stood back, bowed their heads. A breeze had sprung up, fluttered the pages of the prayer book which James held.

Sage had not removed his hat; he stood back, rifle cradled across his chest, his keen eyes scanning the far woods. Not that he anticipated an attack, there was more than enough open ground to enable the party to retreat to safety in time, but constant alertness was habitual.

Ben cradled the twenty in the crook of an arm almost proudly, but Blair experienced a feeling of guilt at being present at a funeral carrying a gun. It was a sacrilege, but the living had precedence over the dead, he consoled himself.

'Let us pray for the departed, that the Lord may take her . . . *and forgive her sins*!' There was an undisguised venom in the missionary's voice. 'One whose life has not been without blemish, one who has succumbed to the temptations of the flesh.' His eyes elevated from the page, centred on Blair. The implication, the accusation was not disguised. You surely would have taken pleasure with her body had I not happened upon you!

Sage cleared his throat loudly, he was not one for lengthy ceremonies.

'Ashes to ashes, dust to dust . . .' He stooped, pitched a

handful of soil down into the grave. 'The Lord hath given, and the Lord hath taken away.'

Sage straightened up. The shovel stuck up out of the mound of excavated soil and stones, the sooner the hole was filled in, the better. He laid down his rifle in anticipation of his imminent duty.

'Abide with me . . . fast falls the eventide,' Victoria began to sing in a flat, unmusical voice. 'The darkness deepens . . . Lord with me abide . . .'

Adele shifted with embarrassment, Blair looked away. Sage stood with his hand resting on the shovel. There was a fanatical expression on Victoria's features, her brother made no attempt to join in with her.

Suddenly they heard a thud, James stiffened, tottered uncertainly, and the Bible and prayer book fluttered from his grasp like butterflies wounded in flight, flapped down into the hole.

He stood there, arms outstretched, miming words with a distraught expression that might have been a belated apology to his departed cousin. His eyes bulged like bubbles on the point of bursting.

' . . . Lord with me abide.'

He was screaming but no words escaped his thin, bloodless lips. Victoria seemed not to have noticed, she closed her eyes, uplifted them to the sky.

The others stared in amazement, watched the preacher's legs buckle beneath him, his body sink slowly down. Then he pitched forward, lay face downwards on the brink of the grave.

Only then did they see the arrow sticking out of his back.

Sage's reactions were fast. In a second he had grabbed up the Hawken, yelled to the rest of them to lie flat on the ground. He dropped to a crouch, they heard the click of the hammer as it was cocked.

A tuft of tall spiky grass some fifty yards away moved, a ragged figure emerged from its scant cover, bent double as it bounded and ran, weaved from right to left in an attempt to present as difficult a target as possible. Clutched in one hand was the bow that had fired the deadly arrow.

Sage did not hurry, he had all the time he needed, he waited just as he might have waited for a jinking snipe to straighten its flight. The long rifle bucked, belched black smoke.

86

The fleeing brave halted in mid-leap, back arched so that his spine might have snapped, arms flung wide, the bow spinning from his grasp. Then he hit the ground, lay spreadeagled, eyes looking sightlessly up at the sky.

'Got 'un!' Sage muttered, making no move to rush forward and check on the Kiote, for he had faith in his own marksmanship. The other was as dead as the body that lay in the grave waiting to be covered. 'Musta bin there since before dawn, snuck up and hid, know'd we wuz going to have us a funeral nearby. Now we got two.' He turned to look where Blair was kneeling beside the preacher. 'Mebbe three.' He blew at the smoke that trickled out of the barrel.

Victoria seemed totally unaware of what had happened. Her toneless singing had moved on to a muttered recitation. 'The beautiful, the beautiful river . . .' Throughout, she stared ahead of her, unseeing.

Blair saw that the arrow had entered James just below his shoulder blades, blood was beginning to ooze out of the rip in the serge jacket. Survival depended upon how far the head had penetrated, what inner organs it had pierced.

'Go back indoors,' he ordered Adele. 'We're sitting ducks out here. Take Victoria with you, give her a mug of hot, sweet coffee.'

'Naw, there wuz only the one,' Sage joined him, 'and he won't be firin' no more arrers. The Bible-puncher dead?'

A soft moan declared that James still lived.

'We'll have to get him inside, Sage. I can't tell at this stage how badly he's wounded but I have to do the best I can for him. Take his feet, go slowly and carefully. He's bleeding a lot.'

A spotted trail of blood followed them right up on to the veranda. Sage kicked open the door.

'Lay him on the table, face downwards.' Blair looked at Adele. 'I'm going to have to operate quickly, best as I can. Boil some water then . . . no, you'll have to stay, it's not safe to go outdoors.'

Once again they had been driven back into the cabin.

Blair used a sharp knife to cut away the clothing, exposed a jagged wound that bled profusely. He selected a syringe from his bag, injected quickly. Very soon the victim's low moaning stopped.

Victoria sat holding the mug of coffee Adele had made her. She seemed oblivious of it, just continued to stare blankly.

'I'll have to get the arrow out.' Blair grimaced. 'Then I'll clean the wound, stitch it. Apart from that, there's not much more I can do in the absence of an operating theatre and equipment.'

'Tell me what I kin do to help.' Sage leaned over the table, looked at the wound. 'Seen wuss, many a time. Remember once I was with a wagon train that got ambushed. Arapahos, they wuz, we drove 'em off but we had more casualties than they did. I helped the doc. I kin recall him as clear as if he stood here now. Doc Wiseman, little feller, allus wore a vest and a stove-pipe hat. Between us we treated more'n twenty wounded, mostly gunshots 'cause Koot and his lot were into gun-runnin' to the Injuns in those days. But this one feller, he'd got an arrer that went through his front and came out back. Real nasty. But it hadn't touched nothing serious, a real miracle. I cut the head off and the doc and I slid the shaft out, fired the wound to purify it. We did a real good job.'

'And the guy lived?' Blair exerted pressure on the arrow, there was going to be a nasty haemorrhage when he pulled it out. He checked that he had bandages and wadding handy.

'Naw, he died.'

'Pity, after all the trouble you went to.' He clenched his teeth, began to pull.

'It weren't the wound that killed him,' Sage chuckled. 'He made it through that afore we got to the end o' the journey, the stupid bugger was messin' with a pistol, didn't realize it were loaded. Blew his head off almost.'

The arrowhead came out in a flood of bright blood. Blair knew then that a lung was punctured; James' chances of pulling through were slim. All the same he worked diligently, stitched the wound, bandaged it, administered another injection.

That was when he became aware of the smell, one that he'd come to recognize. *Gangrene, and it came directly from the arrow wound. Which was impossible in the time.*

'Smells like it's gone bad already.' Sage's senses were keen, he'd encountered gangrene on the wagon trains many times.

Blair shook his head, there were too many unanswered questions around here that sent shivers up your spine. 'We'll let him sleep, that's all we can do.'

'My brother's going to die, Dr Blair.' Victoria had moved across to the table. Blair started because he hadn't heard her. The expression on her face was frightening, a distinct lack of awareness, as if her lips moved, uttered words, like an actress who had learned her lines but did not understand their meaning.

'He has a chance.' He wanted to look away but somehow her eyes held him. 'Whilst there's life, there's hope. Miracles sometimes happen. We never concede defeat in the medical profession until there is no longer any hope.'

'Of course he'll die.' She stood rigid. 'Just as Prudence was destined to be captured by the Indians and punished for her sins. God used the Kiotes to exact His punishment upon her. He used the devil in His own mysterious way, can't you see that? We are all here by God's will and He has decreed that we shall not leave. You and your family have tried, and failed. Do not consider trying again.'

'I . . . I'm afraid I don't understand, Victoria.' She was crazy, of course. Her cousin's death and her brother's imminent demise had rendered her insane. It was kindest to humour her.

'Just that we're all going to die.' Victoria turned, seemed to glide back to her chair in the corner. 'Every last one of us. *There's no way anybody will ever leave here alive.*'

Twelve

James died sometime during the night and secretly everybody was almost glad. Blair had taken a turn at lookout and had been aware that Victoria was standing by the makeshift bed of blankets on which her brother lay.

She remained there motionless, hour after hour. Not once did she kneel by his side nor murmur words of comfort. Even her posture was not that of a grieving relative, she just stood and watched like she was waiting for him to die. It was eerie, Blair smelled gangrene again and shuddered at Victoria's chilling premonition. That had upset Nicola; the child had taken a lot of whispered persuading that the strange woman's mental stability had been unhinged by her cousin's violent death and the certainty that her brother was going to die.

Adele had lapsed into silence afterwards. Blair thought that she might have given up hope and that was bad for all of them.

'We must give my brother a Christian burial.' Victoria spoke for the first time in twelve hours, a statement that was in itself an order. Her eyes were filmed, they centred on Blair.

'Sure thing.' It was Sage who answered. He appeared to have been sleeping but his eyes flickered open. 'Got a grave already dug out there. You kin say a few words an'—'

'*No!*' It was as if the protest came from the very depths of Victoria's soul, a cry of anguished horror that such an idea should ever have been conceived. '*I will not allow him to be buried with that whore!*'

'Ma'am,' Sage raised himself up on an elbow, 'if'n you think I'm gonna dig another hole specially fer him, you're mistaken. Once you're dead, you're dead, an' your body ain't no use to nobody once you're gone.'

'Dr Blair and his son will dig a grave for James, then!' She was petulant, her voice was like a distant echo.

'I'm sorry, but it's too risky being outside for long.' Blair was aware that his voice shook slightly. 'My duty is to protect lives. Sage is right, there's no reason why we can't bury them both together. After all, Prudence is his cousin and he did ask the Lord to forgive her. A double burial would be a sign of James's own willingness to forgive her.' On the spur of the moment it sounded plausible.

He expected another outburst but she merely nodded an unwilling agreement. 'I just hope that James will understand.'

'Kiotes was quiet last night.' Sage helped himself to coffee. 'Worries me when they don't get up to nothin' I kin see 'cause then I start wonderin' what they're doin' that I don't know about. Soon as you're ready, Blair, we'll go and get this buryin' done and hope it'll be the last.'

'*There will be others.*' Victoria was staring fixedly at the wall, as though she was talking to herself.

It was sunny and warm again out in the open. Blair helped Sage to roll James in a blanket and together they lowered him down into the grave, laid him directly on top of Prudence.

'What about that Kiote out there, the one you shot?' A sudden thought struck Blair. He looked out to where the brave had been struck down in mid-flight, but there was no sign of a corpse.

'He'll be gone, Doc, wolves will've had him in the night. If not wolves, then *somethin'* will.'

Blair shivered in spite of the warmth.

'Where's that damn woman?' Sage reached for his shovel, dislodged a trickle of soil and stones down into the hole. 'Or are we just gonna fill this in like it was some pet dawg we wuz burying?'

There was no sign of Victoria. Adele stood on the veranda, Nicola and Ben beside her. Smoke wisped straight up into the air from the stove chimney.

'I'd better go and find out.' Blair's mouth was dry, Victoria was becoming chillingly unpredictable.

'Tell her we ain't waitin'.' Sage spun the shovel, caught it deftly. 'No tellin' after yesterday, might be a Kiote lyin' in the grass. Can't smell nothin' but that ain't to say. They're not like *ordinary* Injuns, give me a Blackfoot or a Comanche any day.'

'Where's Victoria?' Blair resisted the urge to run.

'Inside, I guess.' Adele pulled the children close to her. 'Last time I saw her she was standing staring at the wall like it was a mirror.' *And don't ask me to go find her.*

Blair went inside. God, this place stank of everything that was rotten and decaying. He detected that only too familiar lingering odour of death. That was only to be expected after James had died in here. It was damnably cold, too, in spite of the blazing fire in the stove.

'Victoria?'

There was no answer. He pushed open the kitchen door, looked around the scene of decay and disarray. She wasn't there; his skin began to prickle as he checked behind the door. Maybe she was in one of the bedrooms.

She wasn't. The bathroom, then? But the door was wide open, he could see from here that there was nobody inside. Funny, that shiver ran right the way up his spine, he had never noticed her use the bathroom. Neither Victoria, nor Prudence and James when they were alive. Sage, neither, now he came to think of it. Probably, though, they had all been used to doing their business outside after their trek. In this place you had to come up with a reason for everything, even if deep down you didn't believe it, or else you'd go crazy.

'Wal, we can't wait around.' Sage began shovelling earth down into the grave. 'When I'm done, one or the other of us'll come up with a few words. Done it often enough in the past.'

The oblong mound stood out stark and fresh in the midst of the winter-browned grass. Sage used the flat of his shovel to hammer in the rough cross. An unmarked grave. 'Names don't matter 'cause nobody's interested,' he explained, stood back. 'There's graves along all the trails from the east, nobody gives 'em a glance. More'n half of those travellin' the wagon trains know they'll end up like that somewhere along the way.'

Blair glanced around nervously but there was nobody in sight except his own family huddled outside the cabin door.

'Gittin' edgy?' Sage chuckled. 'Cain't blame yuh fer that. Now, we'd better say somethin' to them folks down there, even if it is only *adios*.' He thumbed the pages of his dog-eared Bible, snapped it shut again. 'Never could find anythin' suitable just when I need it. Don't really need it, though, offishiated nuff times in the past.' He bowed his head. His mutterings were scarcely audible as if he was embarrassed. 'Lord, look after these folks who were spreadin' the Word. Make sure them Kiotes don't get 'em again.'

His words brought a shudder to Blair. The Kiotes had already caused suffering and death to the departed, so why should Sage pray for their safety? It was too frightening to try to make sense of the trapper's words.

Adele and the children were already back indoors. Nobody spoke, there was nothing to say. Their party had been depleted of two of its members and before long night must fall again. There was still no sign of Victoria. Blair tried not to think where she might have gone. Doubtless she had wandered off on her own, distraught by the deaths of her brother and cousin. Well, he damned well wasn't going to worry over her.

Maybe later, if he got a chance to speak with Sage alone, he would try to get the other to agree to some plan for getting them out of here.

None of us will ever leave here alive. He got to thinking about Victoria again.

'Try to eat quietly, Nick.' Blair knew that his nerves were on edge when trivial things irritated him. Sage had gone outside to fetch in a supply of kindling to see them through the night, the others were huddled in front of the stove. 'Close your lips when you chew, you make it sound like there's a pig in here.'

'What are you eating, anyway?' Adele noticed a brown paper bag nestling in the child's lap.

'Candies.' Nicola slurped the word through a sticky mouthful.

'What candies? Let me see.' She snatched the bag, opened it up, held it so that the firelight fell on a mass of sugary humbug-like shapes in the bottom. She shook them, they stuck together in a gooey mass. 'These look like some kind of home-made sucks. Where'd you get them?'

'The lady gave them to me.' There was a hint of embarrassment in Nicola's expression, her lower lip quavered slightly almost as if she'd stolen them from somewhere.

'Which lady?' Adele felt herself tense, she needed confirmation, hoped that she was wrong. 'Prudence before she, she . . . died?'

'No, Victoria.'

93

Oh, Jesus Christ, no! 'When?' The accusation was like a whipcrack in the confined space. She sensed that Blair and Ben were as shocked as she was.

'Just before we went outside to watch the funeral. She stayed back, I was following you, she signalled for me to stay.'

'But you didn't.' Sheer relief.

'No. She gave me the candies, asked me if I'd like to go a walk with her, pick some snowdrops in the forest. I said you wouldn't let me. She tried to hold me back but I ran out. They're nice candies, though.'

'Where . . . where did Victoria go after that?' Blair tried not to make the question insistent but it came out that way.

'I dunno.' Nicola looked puzzled. 'She followed me out, I thought she was standing with us but when I looked round she wasn't there. She maybe went to pick snowdrops on her own, perhaps to put on the grave.'

'She must've walked off, we just didn't notice, we were too busy watching you and Sage.' Adele said it fast just in case anybody had any other ideas.

'Must've done.' Blair was shivering with cold, moved closer to the fire and hoped that Sage would hurry up with the logs. *Nobody had walked across that stretch of open ground that surrounded the cabin, he would have seen them if they had. He'd been scanning for signs of Kiotes the whole time.*

'I hope she'll be all right out there.' Nicola chewed, made an effort to keep her lips closed.

'She'll probably be back soon,' Blair said. *Or else the Kiotes will bring her back tonight.*

'Moon gits later each night.' Sage spoke from his lookout post at the window. ' 'Bout an hour. Comes the night when there's no moon at all. If'n they're gonna risk rushin' us, that's when they'll do it. Meantime they're enjoyin' this, they got two of us. Kinda game for them, one at a time's much more fun than blowin' it all at once. That's as long as there ain't no wagons in the vicinity when they'll be mighty busy. My guess is that folks are skeered at present, holding up in the forts. Then one o' Koot's gang'll come along, persuade 'em that he can guide 'em. Wham!' He smacked a fist into a palm. 'Right into an ambush. In the meantime the Kiotes'll pass the time playin' with us.'

94

Adele looked at Nicola and Ben, saw that they both slept. This kind of talk was scary for adults, terrifying for children.

Soon they would run out of canned food; when she had mentioned this earlier, Sage was puzzled. He could not understand how beans and the like came to be sealed up in cans. Why go to all the bother when you could carry dried beans much easier, kill meat when you needed it; you always had it fresh that way. And if game was scarce, you dried the flesh. He'd show 'em how it was done one of these days. Tomorrow he would set some snares not far from the cabin, catch a rabbit or two.

Tomorrow . . .

'There's somethin' out there,' Sage whispered. They heard him cock the rifle. 'Smelled it . . . not quite right for Injun.'

Blair came off his blankets, joined the trapper. Outside there was total blackness, it was impossible even to discern the uprights of the veranda.

'Don't seem bothered about comin' this way, Blair. It definitely ain't Injun, wolf neither.'

'What, then?'

'Moon'll be up soon.' The mountain man evaded the question. 'If it's still there, we'll see for ourselves.'

An orange sliver topped the far mountain peaks, cast a radiant glow into the sky. Blair stared, the moon rose with amazing rapidity, within minutes half of it was visible; then three-quarters.

'It moves fast. Another minute an' it'll clear the mountains. Then we'll see.'

A soft light spread down the forests, flowed across the valley floor. Now the forest was visible, gnarled trees that gave off grotesque shadows.

'Shit!' Sage's keen eyes had picked out a shape some fifty yards from the cabin, one that knelt with bowed head beside that mound of grave soil, the flowing dress like a shroud, hair knotted on top of the head.

'*Victoria!*' Blair stared in both horror and disbelief.

'Aye, it's her, half guessed it might be.' The Hawken barrel slid forward, the stock was cradled against a fringed shoulder. 'Mercy, I feared it but I never thought it would happen.'

A sideways glance showed Blair that his companion's bronzed complexion was several shades paler; it might have

95

been caused by the moonlight. Did the outstretched hand that steadied the rifle barrel tremble slightly? It could have been an optical illusion.

'*No, Sage!*' Realization why the other was taking a sighting, Blair almost grabbed the gun, threw it upwards so that the moulded bullet would whine harmlessly into the night sky. Except that he was frozen from shocked immobility.

'It's the only way, there ain't no other.' Sage squeezed the trigger.

In that split second before the black smoke obliterated the moonlit scene from view, Blair glimpsed the figure at the graveside jerk, the beginning of her death throes. An unearthly scream was drowned by the roar of the exploding charge. Then, mercifully, the full horror of it all was blotted out by the swirling, thickening powder smoke.

'Oh, God!' Blair leaned up against the wall, the room began to gyrate, he thought he might faint. 'Sage, you've killed her!' Euthanasia was controversial, murder was unforgivable.

'Mebbe,' the trapper was staring fixedly ahead of him as if even he was frightened to go out there, 'and mebbe not. *But not in the way you mean, Blair!*'

Thirteen

Victoria lay on her back, arms outstretched, legs lewdly spread as if to seduce her killers into a mating beyond the grave. Her dead eyes were fixed on them, orbs that glowed like live coals in the soft moonlight, reflected the fury that lived on inside her. She saw and hated them even in death.

Blair found himself backing away. Her lips were frozen into a bestial snarl, trickled blood like a vampire that had just feasted. One side of her skull was shattered, a gaping .54-calibre ball wound which spewed a glutinous grey matter. The torn dress revealed a shapely body that no man had ever looked upon before.

The corpse, the features, bore little resemblance to Victoria, the haughty Spreader of the Word, only just enough for the two men to know that it had once been her. Now sheer evil evaporated from her in nauseating body odours and fetid breath; its putrescence hung heavy in the still atmosphere, a creature of unbelievable malevolence cut down in its prime.

'I killt it!' Sage was muttering his disbelief to himself, shaking inside his hide clothing. 'I daren't think what'd've happened if'n I'd missed.' He stood well back, perhaps fearing that the thing might rise up and vent its terrible vengeance upon him. He prodded at it with the end of the Hawken barrel but it was only the final twitching of the nerves which responded. Victoria was dead, there was no doubt about that.

'For God's sake, man, *why*? *What is happening?*'

'She came back.' His hoarse whisper shook. '*She answered their call and went to them, she was too weak to resist after her brother died. But they sent her back . . . for them.*' He stabbed a finger at the grave. 'Mercy that your li'l girl had more sense'n to go with her.'

'Why did she come back for them? They're dead and buried, no use to anybody.' Blair's senses were reeling, everything that had happened since the Great Storm was beyond his under-standing.

'*To raise 'em up.* They'd've crawled up outa that grave but they wouldna be the same folks as went in. Totem magic, the likes o' which you and me wouldna believe until we saw it, and mebbe not even then. Them two, and her, would've walked back into the cabin and taken the lot o' us. Your gun wouldn't've stopped 'em, Blair. Me, I could've maybe got two or three if'n I'd've used the pistols as well as the rifle.'

'Why *yours*?'

'Dunno for sure, jest the way it is. I've seen waggoners firin' at attacking Kiotes, knocks 'em down but they gets up again. That's the way it is. I only tell you what I've see'd for myself.'

Out there in the icy moonlight Blair did not for one moment doubt the other's word. It was terrifying, but it was true.

'They want me most of all.' Sage paused to scan the open ground, began to reload his Hawken. Maybe it was prefer-able to talk out here than in front of women and children. 'I bin dodging 'em since I fust took to trappin'. 'Cause I killed a few Kiote braves when they's supposed to be invin-cible. Your gun'll mebbe tickle 'em, bowl 'em over, but they gets right back up. Mine drops 'em dead as ever a Kiote is likely to be. Dunno why, jest the way it is. They'd like to torture me till I was screamin' crazy, then,' he drew the flat of his hand swiftly across his throat, 'after that, they'd make me so's I could walk and talk again, shoot 'n' kill better'n any brave or renegade they got. I suspect that's what happened to Koot, why he's so damned bad, but that's only ma figurin'.'

Blair was shaken. 'And what about us, Sage? Wherever this place is, whatever it is, we want to get the hell outa here. Adele can't take much more. God knows what all this will do to the children.'

'There ain't no way out.' Sage stared at the ground as he spoke. 'Coupla days ago when I went scoutin', if I coulda found a way through, I'd've gone, left yuh all. But there weren't none, took me all my time to dodge Kiotes and make it back to the cabin. They got this valley all to themselves and they're keepin' it that way. The whites'll conquer the whole damn country eventually, you mark ma words, but they won't take this valley. *The more the Kiotes kill, the bigger their army'll be. One day they'll make war and slaughter every white in it, take it back for their own.*'

'The valley wasn't like this when we drove into it.' Blair looked back towards the cabin, he was uneasy leaving his family alone. The Kiotes had almost snatched Nicola. 'It was just a nice, peaceful, remote place. Then came the storm, worst I've ever known, blacked everything out. And when we woke up next morning . . .'

'Must've been one helluva while ago.' Sage stroked his unkempt beard. 'I only ever remember one storm like you mention and that was a few years back. I wuz down here at the time, the wagon train I was leadin' had been attacked by Kiotes 'bout thirty miles back. There was a guy and two wimmin, only survivors. Funny thing,' he scratched his head beneath his cap, seemed to have difficulty recalling the distant happenings, 'I believe they wuz Bible-punchers, too. Can't be sure. Anyway, we holed up in the cabin back there, the Kiotes taunted us for 'bout a week, then one night they came howlin' and screamin'. I got two of 'em, mebbe three, I know they fired the cabin. Don't rightly remember what happened to me, they musta dumped me, 'cause next thing I knew I wuz wanderin' the forest same as I allus used to. Never did hear what came o' those preachers but it ain't difficult to guess!' He lapsed into a long silence.

'What is it?' Adele met them at the door. The horses in the hallway were snickering in terror; only Sage's return calmed them or they might have kicked down the door and fled.

'Injun.' The lie came glibly. 'Jest sussin' us out, I guess. He won't be going back to tell 'em nothin'.'

'Oh!' She held Nicola tightly, Ben had the breech of the twenty open, some shells in his hand. 'Can't see properly out there but it looked as if she was wearing a *dress*.'

'Sure was, jest to fool us, I guess, maybe hoped if we spotted him we wouldn't shoot. But ol' Sage ain't fooled by them sorta tricks.'

'Where . . . where'd he get the dress?' Adele asked the question fearfully, maybe didn't want to hear the answer.

'Victoria.' He turned his attention back to the horses. 'There's jest us now.'

They bolted the door, went on into the big room.

'This is crazy, beyond belief and logic.' Adele poured coffee, seemed to have pulled herself together.

'We've talked about it, but there has to be a reason why all this has happened. We arrive at a reasonably normal location situated in a national park. There's a storm and everything changes; the generator packs up, the automobile rusts away like it was thirty years old and virtually every amenity which we've come to take for granted disintegrates. It's like we've stepped back a hundred years or more. I think maybe you know more about this than you're telling, Sage. Native Americans aren't wild any more. Damn it, they're running their own tourist attraction on the Little Bighorn, welcoming whites. They're proud that they defeated the US Army in their biggest victory ever.'

Sage looked perplexed, stroked his beard. 'Don't rightly understand what you're saying, ma'am. Nothin's changed here, not since I've known it, and that's bin a long time. Don't recall the Injuns defeating the whites in a big battle at the Little Bighorn. They've massacred settlers, wagon trains. Heered tell, though, of a big massacre down south, three, four years ago. The Alamo. But it was Mexicans, not the Injuns, that did that.'

'You must have heard of *Custer*?' Ben's eyes were wide with incredulity.

'Custer?' Sage mused, shook his head slowly. 'Nope, cain't say I've heered the name. Who's he, a trapper?'

'A *general*!' Ben stared in disbelief. 'The most famous general in history, he commanded the Seventh Cavalry. They've been arguing about his decision ever since to go on to the Little Bighorn in spite of warnings that there were more Sioux massed there than the troops could handle.'

'Musta happened that time when I was away up in the Rockies for months.' Sage was humouring the boy. 'And jest when did this here mighty battle take place, son?'

'July, eighteen seventy-six.'

'*Seventy-six!*' The mountain man threw back his head and laughed loudly. 'Boy, you are joking! Seventy-six! The Alamo was only in *thirty-six* and that cain't be more'n three, four years ago. By my reckonin', give or take a year, we're in forty right now. You cain't pull one over ol' Sage, you ask them Kiotes – although I hope you never gets nearer enough to talk to the devils!'

'But—'

'Guess we all got a bit mixed up.' Blair silenced Ben with a frown. 'We're not interested in other folks' battles, we've got our own to fight.'

'S'right.' Sage stood up, moved across to the window. 'I'll take first watch. I'll wake you 'bout three hours from now. Had a watch once, lost it that last time I was holed up in here, reckon the Kiotes've got it. That's somethin' else I gotta square with 'em.' He began ramming wadding down the Hawken's barrel. 'Pretty good on timekeeping even without a piece, though sometimes I get a bit mixed up. Jest like you lot ferget which year it is!'

Blair followed Sage out on the veranda. The morning sun had just topped the mountains to the east, and there were all the signs that it was going to be another bright, sunny day.

'Them willers allus used to be full o' doves,' the mountain man pointed with the barrel of the Hawken, 'not now. And that's one reason I know there's Kiotes skulkin' in there. Another, I kin smell 'em and I kin feel 'em. When there's an itchin' in ma scalp I knows I gotta look after it.' He paused, took a steady look all around. 'They'll attack us soon, either late afternoon or on dusk.'

'How can you know that?' Blair's stomach balled.

'Jest know. Sense it. Some mornin's you wake up, feel really good, know it's gonna be a good day. Today I know it's gonna be bad. Real bad.'

'What . . . what are we gonna do, Sage?'

'Wal, we won't just sit around waitin' for 'em to come. There's things that has to be made ready. Good thing I earthed up that roof, did it last time I was tellin' yuh about.'

'But it was timbers the day we arrived.'

'You ain't very observant.' He grinned with his blackened teeth. 'If you'd looked close, you'd've seen that I'd dug up earth jest like I did for that grave, spent three whole days linin' the roof. It saved us from the fire arrers. Course, there's nothin' to stop 'em shootin' into the walls. They didn't bother the time afore when they seed that they couldn't set the roof ablaze. We'll just have to hope on that one. But we'll need slits cut outa the back 'n' side walls, jest room enough to poke a gun through. I did it the last time but some fool's gone and

101

put new timbers in, mebbe didn't like the draughts. You can't have it both ways. I'll soon cut 'em out agin, though.'

Blair was staring out across the flat ground, narrowing his eyes because he could not see what he was looking for.

'Yuh won't ketch a glimpse o' Injuns if they don't want fer you to see 'em,' Sage said.

'I was looking for . . . Victoria.'

'You won't see her, neither.' The trapper smiled grimly. 'They'll've fetched her in the dark afore dawn. They won't be pleased with her, getting' herself shot, 'cause they needed her and the others. Them Injuns'll be so mad they'll mebbe do more things to her even though she's dead. Kiotes are like that. No tellin' what they kin do to a corpse. Jest hope we don't see her agin, that's all.'

'I hope so too.' Blair shuddered.

'C'mon, we got things to do. Should've done 'em before but I guess I was still fool enough to think that we might get outa here. Should've known better.'

Sage busied himself with a small axe on the old pine trunks that made up the cabin walls. With an expertise that never ceased to amaze Blair, he cut out lengths of around a foot long and six inches wide, created slits that were just large enough to allow a gun to manoeuvre but made difficult targets for arrows.

'Pity them Bible-punchers didn't carry guns,' he muttered, 'we could use 'em. You kin use one o' the pistols, Blair, but we'll have to give the others a lesson in reloadin'. That gun o' yours might be useful makin' a bang or two, the boy's too, but the Injuns'll wise up afore long when they only gets tickled.'

'I've dropped more than one buck with it, some high honkers, too,' the doctor snapped. 'The twenty packs a punch as well.'

'I'll have to see it to believe it.' Sage smashed out another chunk of pine. 'Never seed a gun that didn't shoot powder and shot. Why'n hell didn't you buy yourself a Hawken?'

'I'll get one next time I'm down at the trading post.'

'Get them buckets filled with water,' there was an edginess to Sage's voice now, 'we might need 'em if they use fire arrers. Them's strange buckets.' He picked one up, suspended it on an outstretched finger, was clearly puzzled. 'Light as a feather.' He dropped it on the floor, it bounced and rolled. 'Never come across metal like that.'

'It's PVC,' Adele added quickly, 'a type of toughened plastic.'

'What's that?'

'A material from back east, hasn't reached here yet.'

'Wal, I thought I'd seen everythin' till you folks turned up.' Sage returned to his task. 'One o' these days I'll hev to take me a trip to Boston, see what's goin' on over there. But they don't know how to make guns, that's a sure fact.'

'I'll make some more coffee.'

'Fine, and fill them buckets while you're at it. One thing, that ol' well's never run dry all the time I've knowd it. Yuh can't survive without water. And terbaccer.' He pulled out his pipe, began to stuff coarse stranded tobacco into the bowl. 'We'd best get the horses inside, too. Never can tell when an Injun's goin' to attack, sometimes they don't know it themselves.

The sun reached its zenith, began to slope westwards. Sage and Blair stood in the doorway watching its progress. The horses were restless in the confinement of the hallway.

'They knows as well as I do,' Sage knocked out his pipe, began to refill it, 'there ain't much more we kin do now 'cept wait. I'll take the main winder, you the back 'un. Ben kin take the one side, other's blank but at least they can't climb in. If they start hackin' at it, we'll be busy. Li'l girl gotta stop under the table, Adele kin look after the reloadin', she's learned pretty well.' He tapped his rifle. 'Apart from that, we jest shoot at every Injun we got time to. Me, I'd like to get a sight of Black Bear, find out jest how good his bad medicine is!' His lips became a thin bloodless line. 'Koot, too, neither o' them'll come close, jest send in their fodder until we can't shoot no more 'cause we've run outa powder 'n' shot. Don't fergit to save some for yourself, wife an' kids, too.'

Jesus, God, don't let it come to that!

'Now we just wait.' Sage moved back to the window, settled himself down.

Nicola clung to Adele's hand, she didn't understand any more than her parents did but she had given up asking questions. All that remained now were the answers.

Somewhere outside, far away, an owl hooted, and that was strange, indeed, for it was still full daylight.

'Mebbe they'll come on horses, they might come on foot,' Sage briefed Blair, 'never kin tell with Kiotes. Aim for the chest, don't try fancy headshots. No point shootin' horses, riders jest get up agin. Still, won't make much difference either way with that gun o' yours, all it does is make a whump, don't make no smoke, neither. Ain't there no way you kin ram powder 'n' shot down it?'

Blair sighed, it was pointless attempting to explain to Sage about cartridges and nitro smokeless powders. The hunting magazine which they had brought with them had rotted so that it was unreadable. 'No way.'

'Pity, 'cause it sure shoots fast. If'n mine'd fire like that without reloading, them Kiotes'd be wiped out by now.'

The afternoon wore on, so quiet and still that if it had not been for the decay that surrounded them the Lunds would not have thought that anything was amiss.

'Why do I have to get under the table, Mummy?' Nicola was becoming bored, she was overtired, becoming argumentative the way she always did when she got that way. 'It's silly.'

'You don't have to till I tell you. Just keep away from the windows.'

'I'm bored. Everything's all right now, those Native Americans have gone away. It was some kind of game, maybe they're making a cowboy film.'

'I wish they were. I don't understand it any more than you do.'

'Why can't we go home?'

Christ, if you ask that question once more I'll go berserk! 'I've told you, the car's broken down and fallen trees are blocking the road.'

Nicola sat on a chair, lapsed into a sulk. Ben was at the slit in the side wall, had the breech of the twenty open, rattled shells in his hand. He wasn't scared any more, he had a gun and nobody would get close to this part of the cabin, he'd see to that. Blair leaned the Browning up against the wall, there was a shell in the chamber, the magazine was full.

'Be dark in an hour.' Sage spoke softly to nobody in particular. 'Looks like they're gonna leave it till tonight.'

The shadows lengthened, stretched across the valley. Adele loaded some more logs on to the stove, filled the kettle. Everybody could do with some coffee; there were just two cans of beans left in the cupboard; she prayed that those snares which Sage had set would catch. Nicola would doubtless refuse to eat meat, that would be another problem.

They heard Sage catch his breath, the hammer on his rifle clicked back loudly. Outside the heavy silence was suddenly shattered by an unearthly screeching.

'This is it.' The Hawken came up to the trapper's shoulder. *'Here they come!'*

PART TWO

The Ancient Evil

Fourteen

The Kiotes poured out of the willow grove on their half-broken ponies, a dozen or so of them, screaming and yelling. Stripped to the waist, torsos and heads daubed with vivid paint, they brandished lances and bows like wooden totems suddenly imbued with life. Their pleated and waxed hair likened them to Minotaurs, they were crazed with killing lust. Sage was their Theseus.

'Hold yer fire!' The trapper rested his rifle on the sill. 'Let's see what they're gonna do fust.' He glanced behind him to make sure Nicola was under the table.

The ground vibrated with the drumming of unshod hooves; it seemed that the charging tribesmen were going to bear down upon the ramshackle building, overrun the defenders by sheer weight of numbers. Then they wheeled, split into two ranks, began circling in opposite directions, screeching their hate throughout.

'Testin' us,' Sage shouted to make himself heard above the noise. 'Tryin' to draw our fire from afar. They want us to waste powder 'n' shot.'

The Kiotes galloped in opposite circles, weaving, interchanging positions with the ease of horsemen putting on a display. Bareback, their skill would have rivalled any professional stuntman, sliding beneath the bellies of their mounts, hauling themselves back up on the other side. An arrow was fired, embedded itself in the ground a couple of yards from the veranda.

'Testin' their range, too.' Sage's dark eyes never left them. 'Let 'em have their fun, they're only warmin' up.'

Then, as if at some given signal, the riders stopped, reined in their ponies in a cloud of dust, sat proud and motionless, heads turned towards the cabin.

'Show's over, real business'll start soon,' Sage muttered.

'They're angry 'cause we didn't shoot. Now they know they'll have to come in closer.'

The shadows were lengthening, dusk was nigh. The Kiotes' gaudiness was blending into dark silhouettes, horned creatures of the night.

'They'll be closer next time,' Sage prophesied, smoothed a gnarled hand along the barrel of the Hawken.

The riders sat for several minutes, then, as though synchronized, they kicked their ponies into action. Hooves thundered again, the clockwise and anti-clockwise circles began decreasing.

Sage took his time, picked out a galloping brave, followed him with the long rifle barrel, swung through him and squeezed the trigger. The Kiote jerked, his outflung arms loosed their hold on the hide rein, he somersaulted backwards. Through the billowing gun smoke, the watchers saw him roll beneath the hooves of the following ponies and then lie motionless.

'One down!' There was a grim satisfaction in Sage's expression as he handed the smoking Hawken to Adele. He drew his pistols but the attackers would need to be much closer before he loosed off with a .50.

Blair let the full magazine go, he heard Ben's twin reports amidst his own rapid fire. A brave slumped, hauled on the reins to save himself from falling. Then he was upright once more.

It could have been the distance, the .54 had a much greater range and striking velocity than a shotgun. Blair fed the Browning another five cartridges, watched and waited.

The tribesmen were galloping faster, the dust cloud thrown up by the ponies' hooves, together with the gathering dusk, rendered them a blur. Sage held his rifle but he made no attempt to lift it to his shoulder.

'They're makin' a big dust on purpose,' he called out, 'that way we can't see 'em to shoot. One or two'll break away, move in on us.'

The cavalcade continued at a furious pace. The trapper propped his rifle against the wall, drew his pistols, cocked them. Dust clouded in through the window. Adele coughed; Nicola was huddled beneath the table, her eyes closed.

A shot rang out, heads jerked round but it was impossible to see what Sage had fired at.

'Another 'un!' He gave a laugh. 'Watch them winders, there's maybe two or three got in right close.'

Even as the mountain man spoke, Ben screamed. Blair turned, saw a face in the slit between the timbers directly above where the boy crouched. Oh, God Almighty! Those features surely could never belong to a human being, a painted mask in which the eyes burned with unholy malevolence, nostrils that were gaping, mucus-bubbling orifices scenting their prey. The mouth was a slit stretched into a bestial snarl, lips daubed red as if it had gorged itself on fresh meat. A copper-coloured hand was snaking inside, ragged fingernails like claws, reaching for Ben.

Blair screamed, yelled a warning, his terror had frozen him into immobility. He could not shoot, Ben was between himself and the Kiote.

'*No!*'

The lips stretched even wider, the fingers closed over Ben's arm, tightened. The boy's reaction was fuelled by panic, the twenty was held in his other hand, pistol-fashion; the gun was light, easily manoeuvrable. His finger hooked over the triggers, closed on them simultaneously. The double report sounded as one, the shot charges blasted the war-painted face at point blank range.

The Kiote's grip slackened, his hand fell away. Gone were the burning eyes, the sniffing nose-holes, the evil grin. Transformed instantly into a bloody mulch.

The head should have vanished from view. *Instead, it remained framed in the aperture, a morass that squelched its hatred, a scarlet faceless personification of the ultimate evil, functioning without features.*

Then it was gone. The arm slid from view like a retreating snake, only the blood-splashed timbers proof that it had existed outside the tortured imagination of the defenders.

Ben was ashen-faced, he might have given way to hysteria but for Sage's 'Good shootin', boy, thet's one more done fer.' The trapper added beneath his breath, ''Cept that bastard'll go back to fight another day.'

Blair turned back to his observation post, he dared not neglect it. He glimpsed a stealthy shape, fired a snapshot. He thought he detected a cry of pain. The silhouette vanished into the murk.

111

The horses had been remarkably quiet throughout the gunfire. Like they had been through it all before. Blair's neck prickled, everything seemed so familiar for Sage, too. He was probably used to Indian attacks throughout his trapping and wagon-train days.

The sound of galloping hooves died away. Some shots rang out from afar; Blair heard a bullet hit the front wall.

'They got a few rifles, not many.' Sage eased back from the window. 'Took 'em from the wagon trains they looted. Or got 'em from Koot. Injuns are bad shots, allus have been, allus will be. They kin drop a runnin' buck with an arrer but they wouldn't hit it with a gun if'n it sat and waited for 'em. Cain't explain it, jest a fact. But you need to look out fer stray bullets. If they ain't aimin' at somethin', they might jest hit it!'

'It's gone very quiet.' Adele tried to sound optimistic for Nicola's sake, the child must be going through hell.

'Expected it would after the first flurry.' Sage peered out cautiously. 'They've tested us, lost a coupla braves, not that that'll worry Black Bear over much, from now on they'll play it more cunning.'

'We kept 'em out, anyway.' Blair accepted the mug of coffee which Adele handed him. 'They must know by now that we're no pushover.'

'They could've overrun us,' Sage mused, 'lost a few more in the process. But they'll do it different from now on. You won't see 'em till it's too late.'

'They're scared of us.' Ben had regained his composure, recalled how he had blasted that attacker.

'Scared, yep, but not o' you, son. Nor your dad. They got you two sussed. It's *me* they're scared of, that's why they're holdin' back.'

Sage wasn't boasting, his words sent a chill through all of them. He was merely stating a fact. Adele blanched, she didn't understand, she didn't want to know why the Kiotes were frightened of the mountain man. Just that they were had her more scared than she had been all along.

Because Sage wasn't an ordinary mortal, she had long suspected that. He was no different from those savages; her only consolation was that he was on the side of an ordinary family that had somehow found themselves trapped in this valley of evil that had no right to exist in the modern world.

Sage had some terrible secret and maybe even he did not realize it.

Fifteen

Morning came slowly, grey and cold with a low-lying mist across the floor of the valley. The stove had burned itself out, the logs were stacked out back. Adele opened the last can of beans, all that remained on the shelf was a packet of unopened cracker biscuits. She did not bother to tear the wrapper, she new only too well that the contents would be inedible, encrusted with mould.

'That's *it*, the last of the food, and if somebody doesn't fetch some logs in, you'll have to eat them cold.' She glanced meaningfully at Sage.

'I got some jerky to be goin' on with.' Sage noted their puzzled expressions. 'Thet is, some stripped meat, dried and salted ready, comes in handy at times.' He rose to his feet, went through to the hallway where the horses were stamping restlessly. 'If the worst comes to the worst, we'll have to eat our boots.'

'*Boots!*' Adele gasped, Nicola's grimace turned to disbelief.

'Sure, done it a coupla times before, last time was one winter when I was holed up in here and ma supplies ran out, and the snow was too deep for snarin'. Made from animals, ain't they? Skin instead o' meat, lasts longer 'cause it takes some chewin'. Not much flavour but it's better'n starvin'. Or eatin' rats and, come to think of it, I ain't seen many o' them around lately.'

'Our footwear is synthetic,' Adele said quickly. Because Nicola was opposed to wearing anything that might be the direct result of an animal's death.

'Synth . . . what?' Sage was curious.

'It means they're artificial . . . not made from animal hides.'

'Well, I'll be durned!' He scratched his beard. 'Never heard o' boots that didn't come from buffalo or deer. Come to think o' it, them clothes you're wearin' don't look quite right, neither.'

'Anyway, we'd prefer not to eat our footwear.' She silenced Nicola with a frown. 'We'll manage, I'm sure.'

'Depends on how long we're holed up.'

His words carried a chilling implication, made her think of Victoria again.

The Kiotes were still out there. The mist had thinned a little, revealed figures stationed at intervals in a circle which encompassed the besieged cabin, sinister shapes with arms folded arrogantly, just out of rifle range.

'Tryin' to skeer you.' Sage grunted contemptuously. 'They knows they won't skeer me. They're hopin' mebbe you'll panic, make a run fer it or p'raps try to parley. Cain't talk with Kiotes, all they want is to torture and kill.'

'What are your plans?' Blair asked in a low voice, hoping the others would not hear the reply. Right now all they seemed to be doing was sitting this out and there could only be one end to it.

'Don't hev a plan. Never make plans, learned that long ago. Whatever you make your mind up to do, Injuns'll do somethin' different so's you cain't do it. We're stuck here, cain't do nothin' 'bout it.'

'But we'll run out of shells, powder and shot. We're almost out of food as it is.'

'I'll share ma boots.' There was a smile on the trapper's creased features. 'They go further, last longer'n you think. But that'll be after we've finished the jerky and I've got plenty o' that.'

They returned to watching the watchers, the mist dispersed still further. By midday it might have lifted altogether.

'*Look!*' Ben's sudden cry was a half scream, incorporated disbelief and sheer terror. He backed away from the slit in the wall, turned his anguished expression towards his father.

Sage beat Blair to the observation post, moving with the speed and agility of a mountain lion, his head and shoulders restricting the other's view. They heard him suck in his breath, mutter, 'Couldn't be no other way.'

'What is it?' Blair tried to push him out of the way. 'For God's sake, man, what's out there *now*!'

'Nothin' I didn't expect.' Sage only moved aside when he

was ready but even his leathery complexion appeared to have paled a little. 'Better see for yoursel', no point in me tryin' to hide it from yuh.'

Blair caught his breath. What he saw out there on the open ground defied everything which he had learned throughout his medical career. Whilst the fog had enshrouded the still and silent outline it had looked much the same as those which stood to the right and left of it. Tall and sinister, its ferocity in its haughty stance.

But now the grey vapour had lifted to reveal every horrific detail. There was no face, terrible injuries had obliterated the features, replaced them with jagged wounds, cavities that went deep into the misshapen skull, the blood congealed, dried to a black crust. There were no eyes yet the warrior stared and saw; no nostrils but the head was uplifted as if he scented; no mouth yet you sensed the obscenities, the death wish on the one who had brought about his disfigurement. The malevolence was a living force that emanated from the standing corpse.

'*It's the Injun I shot!*' Ben screamed from behind the two men. An eerie recognition that belied logic. Yet it was undoubtedly true.

Blair did not answer, no well-intended lie could have reassured the boy otherwise, there was no disputing that which stood out there. Even if the twenty's twin blast had not inflicted those wounds, whatever their cause, that brave could not have suffered them and still lived to fester vengeance.

'It's like I told yuh, them guns o' yours won't kill 'em, just mess 'em up a bit,' was all that Sage said as he resumed his post at the window.

The dried-meat strip had a flavour all of its own, Blair decided. Meaty, of course. Salty, too. In a way it reminded him of smoked venison. Only tougher. You chewed but you didn't swallow, just the juices which were mostly your own saliva.

'Like terbaccer,' Sage had been watching him with some amusement, ''ceptin' you don't spit. Chew it enough and eventually you'll be able to swallow some. That's where you get the nourishment.'

'Sure,' Blair masticated rhythmically. 'It's really good.'

'Great,' Ben spoke awkwardly through a mouthful. 'Wish we could buy this back home.'

Adele and Nicola had finished the last of the beans. They did not dare think as far ahead as the next meal.

Something thudded on to the roof directly above.

'That'll be an arrer.' Sage barely looked up, he'd obviously been expecting it for some time. 'Jest lettin' us know that they're still there in case we'd fergot. Long range, fired high into the air, gets distance that way but no real force. Bad luck if it drops on yuh, though.'

'Couldn't you reach 'em, with the rifle?' Blair had been attempting to work out the distance from the cabin to the watching braves. It didn't look more than a hundred and fifty yards.

'Might. There agin, might not. Too fur fer an accurate shot. There'll be plenty opportunities fer them later.'

Those opportunities arose towards the middle of the afternoon just after the sun had attempted to break through the dense low cloud and had finally given up for the day. One minute the Kiotes were maintaining a stoic vigil, the next they were running, shrieking, towards the besieged cabin.

Sage's rifle boomed, the ball shattered a brave's chest, hurled him backwards where he lay motionless, spreadeagled on the ground.

It was the one with the shot-blasted face.

Blair heard Ben's gun crack twice, the boy had fired both barrels together. The Browning emptied another magazine. Two Kiotes went down; one began to crawl away, the second clambered back on to his feet, stood there dazed.

'Dropped one!' Blair shouted to Sage. 'He's crawling, bleeding all over.'

Spent shells from the breech-loaders bounced on the floor. Adele took Sage's rifle, handed him back his pistols; she was becoming adept at loading. Nicola was cowering under the table, eyes tightly shut.

Another attacker was bleeding heavily from a charge of 00. An eye was obliterated, he wiped at the empty socket with a hand. Sage felled him with a .50 pistol ball. The brave fell forward; he did not move again.

A hand clutching a knife came in through the wall slit, the Indian had ducked in close, worked his way along the wall.

117

Blair shredded the limb, it was jerked back. The knife clanged on the floor.

The horses were neighing and kicking – up until now the gunfire had not troubled them unduly.

'They smelled somethin'!' Sage tensed as he took his reloaded Hawken. 'An' it ain't jest Injuns . . .'

Something rasped in Adele's throat, there was a different kind of smoky smell this time. It wasn't Blair's cigar, the stench was acrid rather than aromatic. She thought it might have been Sage's pipe; a swift glance told her that he did not have it clenched between his broken and blackened teeth. Powder smoke from the rifle and the pistols, or burned nitro from the shotguns? None of these fitted.

A reverberating blast distracted her for a second. Sage's keen eyes had spotted a Kiote squirming through the broken railings on the veranda. The brave slumped, slid back, half his skull was gone. Sage handed Adele the rifle, the barrel was uncomfortably warm to the touch. He picked up his pistols, checked, his nostrils dilating. He had smelled something, too.

'*Fire!*'

Even as the trapper yelled, Adele noticed thick smoke pouring in through the wall, heard a crackling like when the stove was first lighted and the flames licked the dry kindling.

Blair let off a shot at a running silhouette, knew instinctively that the distraction had checked his swing, the charge was probably a good yard behind it. He looked round.

'*Fire arrer!*' Sage yelled. 'Get buckets o' water on it. Watch them winders, too, they'll use the distraction to rush us.'

Adele grabbed up one of the buckets, hurled water at the place where the smoke had thickened to a billow. A hissing sound followed.

'And another!' Sage ordered, turned back to the window, took a snapshot with a pistol. 'Got 'im, blowed the top o' his head off, horns as well. Keep them buckets fillin', get loadin' too. It's gonna be fast from now on.'

At least the pump was working, Adele thought, and left a bucket to fill under a steady trickle from the tap over the sink. It was probably operated by a gravity fall, Blair had said. She didn't really understand, it didn't matter how the water was drawn so long as it flowed.

Two more thuds came, this time from up above, she looked round in alarm, held the spare bucket in readiness for the first sign of another trickle of smoke through the timber.

'That wuz on the roof,' Sage said as he took back his recharged Hawken. 'Won't burn there, there's a foot o' soil above the rafters.'

Blair reloaded the magazine, slammed it home with the heel of his hand, broke open another carton of shells and filled his pockets. That was the last box of 00. After that was used up there were just fives and sixes left, bird- and rabbit-shot. They gave a denser shot pattern but less penetration due to the smaller size of the pellets. They might perform better if the attackers were closer.

He fired again, saw a brave fall back, lie there for a few seconds then slowly pick himself up. Blair pumped another three at him, had him staggering away until the darkness swallowed him up. It was unbelievable.

Ben fired a single shot. The boy had the sense to shoot sparingly now, they had less twenty-gauge shells than twelves. The fleeing shadow disappeared, he was sure he'd hit it.

And then, without warning, smoke was pouring into the cabin, thick suffocating fumes that might have been fuelled by the long-ago coating of pitch between the timbers. The occupants turned, saw flames beginning to lick through hungrily. A hail of fire arrows must have gone unnoticed in the latest skirmish.

The bucket in the sink was nearly full, Adele hurled the contents in panic. There was a fizzing *whoosh*, a puff of smoke from the doused flames. But within seconds the blaze had caught again, flared up.

'Give me a hand to fill the buckets under the tap, Nick.' Because sheltering beneath the table isn't going to protect you if this place goes up.

The flow of water from the tap was slowing considerably, maybe the well was drying up or else the antiquated system was unable to cope with the excessive demand upon it. Adele said, 'Fuck it,' but, thankfully, it was drowned by a shot from the Hawken.

'Mommy, the water's going to run out soon.'

Of course it is, just like everything else in this place. 'Just leave it running.' She picked up a broom, it had only a stubble

119

of bristles left on it. She tried beating at the flames; the brush head smouldered, began to smoke.

'*Rifle!*' Sage roared at her, his edginess was starting to show. 'Cain't shoot no damned Injuns if I don't hev a loaded gun.' He lined his pistol up on something outside but held his fire. They needed to go real easy with the powder and shot from now on.

The interior of the cabin was becoming unbearably hot. A section of the wall was glowing redly, the way logs on the stove did when the fire was beginning to get a hold. The smoke was denser, everybody's eyes were watering.

A painted face looked in through one of the slits but drew back before Blair could swing his gun on to it. It was as if the Kiote was just checking on those inside; there was no need to take any risks, the flames would do the tribesmen's work for them.

'We can't stay in here much longer,' Blair shouted. 'We'll be roasted alive. We'll have to take our chance out in the open.'

'We don't have no choice.' The mountain man's pistols were belted, he held the Hawken fully cocked, butt resting on his thigh. 'Jest how it was last time, like I told yuh. Injuns burned the cabin down, somebody rebuilt it. They shoulda know'd it'd happen agin. C'mon, let the hosses go, there's too many o' us to ride 'em and I ain't gonna run out on yuh now. Back to back, Blair, you, me 'n' the boy, keep the wimmin between us. Give them Injuns everythin' we got, right up to the end.'

The horses' eyes were rolling, fire was their nemesis. Hardly was the door dragged wide enough before they charged through the gap, bolted into the firelit night.

The Kiotes were just visible beyond the orange-yellow glow cast by the burning building. They stood with folded arms, half men, half beasts with horned heads. Or maybe they were neither, if the legend related by Sage was true; they were evil spirits from beyond the grave intent upon murdering these mortals who had dared to defy them with their puny weapons.

The Kiotes neither screamed nor yelled their lust. They watched, their gloating was only too obvious. The whites were theirs for the taking, they could pick them off at their leisure.

'Too damned many of 'em this time, more'n I thought

there'd be.' Sage halted, signalled to his companions to take up their defensive formation. 'The darkness is alive with 'em. Guess we go down fightin', but don't let 'em take yuh alive. Save a bullet for yourselves an', if I don't manage it, I'd be obliged if one o' yuh would do the same for me.' He smiled wistfully in the firelight, there was just a hint of sadness in his expression.

Blair turned his head away, there was no way he could promise anybody that. Just the same as he'd walked away from the dying Prudence, left the trapper to make the decision and carry it out. He couldn't promise that to Sage, not even to his own family. Because living was hoping. He had once threatened to take his own life; he knew then, standing there in the light of the blazing shack, that his words had been no more than a shallow threat.

God, I don't want to die. I don't want any of us to die.

'You hear me, Blair?'

'I hear you, Sage. We go down fighting.'

He whirled and blazed five rounds at the ring of Kiotes, stabbing flame and leaden shot that was the signal for this night of lurking terror to erupt into mayhem.

A sudden shower of sparks from the inferno drove back the shadows, lighted the scene. Adele covered Nicola with her body, hoped that the child would not see as the menfolk formed a back-to-back triangular defensive wall. There would be no time for reloading the flintlocks, Sage eased the knives in their sheaths around his belt; the end would be bloody hand-to-hand fighting.

A ring of demonic faces surrounded the party, lusted for torture and death with unspeakable things to follow. A slow advance, knives and lances poised, axes swinging from waist thongs, their horned heads symbolic of their Master who was greater than Manitou.

'Shoot whilst you still kin.' Sage's rifle thundered, split open the chest of an advancing warrior, threw him back in a lifeless heap.

The twenty cracked, a Kiote face became an instant polka dot, crimson rivulets obliterating his gaudy paintwork. He checked, just stood there dazed. Blair gave him a charge of sixes and he sank slowly to his knees. He would rise again shortly.

The entire circle sprang forward, the preliminaries were over. Sage's pistols barked from either hand, two more Kiotes crumpled; the weapons were returned to his belt and the Hawken was swung up by its long barrel, its stock arcing in search of a horned skull.

Blair sensed the nearness of an enemy to his right, an attacker who had seized his chance when a comrade created a distraction. The doctor pulled the rest of the magazine, three continuous charges at a range of less than two yards.

The shot blasts took the brave's neck, guillotined it except for a few bloody sinews. The head fell back, hung behind the jagged, bleeding stump. The decapitated body tottered; a step forward, another back, miraculously, horribly, remaining upright.

Adele screamed as Sage lunged, felled it with the butt of his rifle.

Another brave caught the swinging Hawken, wrested it from the trapper's grasp. Sage let it go, pulled a knife and, in a continuation of the same sweeping movement, gutted the other as he would have paunched a jackrabbit. Intestines spilled from the wound like a nest of crimson vipers, squirming and writhing.

Then three more Kiotes were upon their nemesis, sheer weight of numbers bearing him to the ground.

'Keep with me,' Blair yelled to the others. He had somehow managed to reload the Browning; if the gun did not have the power to kill these supernatural foes, at least it was capable of cutting a swathe of mutilation through them.

The fallen kicked and writhed, struggled to rise but, temporarily, they were rendered non-combatant. The others stepped over them, kicked away clutching hands that were slippery with blood, blasted those who were persistent in their efforts to drag the fugitives back.

Adele screamed as she staggered with Nicola hugged to her bosom. A hand fastened over her ankle, lost its grip as she stamped on it. *Its touch was as cold as steak from a cooler.*

There was no sign of Sage. If he had extricated himself from the melee then he had not followed after the others. The blaze from the cabin no longer lighted up the scene; the roof had fallen in as the burning walls collapsed and the soil which Sage had heaped upon it had all but extinguished the fire.

The sky was illuminated by the light of a rising moon which was yet to top the surrounding mountains, a glow that was just enough to see by.

Blair had filled the magazine again but there were no lurking shapes to blast, no death-cold hands reaching for them out of the shadows. No cries of unholy lust.

Just a deep silence broken only by their own stumbling footfalls and laboured breathing. It was as though the Kiotes had never existed, that the Lunds had awoken from some terrible fevered nightmare.

And stepped right into another.

They had reached the tall trees with massive boles and deformed branches. They smelled again that familiar odour of decay which permeated the still night air.

Only then did they realize that their living nightmare continued. Even without the screaming savages it was a terrifying prospect.

Blair found himself on a track that was spongy with decades of leaf-fall, experienced a sinking sensation of déjà vu even though everywhere was deep in shadow. This was the same trail which they had trodden a few days ago, one that began with hope and ended with hopelessness as it wound back down to the valley of no return.

Sixteen

'We'll have to rest up awhile.' Adele spoke for the rest of them. 'We can't go on much further.' Nicola was already asleep in her arms and weighing heavier by the minute.

Blair paused, only the adrenaline had kept them going; under less threatening circumstances they would never have made it this far. His legs felt as if they were about to crumple beneath him, throw him to the soft, stinking ground.

They were in a clearing of some kind, a tract of open ground some fifteen yards in diameter, huge trees all around. On the far side the trails split, one led off to the right, the other to the left. They had best leave it until daylight to make a decision on which one to take.

'We'll camp right here.' We'll doss down, wait for dawn. We don't have anything to eat or drink and we're almost out of shells. Tomorrow we'll probably get lost or else arrive back at that bloody cabin. Only this time it will be a burned-out shell that won't even offer us shelter. And then the Kiotes will show up and we'll start all over again.

They opted for the shelter of a giant poplar, a wind-blasted sixty-foot-high tree that had somehow survived a century or so of storms. It had even defied the Great Storm. It offered scant protection from the elements but there was no other choice.

Blair decided to risk a fire. There was plenty of dead wood scattered around and they needed warmth. The clearing was in a hollow: if they kept the blaze small there was every chance that it would not be seen except by anybody in the immediate proximity. It would be dangerous to expose Nicola to the cold and damp of night; a sleeping person's resistance was at its lowest then, pneumonia could strike with alarming rapidity.

The pile of rotten wood crackled, burned up quickly and

they huddled around it. The shadows which its flickering created were the worst feature, especially for Adele and Nicola; the darkness hid a thousand terrors, dancing flames brought them to life.

'What happened to Sage?' Nicola asked with inquisitive innocence. 'I think he's nice even though he does smell. I was frightened of him at first but I'm not any more.'

'Dunno.' Blair poked the fire, sent the shadows skittering away. 'Guess he . . . well, I can't imagine anybody or anything getting the better of Sage but this time there were a few too many Kiotes even for him. I get the feeling somehow that he might've made it, escaped and is hiding in the mountains.'

'Maybe he's looking for us.' Ben tossed a twig on the fire.

'Could be. On the other hand, he's in no way beholden to us. He fought with us because we happened to meet up and the folks he was guiding are dead.' Blair shuddered at the memory of the missionaries. 'He's free to go wherever the whim takes him.'

'Why didn't the Injuns follow us, Dad?'

'There's no explanation for them or the rest of this whole damned business. They weren't *ordinary* Indians. Sage said so, we proved that ourselves. Sage's gun could kill 'em, ours just knocked 'em about. I guess we just happened to be in the wrong place at the wrong time. I'm just hoping that when it gets light we'll be able to find a way out of here. I never want to set eyes on this place again.'

It was a forlorn hope. But if you stopped hoping, you died.

'We'll have to shoot something to eat in the morning.' Ben's fears were temporarily forgotten by his love of hunting. 'I got about a dozen shells left.'

'*If* there's anything here to shoot.' Blair watched the dancing flames, he didn't even try to interpret their many shapes. 'Apart from the odd pigeon, since the storm we haven't glimpsed a single wild creature. Sage's snares didn't catch either, or if they did, he never told us.'

Eyelids drooped, Blair determined to keep watch as best he could. It seemed a pointless exercise, there was no defence against the evil that surrounded them.

'*What's that?*' Something catapulted Adele out of a deep sleep into instant wakefulness. The fire had burned down to a dull glow, she felt the warmth from the embers but it cast no light. There were no shadows, just impenetrable blackness all around.

'What's what?' Blair murmured, stirred.

'I . . . I heard *something*.'

'Can't say I did.' He reached out, threw some more branches on the fire. They smouldered, then burst into flames and the shadows came flitting back.

'I *thought* I did, anyway.' She felt slightly foolish, apprehensive, too. Sometimes you heard noises in your sleep and they woke you but you could not remember exactly what you had heard. You had to wait for the sound to come again. Adele prayed that this time it wouldn't, that whatever she'd heard had been in some disturbed dream.

'There it goes again! Did you hear it this time?'

'Yes,' he whispered, listened. He heard a movement back in the forest somewhere, a soft footfall on a leaf-carpeted track, a dead twig snapping. His hand reached out and the feel of the Browning was comforting.

'What is it, Blair?'

'How should I know? Keep quiet, just listen. There it goes again.'

It might have been a Kiote but somehow the sound was wrong. Wrong for Sage, too. It had to be an animal of some kind. The tread came again, it was too heavy for a rabbit.

'*Look!*' Adele half screamed, pressed herself back against the trunk of a poplar. A huge shaggy shape stood on the far side of the clearing; without the glow from the rekindled fire it would have remained mercifully hidden from her view.

It was twice, maybe three times, the size of a Labrador dog, jaws agape menacingly and pointed ears erect. Its rough coat had a greyish tinge that in the half-light created a ghostly illusion.

'A *wolf!*' Blair grunted, raised the gun slowly, careful not to startle the animal. One leap and it could have been upon them. He recalled the last time he'd shot at wolves and they had not seemed even to notice.

It continued to watch them, its unblinking eyes glowing redly in the reflection from the fire, twin orbs of sheer evil. Adele was relieved that Ben and Nicola still slept, she prayed that they might be spared this latest horror.

126

'Is . . . is it *real*?' She breathed.

'Is anything real in this hellish hole?' He eased a shell into the breech, hoped that the metallic sound would not antagonize the animal. 'Real or not, the inhabitants of this place aren't exactly friendly towards us.'

The fire burned up even more brightly. Wild animals were supposedly afraid of fire; this one seemed undeterred, totally oblivious of it.

'Shoot it, Blair,' Adele pleaded.

'Not yet.' He would never forget that night when he had blasted the pack, sprayed them with heavy buckshot and not a single one had reacted. They might just as well have been wooden silhouettes on a shooting range where the tip-over mechanism had jammed. 'Not unless I have to.'

Nicola stirred, muttered something incoherent in her sleep. She was having a nightmare. Theirs was for real.

The wolf moved forward like it was merely easing its position, loosening cramped limbs. Its hindquarters tensed, it might be making ready to spring. Blair had the automatic resting across his knees, the barrel centred on the beast, his finger took a slight trigger pressure. He was tempted, this one was real close, much closer than those others had been.

Its eyes were its most terrifying feature; the way they glowed, you felt evil in them. It wasn't in any hurry. Maybe it had already fed and wasn't hungry any more. But it would kill because that was its nature.

'Hi, boy!' Jesus, it sounded stupid, anywhere else you would have creased yourself laughing. But not here. Maybe a soothing word, the tone, would reassure it and it would just wander away. It was worth a try, Blair was prepared to try anything.

The wolf heard and growled low in its throat. Blair sensed every muscle in its powerful body tautening, a spring that would uncoil without warning. He winced at the prospect, braced himself.

Adele screamed loudly as the wolf leapt, became airborne with an agility that belied its size. Blair's finger tugged the trigger. Three shots rolled together, vivid flame lighting up every corner of the clearing.

He closed his eyes, felt Adele clinging to him. No way could he have missed at that range. They braced themselves for the tearing fangs, prayed also that they might hear the thud of a heavy body hitting the ground; dead in the air, limp on the leafy floor.

Or it would land on top of them, maddened with pain and rage, venting its wounded wrath upon them, ripping at their flesh.

Neither happened. Nothing happened at all. Only when the rolling echoes of the gunshots had died away did they summon up the courage to peer out from beneath trembling eyelids. *There was nothing to be seen, not so much as a leaf stirred in the deserted clearing. The wolf had appeared before them, it had disappeared as mysteriously and as silently as it had come.*

'What is it, Dad?' Ben scrambled awake, grabbed for the twenty. Nicola came sobbing out of her bad dream.

'A jackrabbit.' The lie came convincingly on the wings of sheer relief. 'And I damned well went and missed it!'

It was daylight, time to move on.

They were cold and stiff but somehow their exhaustion seemed to have receded; sheer desperation to find their way out of the valley had provided them with an extra reserve to draw upon.

'Any idea which direction we're going to head in, Blair?' The forest looked much as it had the last time, tracks that wound back on themselves, forked and created added confusion.

'We just keep going.' He checked that the gun was fully loaded, slung it on his shoulder. 'One day's much the same as another. This time we just trust to luck, we don't have anything else.'

The wood seemed much bigger than the last time. As they emerged from yet another clearing they saw how the poplars and redwoods were spaced; there was distance between them as if they had originally been planted or else Man had maintained some form of forestry management. Trees and more trees, there was no welcoming view of an open landscape beyond.

'It's like the whole country has been planted with trees,' Ben surmised. 'Nothing but trees.'

'At least it's not a dense jungle that we've got to fight our way through. Look!' Blair pulled up suddenly, pointed ahead of them. *'Somebody's been felling timber!'*

128

They stared, saw stumps where tree trunks had been cut with axes, snapped branches where they had crashed down. All around the ground was churned up where the timber had been dragged away.

'Pulled with horses, not tractors.' It didn't need a backwoodsman of Sage's experience to read the tracks, piece them all together. 'Some homesteaders still use horses for work. Well, that's encouraging, we can't be too far from a habitation of some kind.' He checked his rising euphoria. In this place one learned to reserve judgement, hopes were dashed with frightening frequency. But at least the felling was recent, the sweet aroma of sap and sawdust was like nectar in the air. He breathed deeply, let it out slowly. 'If we follow these tracks we're sure to come out wherever the timber's been transported to.'

A loggers' camp, possibly, Blair decided. A colony of lumberjacks who worked in a remote forest, moved on when they had cut their quota of trees. Any *human* habitation would be welcome after what they had been through these last few days. Or was it weeks? Months? *Years*? Their only timepiece had stopped with the storm. When that happened you counted dawns and dusks but eventually you lost count. Then the passing of time lost its meaning.

'Blair, I think I can hear somebody coming.'

Blair's pulses stepped up a gear. Instinctively he unslung the Browning. Out here you didn't take any chances, every twist or turn was fraught with danger.

'It might be Sage caught up with us.' He spoke the possibility aloud for all their sakes. 'Or perhaps it's somebody from the lumber camp or settlement, or whatever they're building with the timber they've cut down.'

Heads turned with his own, they stood there looking back the way they had come. At any moment whoever it was who followed them would hove into sight over the top of the bank which they had just climbed.

A heavy tread, loggers were mostly big and strong, they had to be. Sage was powerfully built, too. Except that he had perfected the knack of moving stealthily, his tread was barely perceptible. It had to be in a place that was infested with wild tribesmen.

Dead branches snapped loudly, no attempt was being made

129

to move quietly. Maybe that was a good sign, Adele thought, at least they weren't being stalked. All the same, her heart pounded madly.

Any second now they would see whoever it was . . .

Nicola moved nearer her mother, Ben stood alongside his father, pushed the safety catch forward on the small shotgun.

They knew by now it wasn't Sage. It *had* to be a lumberjack, they willed it to be. Then they glimpsed a head coming over the top of the bank.

It was neither Sage nor a logger. Nor a homesteader. Adele screamed, Blair gasped with shocked surprise and lifted the gun to his shoulder.

It was a giant of a grizzly bear.

The bear had been travelling on all fours, now it reared up on its hind legs, towered seven or eight feet tall, claws that were capable of disembowelling a human being at one slashing stroke lifted menacingly. Its small eyes regarded these trespassers in its domain from beneath its shaggy fur. Its powerful body tensed, one hug from those arms could crush them to a much.

'Bastard!' Blair pushed the gun barrel at it, the range was no more than three yards, held the trigger back. Five shots exploded in as many seconds, he had a close up view of the charges obliterating the beast's face; the open jaws spewed claret as they were morassed, the snout was mashed to a dripping mulch. The eyes disappeared into a raw and bleeding cavity.

But the bear still stood, lashed out blindly with its claws.

'Run!'

Then they were fleeing breathlessly, afraid to glance behind them, the lumbering of huge paws vibrating the ground. The decimated monster roared and vomited blood as it charged blindly in pursuit.

Its cries resembled an erupting volcano, liquid ferocity as it crashed sightlessly from tree to tree, intent upon a terrible revenge upon those who had stricken it.

It showed no signs of slowing. If anything, its momentum gathered a pace, a trail of blood-splattered boles and branches in its wake.

The Lunds left the track, zigzagged through the trees, running hell-bent on finding some place of safety. Blair thought of grabbing an overhanging branch, lifting the others up out of reach; there wasn't time. And, anyway the beast would probably have settled itself down below and waited them out.

They passed a stack of felled tree trunks; seconds later they heard it avalanching as their enraged pursuer blundered into it. The bear didn't even check its pace.

The grizzly was sightless, scentless, blood gushed from its mouth, yet it showed no sign of slowing.

Adele's foot caught in a protruding root, threw her. Ben helped her up, Blair grabbed Nicola. The flight continued.

Timber stacks were becoming more frequent now. Once the fugitives fled along an alleyway of tree trunks, piled high on either side of the track. Again logs rolled, cascaded, as the infuriated creature bumped from side to side. It was steadily catching up on its intended prey. Nothing would halt its crazed charge.

The ground was trodden flat from here on, worn level by the constant passage of beasts of burden dragging trees from the forest. The overhead sky was no longer obstructed by entwining branches.

Blair and his family had finally made it out into the open.

They staggered from the wood, found themselves standing upon a hillside that sloped down to a cluster of shacks below. It was a small valley but certainly not the one from which they had fled.

They stared in disbelief, people were moving about, wagons were parked at the rear of the buildings, horses were tethered. Smoke wisped up from a dozen or more chimneys. It was some kind of settlement.

Blair glanced nervously back at the forest. There was neither sight nor sound of the rampaging grizzly bear that had chased them. Like the timber wolf, it had disappeared as if it had never even existed.

Seventeen

It was the kind of township that might have been used for a set for one of Ben's favourite videos. There were about twenty cabins in all, of varying shapes and sizes; some stout and well constructed with tree trunks from the forest, others ramshackle as though the occupants had more important tasks to occupy their time.

Blair's feet dragged, Nicola was heavy in his arms with exhausted slumber. Adele staggered, held on to Ben for support. The smell of wood smoke was sweet in their nostrils.

One of the buildings had a veranda and an overhanging roof. A man walked unsteadily from out of it, fell down the steps and lay in the dusty street. Shouting and coarse laughter came from within; it was obviously some kind of bar.

Where the street began, a group of men were huddled in conversation, every one of them clad in that now all-too-familiar clothing fashioned from animal skins. Bearded faces looked up at the approach of strangers, the curiosity turned to hostility.

Blair thought, Shit, this isn't a *normal* place, either. Tiny icicles touched his spine. The morning sun had suddenly lost its warmth.

'What kind of people are they, Blair?' Adele was uneasy too.

'Loggers, I guess. Maybe traders.' And I don't damned well like the look of them.

More men emerged from the cabins, stood out in the street, shaded their eyes from the glare of the sun. Quite obviously the arrival of strangers wasn't an everyday occurrence and they didn't like it when it happened.

'Good morning.' Blair stopped, glanced from face to scowling face. There were no smiles, not so much as an answering nodded greeting. Just stares. He saw that every one

132

of them carried pistols and knives in their thong belts. He might have been looking at a score of Sages, except that Sage had always been friendly.

The doctor was aware of another smell that began to permeate the wood smoke. He caught his breath, it was an odour that the Kiotes had worn, the missionaries, too. Even the mountain man stank of it.

The stench of rotting. And death.

'We got lost in the forest, happened upon your township. We'd appreciate some food and a rest. Then maybe you'd be kind enough to put us on the right road to . . .'

'Tuh *whair*?' A bull-necked bearded head was thrust forward, the dark eyes suspicious. 'Whair're yuh headed, mister?'

'To the . . . main highway.'

'The main . . . *highway*? What's thet? Where's thet?'

'I . . . I'm not quite sure. You see, we got lost. We've been lost for several days. Ever since the big storm.'

'Storm? Ain't bin no storms since last winter.' His eyes were almost closed as if he tried to hide his suspicion from them. Other hide-clad figures moved slowly, furtively. Suddenly, the Lunds were surrounded. 'Where yuh from?'

'Back east. New York.'

'Nooo York.' He dwelled on the name like he'd never heard of it before. 'What're yuh doin' hereabouts then, stranger?'

'It started out as a hunting vacation.' Blair swallowed nervously. Whatever he said, these guys weren't going to believe him.

'Huntin', uh?'

'That's right.'

'Headin' west like everybody else, huh?' His eyes gleamed, his companions were crowding the newcomers now.

'We came west, yes. From New York.'

'Injuns attacked the wagon train, I guess. You escaped.'

'All right,' Blair sighed. 'We were attacked by Indians. We were lucky, we got away.' It was all true, anyway. It might be easier to go along with that story.

The men exchanged glances, a couple at the back were muttering.

'I'm Jason. The boss is away right now, mebbe he'll be back tomorrow, day after. Never kin tell. His name's *Koot*.'

133

Blair went cold. 'I've never heard of him.'

'You got any money?' Their eyes switched from Blair to Adele. There was no mistaking their expressions. One of them licked his lips as if he'd just smelled a freshly cooked steak and fries.

'Not a lot.'

'It'll cost yuh to stay here.' Jason was looking fixedly at Adele. 'This woman yours or did yuh pick her up on the wagons?'

'She's my wife.' Blair's grip tightened on the Browning; he wondered how fast he could unsling it and fire. No chance, these bastards had crowded him too close for movement. They'd grab the gun, jump him at the first sign of trouble.

'Now, Koot, he'd ride from here to Texas 'n' back to get hisself astride a white woman.' The leer behind the thick beard had Adele cringing. She backed away a step, bumped into a logger who was standing close. Too close. His calloused hands strayed to her buttocks, she dared not knock them away. She closed her thighs tightly just in case those rough fingers might stray elsewhere. One of the others sniggered. 'Me, I prefer an Injun. Give me a young squaw any day, younger the better, preferably Comanche. Comanche gels have so much fire in their bellies. And they're hot other places, too.' His words brought a chorus of guffaws.

Blair noted with no small amount of alarm that Jason's fingers were stroking the barrel of the automatic, curling round it.

'Koot'll sure like bein' introduced to the lady.' Jason grinned and Blair saw that he had no teeth, just blackened gums. 'Sure will. Take my advice, mister, don't try to stand in his way. If'n he takes a shine to your woman, it might be a good thing for you, too. Koot's a strange guy, allus gets what he wants, takes it if folks refuse to hand it over. More'n one got kilt that way.'

Blair's heart missed a beat, one of the men had taken the twenty from Ben, was examining it with no small amount of curiosity.

'Strange gun, never seed one like that before.' The man unhitched a ramrod which had been hanging from his shoulder. Another produced a powder horn, a bullet pouch rattled. 'Purty little Bess, depends how she shoots, though.'

Powder trickled down the barrels, some wadding was rammed after it.

'No!' Blair protested. 'You don't load it like that, you—'

'Mister,' Jason's animal snarl was only inches from the medic's, the logger's breath was as fetid as an opened grave, 'you got no say in this. How'd you like to see that woman o' yourn stripped right now an' every man in this town take her, right before yer eyes. Yuh reckon she'd be much good to yuh after?'

Blair did not resist as Jason took the Browning from him.

'Stoke 'er, Ned, try 'er on that post yonder. A noggin o' whisky says yer don't hit it.'

'I'll hit it.' The lean man's face twisted as he thumped the charge hard. 'You see if I don't.'

'It's a breech-loader!' Blair shouted, and strong hands seized him.

'Shaddup, dude. You reckon you knows more 'bout guns than us who lives by 'em?' Jason spat on the ground. 'One more squeak outa you and you'll be the target practice!'

'Dad, the twenty's got shells in!' Ben protested. The flat of a hand struck him across the face, his lip began to bleed. Blair was proud of his son because he didn't start to cry.

'Give 'er a go, Ned!' A chorus of encouragement came from the half-dozen men who stood around the one called Ned.

The gun was at Ned's shoulder, looked almost trivial against his mountain attire. He was tugging at the trigger, cursing. 'Fuckin' thing don't shoot!'

All eyes turned on Blair. Their expressions said, 'You'd better show us how, stranger.'

'Push the catch on the action forward.' He spoke in a trembling voice. 'But I warn you, there's shells in that gun, and with your powder charge it'll—'

Jason's fist took him in the mouth, sent him sprawling backwards. There was a kaleidoscope of vivid colours before his eyes, he tasted the iron flavour of blood.

'Blair!' Adele would have rushed to her husband except that the man holding her pulled her back roughly. 'Are you OK?'

'I'm OK.' He struggled up to a kneeling position. 'But that guy won't be when he pulls the trigger. I've just instructed

135

him on how to kill himself. I feel like an executioner who's just pressed the switch.'

Ned squinted along the barrel, muttered that it was 'too fuckin' short'. His stumpy finger curled round the trigger. Pulled.

It was as though a stick of dynamite had been detonated in the midst of the gathering. Blair saw the twenty-gauge barrel burst, transformed from smooth steel into twisted metal instantly, its debris flying in all directions. There was a jet of crimson as a severed hand became airborne.

Ned staggered backwards. His features were awash with blood, an eye hung by a thread, an ear was gone. He screamed gutturally; others were screaming, too.

Even in those first few seconds Blair knew that the injuries to Ned and those standing close to him were too terrible to contemplate. Two shells, ignited by a charge of black powder, had strained the barrel pressure beyond its generous designated limits. Two men had crumpled to the ground, the staggering Ned fell over them, lay still. Another's cap was gone, revealing a completely bald head, the top of which had been sliced off. He, too, collapsed.

Others who had suffered less serious injuries were yelling where the split charges of birdshot had sprayed their bodies. One was holding his groin, bloodied fingers vainly trying to staunch the wound.

Jason whirled on Blair, murder in his eyes. His thick lips moved, growled. 'You done this to us, stranger. You're an army spy, the government sent yuh here to blow us to hell with that trick gun. Grab 'em all, take 'em to the cell to join Brock. Brock's gonna hang when Koot gits back and I reckon these folks'll be joinin' him in a necktie party!'

The survivors of the blast rushed to the strangers. Blair was hauled to his feet, kneed in the groin. Lecherous hands explored Adele once they had grabbed her hands and feet, prevented her from kicking and slapping. Her captors laughed, their wounded comrades already forgotten as they pulled and fondled her down the street.

Ben was cuffed over the head, made to walk in front. Nicola was dragged screaming by her hair. Dust clouds rose beneath the unwilling, scuffing feet of the captors.

Jason brought up the rear; he had left the Browning five-shot where it lay. He wasn't going to touch *that*, it was sure to be another government trap.

'You lot're gonna hev your necks stretched.' He pointed to a makeshift gallows that stood starkly behind the line of buildings. 'There's a few swung on that, I watched 'em dangle. Koot's a hangin' man, he'd sooner hang yuh than kill yuh seven different ways from Sunday. You see if'n I ain't right, you'll hang. 'Cept mebbe the woman when Koot sets eyes on her. Lady, if I wuz you, I'd pray that he has a mind to hang yuh instead.' He burst into laughter. 'But that'll be *after* he's done to yuh what he allus does with women, specially whites!'

Eighteen

The room was roughly nine feet long and six wide, a separate building that stood behind the others, built from the stoutest tree trunks the forest had to offer. The door was reinforced, the huge bolts fashioned by a blacksmith, and a bar that dropped across the outside ensured that it could not be broken down by those it confined.

The only light came from a slit cut in the high roof, barely wide enough for an arm to be pushed through. A prisoner standing on a comrade's shoulders might just have been able to reach it with his fingertips. The earthen floor directly beneath it was muddy from the last rainstorm.

There was no furniture of any kind; you sat, slept, ate on the floor. The stench from a bucket in the corner was nauseating.

'You jest make sure you use that,' Jason growled. 'We don't do no muckin' out here. If'n you shit on the floor, you can clean it up yerselves. An' we don't allow prisoners to use shovels! You'll stay here till Koot gets back. Make the most of it, pray each mornin' that he won't come today!'

They heard the bolts being shot, the thud of the bar as it was dropped into place.

Adele held Ben and Nicola to her, they were sobbing with shock. Blair stood there dazed, felt at his mouth, his lips were swelling. His head ached, it was all he could do not to throw up.

'What is this place?' Adele asked.

'Dunno, maybe some of the early pioneers decided to settle here, built themselves a bit of a shanty town, even built a jail house with the idea of enforcing law and order. Then the renegades took it over.'

'S'right, jest what happened.'

The cracked, rasping voice from the corner made them jump.

138

They whirled, their eyesight was not yet adjusted to the deep gloom of the cell; they could just make out a huddled form in the corner. Adele caught her breath, pulled the children away.

'Frightened you, did I? There's no need to be afraid of ol' Brock, he never did nobody no harm.' The figure shifted its position with difficulty, they saw an emaciated body from which ragged clothing hung.

Barefooted, his toenails curled like a hawk's talons, his near-skeletal hands were deformed, too. As a beam of light from the overhead aperture fell on his features it was all that Adele could do not to scream.

He was hairless and yet he wasn't bald, a kind of dried crust covered the top of his head in an almost symmetrical circle. His eyes were sunken into black hollows, parchment skin stretched across the cheekbones, giving him a skeletal appearance. The nose had been broken at some time and not reset. The mouth was a toothless slit that dribbled saliva every time he spoke.

'Name's Brock.' He had a lisp, Blair thought it might have been due to his having no teeth. 'Scout fer the army. Leastways, I wuz until the Kiotes ambushed me. That wuz . . .' He might have closed his eyes, it wasn't easy to tell, 'Lose track o' time when you're shut up in here, day after day. I reckon' it was thirty-seven, can't be sure. Must've bin here three months, at a guess. Wish the Injuns had finished me off, would've done if Koot hadn't bargained with 'em, fer me. See – ' a bony finger tapped his head – 'they *skelped* me.'

Ugh! Adele looked away.

'Thirty-seven, you say?' Blair caught his breath. He might have guessed, they had escaped from one danger, walked straight into another. Time had not moved on for these folks, either.

''Bout then, I know it's after the Alamo.'

'What *is* this place, Brock?'

'They call it Dark Pines. A few settlers stopped off here in the beginning, I guess they'd had enough o' Injuns and renegades, decided not to go further. Then along comes Koot and it's just what he's a-lookin' fer, valley that even the army don't know about. They would've, 'cept I never got back to tell 'em. The settlers are dead and gone, Koot seed to that!' The toothless mouth pouted. 'Koot's gonna bring about the biggest Injun uprisin' there ever wuz. He's runnin' with the Kiotes and the Kiotes have *power*. I seed things that I wouldna tell yer, you wouldna believe me, anyway. Black Bear is the devil himself, come back to earth like the Bible says he would. Soon he'll have all the tribes joinin' forces with the Kiotes; Blackfeet, Gros Ventres, Comanches, the whole damned lot. They'll drive the whites out o' this country, for sure. Then Koot 'n' Black Bear will take over.'

'I see.' Blair did not disbelieve the other. In this crazy set-up nothing was too crazy.

'How come you folks ended up here? Survivors from a wagon train?'

'In a way.' It wasn't worth the effort of trying to explain. 'We were with a guy called Sage. Last we saw of him there was a bunch of Kiotes pinning him down.'

'Sage!' Somehow Brock found the strength to sit upright. 'Y'mean . . . *Rufus Sage* as used to ride with S. E. Hollister?'

'*S. E. Hollister!*' Ben's eyes were wide, his mouth dropped open. 'He killed a grizzly bear all on his own with just a Bowie knife.'

'Sure did, son. Must be the same Sage, cain't be no other. Even if the Injuns did get him at the siege of Bent's Cabin. That don't mean nothing in these parts, not since Black Bear forsook Manitou and found somethin' a lot more powerful.' His voice was a whisper, scarcely audible. '*Just 'cause you die don't mean you're done for. Me, I'm hopin' they'll let me stay dead after they've hanged me, but I don't reckon they will. Folks are more use to Koot an' Black Bear when they're dead!*'

'Where is Bent's Cabin?' Blair crouched close, steeled himself against the old man's fetid breath.

'Few miles up the valley from here. They say Bent lived there once, don't know if it's true. A lotta guys've wintered there over the years. Rufus Sage, so the story goes, was runnin' from the Kiotes, got a bunch o' missionaries with him. The Kiotes caught 'em at the cabin, the siege lasted several days, and Sage, he sent a few o' them braves to the happy hunting grounds. They say he could shoot the pip out of the ace of spades at a hunnerd yards with his old Hawken. But the Injuns set fire to the cabin, Sage and the others came out shootin' but the Kiotes wuz too many for 'em. Never heered exactly what they did to Sage but nobody seen him after that. They do say, though, that somebody rebuilt Bent's Cabin, cain't think what fur with it bein' right outside Koot's back door.'

Adele had moved as far as she could from their fellow prisoner. Nicola was cowering behind her, she could tell that Ben was very scared. The occupants of Dark Pines were terrifying in themselves, the Lunds' fate did not bear thinking about. But there was something about Brock that went deeper than revulsion. Sage was a friendly uncle by comparison.

'They'll hang me fust.' Brock's voice had faded with talking to almost a mime. 'Soon as Koot returns.'

'If it's so long since you were captured, why didn't they hang you right away?' Blair was curious, it did not make sense.

'Hangin' takes mebbe three minutes.' The thin lips parted into a hideous grin. 'Not as quick as shootin' but too quick for Koot. He'll hang yuh, mister, but it won't be for a long while. Best for yuh if he did, but he won't. Not till you're outa your mind and too weak to stand so's they have to lift you up on to the gallows. There's lots o' things they'll do to yuh in the meantime but p'raps it's best I don't tell yuh 'bout thet!'

Ben was clinging to Adele now; Blair saw that his body shook with sobs which he was no longer able to contain.

'Sometimes a party of Kiotes comes to town by Koot's invitation. He lets the Injuns have a bit of fun with yuh, but they're careful not to go too far and kill you. Best if'n they did. And Koot's got hisself a Bible-thumper now.'

'A preacher!' Blair's eyebrows raised. 'Surely a man of the cloth wouldn't tolerate torture.'

'This'n does.' Brock's lungs wheezed, he was laughing in the only way that was left to him. 'Not a man o' God, even if he once was. More like a priest o' Satan. Sometimes his visits are worse'n what the Injuns do to yer. Don't know his name, didn't ask 'cause he wouldn't't've told me and it don't matter, anyway. *He tells yuh what it's like when you're dead. Accordin' to him yuh don't jest go to sleep for ever. No, sir! The Master, he calls him, raises you up so you'll walk better'n you did before, 'cept you gotta do what you're told. He makes*

141

yuh kill and torture, do things to others like they've done to you!'

'You're ill, Brock.' Blair spoke aloud for the benefit of Adele and the children. 'Delirious.'

'Deliri . . . what?' Brock attempted to move but he was too weak. The smell that came from him had Blair heaving.

'How long is it since you moved, crawled even?'

'Don't remember. A week, mebbe. Used to be able to get to the bucket, cain't now.'

'And you're in pain?'

'Guts. Not as bad now as it was a couple of days ago. P'raps 'cause I ain't eaten nothin'.'

'*Le mal de vache.*' Blair spoke his diagnosis aloud. 'In other words, a bad form of dysentery.'

'Had dysentery afore, several times.' Brock mouthed the words with fetid breath. 'Yuh don't eat for a few days an' it goes away.'

Not this variety, Blair thought. He said, 'I'm a doctor. Unfortunately my emergency bag was lost when the Kiotes attacked us. Otherwise I could have injected you.' Morphine was all he could have offered, nothing would save the old man at this stage. Euthanasia would have been kindest of all. 'Some clean water would help.'

'Water's all yuh get to drink here.' Brock's eyes might have closed, it was difficult to see into those deep, dark sockets. 'They bring yuh a drink with yer food. Water ain't clean but when you're parched you don't give a cuss. Food's mostly their own leftovers, remains of meals served in the bar room.'

God almighty, Blair's expression was grim. As likely as not they would all have *le mal de vache* within a few days. This chronic form of dysentery was prevalent in pioneering days, it was usually fatal, accounted for more lives than Indians and renegades put together. Dirty water was the main cause.

'Try to sleep if you can.' It was all he could offer under the circumstances. He felt so helpless, his professionalism screamed at him, rebuked him because he had to stand and watch a patient die.

'We're all going to die,' Adele sobbed in his ear as he held her to him. 'Degradation, torture . . .'

'We'll find a way out!' Empty words, he couldn't even muster any conviction.

'How,' she suddenly screamed at him, 'for Christ's sake, *how*?'

There was no answer to that. His arms went around them, together they sank down into a corner, huddled together. And finally, mercifully, sheer exhaustion brought sleep.

Blair awoke, stiff and cold, just as the grey dawn light was seeping in through the overhead window. Waking brought back all the memories of yesterday. With some difficulty he extricated a numbed arm from the huddle of sleeping bodies. Nicola and Ben had their faces buried against Adele, her head had fallen forward so that he was unable to see her sleeping expression. Even in slumber it would be anguished.

He stood up slowly, his joints creaked and cracked. God, it stank in here! Brock's slumped form was still in shadow in the opposite corner. He managed to muster up some pity for the other because of what the scout had suffered. Whether it had happened yesteryear or yesterday, it made no difference. Man's inhumanity to man was inexcusable.

Even as a prisoner of outlaws who should have died a century and a half ago, Blair's professional training surfaced. He was a doctor, he had a duty to tend the sick, no matter how, where or when. There wasn't much he could do for Brock, he had no medication of any kind with him. At the very least he could try to make him more comfortable.

The stench was the worst he had ever smelled; if he had not had an empty stomach he would have vomited. Urine, excrement, sheer filth and . . . the smell of death.

Brock was dead, all right. Even in the half-light of dawn, the doctor knew a corpse when he saw one. The limbs had become rigid with death, then loosened in the posture in which it had occurred. The legs were splayed stiffly, the back against the wall, his head had fallen forward on to his emaciated chest.

He could have accepted that which his eyes saw, confirmation was a mere formality which benefited nobody. There was no death certificate to be signed, no formalities. He laughed softly to himself; those who lusted for a macabre execution had been cheated at the final hour. Brock had found his own way out of here.

Yet, Blair's rigid self-discipline prompted a final examination of the corpse, verification of death for his own satisfaction.

Le mal de vache was undoubtedly the cause of death but he needed confirmation. He must examine the corpse.

He turned his head away, took a deep breath, crouched down. His probing fingertips touched parchment-like flesh that could in no way have retained any vestige of life. There was no pulse. He did not have to check for a heartbeat but he did.

The rotting garments had adhered to the other's body, ripped when Blair attempted to unfasten the knotted thongs. The skin beneath was dry, encrusted with years of filth, a mass of blackheads was abrasive to his touch.

There was no heartbeat. The coldness of the flesh reminded him of that severe winter when he had treated a party of survivalists for frostbite. Or when he scrabbled in the freezer to find a pack of hamburgers for dinner. He snatched his hand away; there was no need to continue the examination. He was satisfied that death had occurred some time during the night hours, probably early on. It was up to the jailers to remove the body and bury it.

The others were awake, he sensed their movements, the easing of their limbs, but they still huddled in terror.

'Brock's dead,' he told them.

They shied away, they didn't want to see.

It grew lighter by the minute. Outside, they heard people moving about, voices that grunted unintelligibly, a horse whinnied. Heavy footfalls, but they did not come towards the cabin. Evidently the prisoners' breakfast was not a priority.

'I wonder if we're allowed to exercise.' Blair spoke his thoughts aloud.

'If we are, perhaps we could make a run for it,' Adele whispered. 'Better to risk it than wait in here for whatever they plan to do to us.'

'We'll see.' He was unwilling to commit himself to a rash promise. 'I've been thinking. Undoubtedly that storm caused a freak time-warp that even scientists would be at a loss to explain. So we find ourselves thrown back a hundred and fifty years or so in time to eighteen forty. We haven't changed, neither have those around us. But does this time-warp exist only in this valley or is it nationwide, worldwide? If we get out of here, what are we going to find beyond? So far we haven't come to any real harm,' he rubbed his aching jaw,

144

'but our guns haven't been able to kill the Kiotes, just knock 'em about a bit. Maybe they can't die except by the means they once died. But are we vulnerable or are we just trapped for ever in the middle of the nineteenth century? Or is there some much more sinister reason why the Kiotes and outlaws are still alive?'

'You mean this . . . this Black Bear fellow?' Adele's voice shook.

'Maybe. I read a book once on devil worship, the left-hand path as they call it. I've always had an open mind about it.'

'Oh, God!' she said.

'Got the feelin' Koot'll come today.'

Adele thought for a moment that it was Blair who had spoken, maybe a hoarse whisper that had somehow magnified in the confines of their prison. But the voice was old, strained to make itself heard, lungs wheezed under the effort. She sensed, rather than heard, a movement in the far corner. She glanced quickly round, could not hold back the scream that rose in her throat.

Brock had somehow managed to draw up his legs, his skeletal hands were folded on his lap. And the toothless mouth was moving as he struggled to speak.

'Yep, I git a feelin' Koot'll be back afore sundown.'

Blair backed away with the others until there was nowhere left to go. They bunched up against the wall, staring in disbelief at the decrepit form that tried to rise but had not the strength. The pulse and heart had stopped but he breathed once more, stared at them with sunken eyes.

And the smell of death was overpowering.

Nineteen

Some time later one of the outlaws brought the prisoners' breakfast, a bowl of half-cooked beans and a jug of water. Even from where she stood Adele could see that the water was brackish; it had probably been scooped out of a dew pond or one of the horse troughs in the dusty street.

'You'll hev to help *him*.' The man had lost an eye, it created an illusion of winking as he inclined his head towards the slumped figure of Brock. 'Don't let him starve to death else Koot'll get in a ragin' fury. Wuss than usual!'

Adele felt her intestines balling as if preparing to vomit. The very prospect of assisting Brock to eat was the ultimate revulsion.

'He needs help,' Blair spoke softly. 'He's got dysentery bad. He'll die.' Like he appeared to have done earlier.

'Sure he will,' the other growled. 'On the end o' a rope. Don't let him die before, like I said. You'll all hang. Eventually. Except mebbe the woman. Koot'll want her for hisself, no doubt about that.'

Blair had not failed to notice how the man's hand rested on his belted pistol. He wondered how fast the fellow could draw and shoot; there did not appear to be anybody else with him. It was just a thought, which he dismissed as quickly as it had come. Any attempt to escape from here must not be done on impulse, it needed careful planning.

'You jest make sure he lives.' It was as if the other read Blair's thoughts. 'An Injun jest rode in to tell us Koot's on his way.' He stepped back, the heavy bar dropped into place. Brock had surmised right.

Adele stared aghast at the victuals which had been set down inside the door; a mush of dried, partly soaked, half-cooked beans; you were supposed to eat them with your hands, feed like a dog. The water jug had a rime of congealed saliva around the rim.

146

'No knives, forks or mugs.' Blair put her thoughts into words. 'Not that I expected any here.'

A series of unintelligible grunts interrupted them. Brock was demanding attention, his voice box had maybe given up under the strain of talking yesterday. Or dying.

'I'll feed and water him first.' Blair had a moral duty to administer to the sick whenever and wherever he found them. Adele turned the children away with her, this wasn't going to be a pretty sight.

The toothless mouth was agape as wide as it would stretch, the eyes seemed to have dropped out of sight in the deep sockets. Water was a priority. Blair lifted the jug, poured carefully into the open mouth.

The cavity filled like a water hole with the first deluge after a lengthy drought, glugging, overflowing the cracked and blistered lips, trickling down the wasted chin. Swirling muddied water that finally found an outlet, gurgled as the level dropped. Only when the mouth was empty did the eyes pop back into view.

'That better, old timer?'

The scalped skull nodded its thanks.

'Food?'

Jesus, he wanted to *eat* as well! Blair popped a couple of beans into the open mouth, the hardened gums squashed them, masticated noisily. A sudden belch, it smelled vile. The lips parted, grunted. *More!*

Blair's trembling fingers touched Brock's hand, it was as though the leathery skin was frosted. The doctor steeled himself. 'I'd like to check your heart and pulse again, Brock.'

Brock gave no sign that he had heard, he was too preoccupied with the offering of finger-fed beans. He did not appear to be aware of the slender touch that probed for a pulse, trembled as it went in search of a heartbeat.

Blair did not find either.

'I think that'll do for now, Brock.' Blair snatched his hand away; it tingled with the cold of a body that should have lain on a mortician's slab.

The lips pouted, sucked noisily at the remnants of the bean juice that adhered to them. The flicking tongue reminded the doctor of a Gila monster.

'That's berrer.' Brock suddenly found his speech, broke

wind loudly. 'Nothin' to beat beans for givin' yuh strength. Fust good night's rest I've had in many a while. Slept like the dead.'

Blair shuddered involuntarily. 'Good, now you just stay right there, don't try to move.' He turned away, put the bowl and the vessel of water down on the floor. 'Any of you lot fancy some, just help yourselves.'

Nobody took him up on the offer. It looked like being a long, hungry and thirsty day.

They lost all track of time; although there was a restricted view of the sky through the aperture in the roof, without any background it was impossible to follow the sun's course. Daylight, dusk and darkness were the only certainties.

It was still bright enough to be the middle of the day when they heard footsteps approaching and the door unbarricaded.

Adele pulled Nicola and Ben to her, embraced them protectively. The only way her children would be taken from her was over her corpse. She shied from the open door, it could only be another of the filthy inhabitants of this shanty town come to gloat over the prisoners.

The sudden bright sunlight had Blair squinting; he could make out a silhouette framed in the doorway, a wide-brimmed hat and clothing that had been tailored, not hacked out of the skin of some luckless creature felled by a musket ball.

The features were in shadow; he sensed their expression of contempt. Another figure stood behind the first one, female in shape, a long dress trailing on the ground.

'It's *them*, all right, my dear.' The man spoke to his companion. 'Who else could it possibly have been out here?'

'Good.' Her voice was familiar. 'Is Sage here, too?'

They both stepped inside, their searching eyes burned like lasers, there was no mistaking their anger. Their *evil*.

'I had hoped that I might find Sage with you.' The tone embodied disappointment, frustration. 'It must be true what they say, the savages got him, after all. Such a shame, I was looking forward to meeting him again. Perhaps, though, it might still be possible.'

The man moved to one side and a sunbeam washed over him. Adele managed to stifle a scream of shocked recognition; Blair stared uncomprehendingly. Once again the impossible had proved possible, defied Nature and everything that he had studied at medical college.

'I told yuh, it's the preacher an' his woman.' Brock unlocked his voice, rasped an introduction.

Sure enough, it was James, the missionary, and his sister, Victoria, who surveyed the prisoners with gloating on their disfigured features.

'Well, well, if it isn't Dr Lund and his charming family.' James appeared to walk with difficulty. 'How nice to be re-acquainted, and under such different circumstances. I do hope that you are going to cooperate with me.'

Blair noticed that the other's clothing was still ripped where he had torn it away to remove the arrow.

'The brats are somewhat more subdued, I perceive.' His leer had Ben and Nicola darting back behind their mother, sobbing with fear. 'The girl still wails, but much more quietly, and the boy has lost his arrogance along with his gun. However, your own refusal to yield to an impossible situation is still apparent, Dr Lund.'

'I appeal to you as a man of the cloth to do something about these appalling conditions.' Blair's tone was firm yet cautiously respectful. 'This poor wretch over here . . .'

'Will hang before the sun sets.' James made no attempt to disguise his gloating. 'You will all be taken out to watch.'

'Not the children, I hope.'

'But of course.' James's lips stretched mirthlessly. 'They must witness the demise of a traitor. Brock would have led the army here in a futile attempt to destroy the Master's humble followers. But others would have taken their place, it would only have been a temporary setback. Nevertheless, Doctor, the sooner you take the oath, the better for all concerned.'

'The oath?'

James thrust his head forward, his features were scarcely recognizable from those which the others had known back at the cabin; he was like a demon risen from the flames of hell. 'Allegiance to the Master.' He thrust out a Bible, his other hand held up a small wooden cross, his forefinger and thumb dangled the crucified figure upside down. '*Deny Jesus Christ. Spit upon his false image and upon his book of lies!*'

The darkened room spun before Blair's eyes for a moment, he had to wait for it to steady.

'*Deny Christ, and spit upon him!*'

'It wouldn't make much difference if I did.' Blair tried to sound casual.

'Why . . . not?' James was clearly taken aback.

'Because I'm an atheist. I don't believe in Him, anyway, so it's a pointless exercise.' In latter years Blair had decided that he was agnostic. During boyhood his parents had forced him to accompany them to church. After he was old enough to please himself, he hadn't bothered. All the same, he considered it blasphemous to spit upon the image of Christ and the Bible when he hadn't really made up his mind. He would do so, reluctantly, if it might save them.

'Well, that is a good foundation for conversion to the left-hand path.' James's eyes glowed, switched to Adele. 'And her?'

'I'm an atheist, too,' she lied glibly, hoped her voice did not quaver.

'You told us that the children attended Sunday School!' Victoria spat, saliva swung from her snarling lips.

'I lied because I thought you were preachers.'

'*Do you go to Sunday worship?*' The scream was directed at the cowering children.

'No . . . not since we were very young.' Ben shook visibly. 'It was boring.'

'Well, we seem to be progressing.' James was suddenly smug, the way he had been when they last knew him. 'In my foolishness I once tried to preach God to the natives. The Kiotes enlightened me. My sister and I have now been granted eternal life, raised from the dead by Black Bear, who is a disciple of the Master, awaiting his coming again on earth. Those who believe and serve him shall be saved, rule the earth. Those who deny him shall be cast into everlasting torment. Satan has already returned to earth once since he was cast down. In Massachusetts, so Governor Winthrop wrote in his Journal in sixteen hundred and forty-eight.' James paused, drew himself up to his full height. 'He chose the Indians near Aquiday as his disciples. *He came to them in a tempest, took five of them away to teach them his ways. Almost two centuries later he returned one of them, Black Bear, to lead the Kiotes away from the Blackfeet and the Gros Ventres. The tribes will unite, destroy the white invaders who attempt to turn them to*

God. I give you a choice, join myself and my sister in serving the Master and spreading his word, or be hanged with this wretch and condemned to everlasting torment!'

'I guess we'll go along with you,' Blair stalled, heard Adele's sharp intake of breath.

'That is sensible,' James's expression hardened, 'but the decision is not entirely mine. Koot will arrive soon, I understand that he is bringing Black Bear with him. Doubtless there will be a price to be paid for your lives. But remember the gospel of the Master. *Do as you will, spread evil before you.'*

The door closed behind them, plunged the room back into gloom.

'Oh, Blair,' Adele slumped against her husband, heard Nicola and Ben sobbing, 'what's going to happen to us? Why are James and Victoria alive again?'

'I don't rightly know.' He clung to his sanity with grim determination. 'I guess the Kiotes dug James up, resurrected him like Sage said they would. Victoria too. Maybe Prudence is also somewhere out there. There are things I can't explain and probably nobody else can, either. I know that witchcraft has been a growing menace in the States for a long time, and this valley appears to be the heart of it. If what James says is true, and that Satan came to earth on a tempest in the seventeenth century, then my guess is that he did it again recently and it was just our bad luck to be caught up in it. Well, we're here and, apparently, there's no chance of us going anywhere else for a while. Our only hope is to play along with this lot, wait our chance.'

'It's awful!' Adele sobbed.

'It could be a damned sight worse if we get on the wrong side of this bunch. Our priority is to get out of this jail, which we might just do when the big shots arrive on the scene. Then we'll play it from there. No wonder our guns didn't do much more than knock the Kiotes about a bit. Sage's dropped 'em. *Because he's one of them except that he seemed to be fighting them. They're desperate to get hold of him and make him one of them. Maybe they've already done that but the news hasn't reached Dark Pines yet!'*

'How can he be one of them and yet not one of them, Blair?'

'I dunno, exactly. I guess he's got caught up in the immortality but he's not evil. Yet. I'm just guessing.'

'So even in this time-warp, or whatever it is, they're all . . . *dead but still living. What they call in the movies . . . the living dead!*'

'Yes,' he muttered softly. He refrained from adding, '*Zombies.*'

It was a man, all right, six feet tall, perhaps more, muscular inside the loose-fitting clothes he wore. The garments were made from some kind of animal skin, fringed at the shoulders and fastened with thongs. From beneath the low-crowned wool hat, coarse and bushy hair, flecked with grey, spilled down to his shoulders. A thick beard hid most of his lined and weathered features, and when he grinned Blair saw that a couple of front teeth were missing; the rest were yellow, either he didn't clean them or he was a heavy smoker. A pair of soft calf-length boots was made from the same hide as the rest of his clothing.

It was everything that either hung from their nocturnal visitor, or was affixed to him, that had Blair staring in astonishment. The leather belt encircling his waist had two flintlock pistols shoved behind it, there were at least four knives of varying sizes in sheaths. A leather pouch was suspended from his thick neck, doubtless containing bullets; a powder horn was hanging from his shoulder along with a ball-screw, wiper, awl, cleaning rod and an obviously home-made ramrod. Blair recognized them all, one by one, for they were depicted and accurately described in that book which held such fascination for Ben.

The other watched him with obvious amusement, leaned on the longest rifle that Blair had seen outside a museum.

'You done, mister?'

A horse stood patiently beyond the veranda, a big black, its flanks flecked with sweat like it had been ridden hard. It was heavily loaded, boxes and sacks strapped on to it, probably its role was as a pack horse, it was accustomed to being led rather than ridden.

'I smelled your cawfee afore I saw your lights. Damn dangerous showin' lights at night.'

'We don't have any power. The storm took it. Just candles.'

'Nothin' wrong with candles, lamps're brighter. Kin use a fire, though, too risky to light one out thar.'

He's crazy, Blair thought, some old coot who's lived out here all his life, doing what Ben would do if we gave him the chance. Or else he's one of those freaks who play at it and this guy's really gone to town on the part. There's ranches for dudes, no reason why they shouldn't have a centre for would-be mountain men. Easy money for somebody, give 'em a bundle of hides to dress up in, let 'em loose in the mountains. Eat what they kill, that way you don't even have to feed 'em. Probably they sleep rough, too.

'You gonna stop pointin' that musket at ma belly? Cain't say I've seen one like that afore.' The head was thrust forward, the dark eyes were wide with amazement. 'Where'd you get that? Never see'd one in the tradin' post – mostly Hawkens, everybody shoots Hawkens. Accurate at two hundred yards, drop a buffalo so's he don't even twitch.'

'You'd better come inside.' Blair moved back into the hallway, lowered the Browning. 'Go through into the living room, there's coffee on the stove. My wife will pour you some.'

'Keep that door shut.' The stranger dragged it closed behind him. 'Best not show too many lights, not tonight, nohow. Outside ain't no place to be right now but my hoss'll warn us if there's danger.'

Blair's spine prickled right the way up into his scalp.

Ben stared open-mouthed, his gun forgotten. This guy was just like a picture out of his book, one that had suddenly come to life and stepped right out of the pages.

Adele was on her feet, she had backed away, Nicola went with her. The stench was almost suffocating.

'Can you fix some coffee for our visitor?' Blair stood in the doorway.

Nicola's expression was one of sheer terror as the candle-light fell full upon the stranger. Disbelief at first, then her mouth shaped up for a scream but it was some seconds before she managed to get it out.

'*Daddy, that's the man who was in my bedroom!*'

Seven

'I think you've got some explaining to do, mister, whoever you are,' Blair stood in the kitchen doorway, the barrel of the Browning swung up to centre on the strange and frightening buckskin-clad figure.

Ben had moved back, there was an ominous click as the safety catch on the twenty was pushed forward. On this occasion his father surely would not be angry about it being loaded indoors.

Adele pulled Nicola behind her, the child was crying hysterically. Even the shadows appeared to have backed off this nocturnal visitor. It was deathly cold in the room.

'I kin use some cawfee, bin ridin' since nightfall, only time it's safe to move out there. Allus travel after dark lately.'

'*What's your name?*' Blair yelled, he had done with pleasantries, there was something decidedly sinister about this man.

'Told you once. You forgotten already? *Sage*. An' I kin spell it, too, if'n you're hard of hearin'. I'm a readin' man.' He tapped a pocket that bulged square and solid. 'Shakespeare. Sometimes I read the Bible. Depends. When a man's holed up for a long winter he has to do somethin', else he'd go plumb crazy. Me, I read. Many's the winter I've spent in here, afore Christmas till the thaw comes in spring. Sometimes go out with ma snowshoes to try get some fresh meat.'

'You've been here before, then?' Blair's mouth was dry.

'More times'n I kin remember. Allus heads for here come late fall.'

'It's *spring* now!' Blair's tone was challenging. 'The snows are gone.'

'S'right. I was headin' down towards Yellowstone, lumbered with some dudes from back east, when a bunch o' Kiotes got on ma scent. Kiotes alone are bad news but when Koot an' his gang're ridin' with 'em, that's double trouble. I holed the

49

dudes up in a cave, hope they'll be safe, pushed on. Mebbe I'll go back for 'em, bring 'em here. This is as good a place as any to stand off Kiotes if it comes to it.'

'*Coyotes*?' Ben echoed. 'Coyotes don't attack you, they're scavengers, but we saw wolves last night.'

The man looked puzzled. 'Allus wolves in the mountains, they're no trouble 'cept when food's scarce. Me, I'd sooner tangle with a pack o' wolves any day than run in with Kiotes. They're worse'n the Blackfoot and the Gros Ventres, got the bad blood o' both tribes in 'em and more besides. And when you got the likes o' Koot stringin' along, you make sure they don't ketch you.'

'Coyotes?' Ben was still confused.

'*Cauites!*' Sage threw back his head, bellowed coarse laughter. 'Boy, you ain't bin in these parts long, I kin see. Damn my luck to find another lot o' dudes just when things're gettin' too hot fer comfort. *Cauites* aren't *Kiotes*, and don't ask me to spell it 'cause I never see'd it writ down. Kiotes are Injuns, least folks here around *thinks* they are but I reckon I knows better. Injuns they might've bin once but they come from the fires o' hell and if they ketch you . . . don't let 'em! Turn that gun o' yourn on yersel' fust. And there's Kiotes and Koot out there in them woods right now, so the less light you show, the better. Now, how about some o' that cawfee?'

Blair walked over to the stove, poured boiling water on some instant coffee. The man called Sage looked on in astonishment.

'Wal, I never did! Don't you know how to boil up cawfee beans? What's that 'un there you got, looks like sand to me.'

Blair ignored the question, pushed a steaming mug across the table. 'Where are you from, Mr . . . Sage?'

'Jest call me Sage. Never did find out ma other name, mebbe never had one. Me, I'm from Virginia but that was long time ago, scarcely remember it. I've travelled just 'bout every trail hereaparts, some that folks know, lots they don't and prob'ly never will. Started out ketchin' beaver. Good money if'n you kin ketch enough 'cause they don't pay a lot for furs. The more you trap, the more you earn. Done tolerably well but the furrin's gettin' harder, too many at it since the likes o' me opened up the trails. Don't do much now, more money in guidin' folks west, wagon trains mostly. There's

Twenty

The sun kissed the far mountain tops beyond the big forest, a radiant ball of fire that bathed the valley in its dying golden glow. The shadows prepared to creep forward, create silhouettes and obscure detail.

Adele spread her arms to shield Ben and Nicola from the spectre of the gallows and those who gathered around it. There were maybe fifty people in the crowd; the Kiotes stood apart from the inhabitants of Dark Pines. Old habits died hard, even beyond the grave.

Thronged by a group of ragbag guards, Blair surveyed the scene around him. There was no mistaking Black Bear even from a distance of fifty yards. Tall and majestic, he wore no coloured paints, the deep scars patterned on his cruel face were sufficient in themselves to etch him with a malevolence that transcended any markings of evil worn by his followers. His dark eyes burned redly, though it might just have been the reflection of the setting sun; flared nostrils had been distended with plugs of mud as if his breathing requirements were greater now than in a past life. The corners of his mouth had been slit with a sharp blade to extend his leer. And those horns were surely not just pleated and waxed hair but grew from his skull as a living symbol of the Evil One.

His tribal robes were black, adorned with strange markings, shrouding him in darkness that would render him invisible when night fell.

Those around him, red and white, cast furtive glances in his direction; their fear was only too apparent. He ruled supreme over his followers. Soon he would rule this whole land.

Beyond him stood the one who could only be Koot, traitor to the white invaders, torturer and murderer of innocent families who trekked in search of a new life but found only death in its most terrible form.

He was tall, too, but a few inches shorter than the Kiote chief. There was nothing majestic about his attire, animal-skin clothing that was stained with filth and blood. When the soft breeze wafted, those near and far smelled his vileness, the ultimate stench of evil.

A black beard was patchy with mange, hosted swarms of lice. The over-size hooked nose was clogged with mucus that bubbled in time with his breathing. Bushy brows concealed small eyes, gave him the appearance of a sightless subterranean creature.

He was an arsenal that moved with a shambling gait, broad shoulders that hunched beneath the burden of half a dozen belted pistols and a slung rifle of such weight and length that it dwarfed the much-favoured Hawkens of the occupants of this strange settlement. Accessories hung in abundance upon one who lived by the gun but would never die by it.

His cap had been shrunk by the elements to reveal a baldness that added to his awesome appearance, a skull that was encrusted by blackheads like barnacles upon a rocky coastline, a natural revulsion that might have spared him the scalping-knives of fierce tribesmen in the past. A trader at the Hudson's Bay Company had once remarked that he was 'as bald as a coot'. The man had died as a direct result of his insult but the name had lived on to become a fearsome legend.

The rest of this gathering of mountain men paled into insignificance by comparison with their leader.

The gallows dominated the scene. Blair saw that it was a much more intricate and well-built structure than any of the rough and ready edifices in this place. The timbers had been cut to a symmetry, the main stanchions were buried deep in the ground. Far from being a crude gibbet to suspend a body pulled by the neck from a horse's back, in the manner of a lynching party so common in the nineteenth century throughout the States, the design had clearly been copied faithfully from some 'official' contraption of execution; the platform was hinged and was worked by a lever. It had a decidedly sinister look about it. Death by design, a grim finality.

Brock had to be carried from the jail, rough hands lifted him up on to the platform, supported him whilst the noose was draped around his neck, for he had not the strength to stand unaided.

James was clad in his dark attire; at a cursory glance he might have been a minister of religion about to comfort the condemned and pray for his soul. Except that the clerical collar was not in evidence. The implication was not lost upon Blair. Death became an even more dreaded prospect.

Victoria stood by her brother's side, her long hair freed from its bun so that it straggled around her shoulders. Her torn and dirty dress fluttered in the breeze, reminded Blair of a childhood portrayal of a witch at Halloween. He shuddered.

The attempt to create an official termination of a human life added to the sheer brutality of it all. The knowledge of preceding events threatened one's sanity.

Black Bear and his braves watched impassively. This was not their mode of killing, their preference was for one which prolonged the procedure.

Koot detached himself from the gathering. His stride was calculated, every movement chillingly deliberate. Blair tensed, felt Adele and the children pressing in on him, seeking futile, fragile protection. They, too, had noticed what was only too apparent to himself. *Koot was headed towards them.*

He came to a halt in front of them, towered above them. They were dwarves before a giant.

'Heered 'bout you lot.' His voice seemed to rumble within him, the thick lips curled. 'You're a doctor, huh?'

'That's right.' Blair fought to control his fear.

'Yuh might be useful.' A deliberate, mocking pause. 'Depends. There's pox back beyond the Yellowstone, Injuns are droppin' faster'n the waggoners could shoot 'em. It might wipe 'em out. It might travel on here. You got a scratch needle with yuh?'

'I did have. I lost my bag in a Kiote raid.'

'I'll hev 'em bring it to me.' He wasn't boasting. 'So yuh know how to keep folks alive. Yuh also know how to kill 'em.' The eyes were invisible in the lengthening shadows that preceded dusk.

'I guess so.'

'We kin do with a hangman, make it . . . official.' He gave a low laugh. 'One brought in to do the job, not just a necktie party. Somethin' folks'll remember. Doc, I jest appointed you hangman o' Dark Pines. We hang traitors and spies . . . and others! Step right up and show us what you kin do.'

Jesus Christ! Blair's brain reeled, his vision blurred, distorted the man who stood over him, created a fairground-hall-of-mirrors image of an ogre that had kids fleeing and screaming. Adults, too, like himself. *Step up and become a murderer, Doctor Lund.*

'I . . . I've never hanged anybody before.' He sensed Adele and the kids pulling at his shirt, trying to tug him back.

'Always a fust time. Do it right an' you might get the job reg'lar, there'll be plenty more.' Koot's gaze moved on, came to rest on Adele. Beneath the hooded eyebrows gleamed his invisible lust.

'Surely we have to have a trial . . .'

'Bin and done. Guilty. Sentenced to hang. Pronto.'

Blair was aware that he was moving, walking unsteadily in the direction of the gallows. For his family's sake. The ladder creaked and bowed under his weight, he clutched at a rung whilst a wave of vertigo passed.

Then he was standing up on the high platform, aware that everybody watched him. The ripple of muttering from all around had faded to an awful silence. He sensed them urging him on. Kill the old man for us, Doc, we're all gonna *enjoy* it.

James turned, his features exuded the evil that had replaced his former godliness. He stank of the grave from which he had been exhumed, his cheeks were streaked with soil. 'The Master awaits his soul, Doctor. The Indians await his body. Everybody is waiting for *you*.'

Brock was slumped in his captor's grasp. Slowly, every wasted muscle in his skeletal frame made a supreme effort and his head was uplifted, rested heavy upon his shoulders. Blair caught his breath, recoiled from the countenance that looked up at him.

'You gotta hang me, Doc.' There was no hint of pleading in the dulled eyes, no whine in the voice. No plea of innocence.

'I have to check you over first, old-timer.' It took a determined effort to advance upon the living cadaver.

'*Why?*' James spoke sharply.

'Part of the procedure.' Blair's temples were pounding. 'It's law in some states. Texas and Massachusetts, Missouri, too.'

156

He could not remember exactly if the death penalty still existed elsewhere. He had once met a doctor at a seminar who worked on Death Row. Those going to the execution chamber had to receive a thorough medical check to ensure that they were fit to die.

'Hurry.' Permission was granted.

Blair's probing fingers shook, contact had his skin prickling. But he had to be sure.

Oh, thank God, there was neither heart nor pulse beating. At least it would not be murder.

'Finished?' James's foul breath fanned the back of Blair's neck, an icy blast.

'He's OK.'

'Good.' The preacher moved close to the condemned man. 'Do you, Brock, pledge your soul to the Lord of Darkness?'

A nod, a noise, as phlegm wheezed in the lungs.

'Go to the Master in filth and wickedness.'

That was the only time Blair saw terror in the old man's eyes. If he protested, pleaded, then his gurgled cries were stifled by the tightening of the noose. His body went limp, it only remained upright because the two men supported him at arms' length, ensuring that they stood well clear of the trapdoor.

'*Hang him!*' The order was growled in Koot's tone from down below in the gathering darkness.

For a moment Blair thought that he might pass out as a red haze shimmered before his eyes; he felt beads of icy sweat all over his body.

'Hurry!' Victoria's whisper was loaded with lust.

Blair's hand found the lever, an iron bar attached to a swivel. It vibrated to his touch as if an electric current surged through it.

Somewhere, in the far distance, he thought he heard a rumble of thunder.

Suddenly, the slight breeze became a strong wind. His hair ruffled. He glanced around, saw that James was holding on to his hat, Victoria's filthy, matted hair streamed. The weather was changing.

'God be with you, old man.' Blair mouthed the words, hoped that none of them could lip-read. Dusk had become darkness.

He felt the trapdoor go before he heard it bang against the hatch. The lever hung limp; Brock was gone and against the approaching storm clouds the doctor glimpsed the rope, taut and twisting, swivelling one way, then the other.

Wild cries filled the night air, throaty roars that might have come from the wild beasts of the neighbouring forest. The watchers surged forward, a black mass that spilled and over-flowed. They were fingering the dangling corpse, stroking it, talking excitedly. Blair nearly threw up.

'Well done!' The praise came from James, he was shaking, it might have been because of the sudden drop in tempera-ture. 'The Indians will cut him down. He's theirs now.'

God forgive me. Blair prayed for the first time in years to a God whom he didn't even know was there. At least it wasn't murder. You couldn't kill somebody who was already dead. At the very worst it was euthanasia. That eased his conscience.

He descended the ladder with difficulty, held on tightly because his shaking legs threatened to throw him down. In the darkness bodies pushed and jostled, their thoughts were only for the wretched thing that twisted on the end of a rope.

Touch it, feel it, stroke it before the Indians take it.

The wind howled down from the mountains as if this unspeakable deed had stirred its wrath. Blair thought a rainspot splattered on his cheek. Half-silhouettes all around, pushing him in their eagerness to get beneath the gallows; he almost fell.

'*Adele!*' The wind whipped the name away before it could have been heard.

'*Ben! Nick!*'

The only answer was the laughter and growls of creatures that had no right to walk this earth. He tried to push his way through them but it was impossible.

If he could only find Adele and the kids, they'd make a run for it, take their chance in the forest and mountains. The terrors which the wild held were as nothing when compared with those of Dark Pines.

'*Adele!*' He screamed her name, the wind threw it back at him. Everybody around him was laughing, they did not appear to notice him. Except the man whose hand closed over his arm like the grip of that grizzly bear that had chased them through the trees.

'Dr Lund!' It was Koot, tall and terrible against the night sky. 'You'd best come with me.' Obviously Blair had no choice in the matter.

'My family,' Blair yelled, struggling was futile. 'Where are they?'

'They have already been taken back.' An unbelievable strength for a human being began dragging the doctor along. 'Mebbe it's better fer the kids not to see what the Injuns'll do to Brock. See, they lit their fire already. Yuh hanged him well, you kin stand 'n' watch with me!'

'I don't want to see!' He screamed his protest but Koot appeared not to have heard.

An eerie glow lit up the sky as the wind fanned the flames of the fire which the Kiotes had lit at the head of the street. Behind it, Black Bear stood motionless and impassive, he might have been a black-cloaked horned totem, a carved effigy of the Evil One. Shapes flitted to and fro, the mountain men had bunched to one side. Was that fear in their expressions or was it an illusion caused by the dancing firelight?

Blair resigned himself to the role of an unwilling spectator. He could always shut his eyes, he did not have to watch. Koot was still gripping him but seemed unaware of his presence, so intently was he staring at the scene before him.

Some of the Kiotes had cut Brock down, they were dragging him on the end of the frayed rope. His scrawny neck had chafed, elongated under the pressure. Any second it might be pulled right off.

Blair wanted to close his eyes, shut out the bizarre sight. It was as though his eyelids were stuck open with superglue. He tried to turn his head away; his neck refused to move.

Watch, Dr Lund, because Brock's fate might become your own.

Blair thought that they might be going to burn the dead body, cremate it. That might have been almost decent. But they dragged it past the fire, lashed it to the wheel of an uncovered wagon. The scalped head fell forward, they jerked it back up, roped it to the spokes. Brock stared fixedly, the eyes *saw*, bulged their terror.

Brock's mouth was open, he was screaming, but his cries went unheard against the chanting of the Kiotes and the howling of the braves.

One of the warriors appeared with a can, upended it. Liquid splashed over Brock's head, dripped. Blair guessed that maybe they were trying to revive him. Here in Dark Pines anything was possible.

Koot was tense, trembling with excitement. The mountain men pushed forward, drew back again. They lusted for inhuman torture but they were scared, too.

Then, without warning, Brock's head was alight, a fiery ball that screamed from the depths of its tortured soul. The wretched body writhed, strained at the ropes. Now they all heard its screams, bunched in terror.

Except the Kiotes. Their dance stopped as if at a signal from Black Bear, who appeared to glide forward. He stood there, seemed to grow in a dreadful majesty, his features those of a being Man had no right to gaze upon. His slitted mouth extended, frothed as the lips moved. His nostrils breathed deeply and his eyes glowed dull red. He was chanting but none heard him, even his own followers had thrown themselves upon the ground.

Brock's skull blackened, flames licked from his orifices. The ropes that bound him fell away but still he remained upright against the charred wheel.

And then he began to walk unsteadily away.

Blair was sure that his mind had snapped, that what he saw was the figment of a crazed brain. Brock staggered, tottered, somehow kept his balance. Black Bear stood with folded arms, watched him go until the darkness swallowed him up.

Only then did the watchers move, slinking back to their hovels until only Koot and Blair remained out on the street.

Blair was unaware that Koot was leading him, pulling him roughly by the arm. The other growled something, it sounded like 'hurry'. Maybe even Koot was afraid this time.

Blair was aware that his clothing was wet, it must have been raining for some time. A gust of wind buffeted him with a force that might have toppled him had not the other been holding him.

A now-familiar square shape loomed up out of the night: it was time to be locked back into the stinking jail. Right now there could be a lot worse places to be, Blair thought. And a few better.

'Favourite Injun torture.' Koot inclined his head back to

where the wind was whipping the fire into an inferno, sparks flying like a fiery blizzard. 'Cook yer brains, yer don't feel much after that! Now they'll do to him what they have to. They'd do it to you if'n I'd let 'em.'

'He was dead before they started.' Blair would have run for the building if the other had not been holding him.

'Not fer long.' Koot laughed, the wind gusted at him as if it was trying to drown his words. 'He'll be back. Resurrected in hell's fire, like you saw. *Like most around here.*'

The heavy bar was lifted, the door eased open a little. Koot's hand loosened its grip, shoved Blair so that he staggered inside. Then the bolts were shot. The wind buffeted the building, it was impossible to hear anything outside.

The interior was in stygian blackness. Blair heard Nicola sobbing. Her hand found his, clutched it tightly. Ben grabbed him, too. He held them close, felt how they shook. God, what they must have been through didn't bear thinking about!

'Adele?' He called into the darkness.

There was no answer.

'Where's . . .' Blair sensed panic rising inside him.

'Mommy's not here,' Nicola screamed hysterically. '*Some of those men took her away!*'

Twenty-One

Koot eyed Adele. He hadn't bothered bolting the door, there was no way she was going to dash outside with those Kiotes going crazy, screaming and yelling. He had all the time in the world.

'You're a real looker.' His lips scarcely seemed to move as he spoke. 'Better'n any mover I've seen for a long while, and we've raided a few trains, I kin tell you.' His eyes narrowed. 'Injuns allus demand the wimmin, no amount o' parleyin' will make 'em change their minds. You know what the Injuns do to women?'

'I . . . I really don't want to know.' Adele had slumped into a chair by the table. She was reminded of Sage's advice about saving a bullet for yourself if there was no chance of escaping. She wished that Blair had shot them all, her greatest worry was what might happen to Ben and Nicola. 'Could you . . . could you see to it that my children aren't harmed, no matter what happens to me?'

'Cain't guarantee it.' He moved behind her, she cringed at his icy touch on her shoulders. 'No tellin' what'll happen to them. Now *ordinary* Injuns, sometimes they'll take kids for themselves, bring 'em up as Injuns. Other times they jest kill 'em straight off, babies they usually swing by their legs, crack their skull on a rock or agin a wagon wheel, anythin' that happens to be handy. But Kiotes, they're different, never kin tell. Black Bear makes a lot o' human sacrifices to his Master, slits the victims' throats and his followers drink their blood. Had to do it myself on a coupla occasions.' He smacked his lips noisily. 'Cain't say I really like the taste.'

'It's . . . awful!' Adele was nauseated, her stomach knotted. 'Please . . . if there's anything you can do, I'll . . . well, I'll do anything you want, Mr Koot.'

'I guess you'll do that, anyway.' His hands slid beneath her

162

denim shirt. His thick fingers fumbled for the buttons, popped one. She heard it ping on the floor. 'You got a real pair there.' He squeezed roughly, she gave an involuntary cry.

A gust of wind shook the building, rattled some loose timbers.

'Storm's gittin' up.' He ripped her shirt from her, snapped her bra strap. 'But I guess that won't worry us, lady. Hey, no good sittin' at the table, there's a nice comfortable bunk over there, plenty o' room for both of us.'

She froze, movement was denied her. Her stomach churned, if it had not been empty she would have vomited. She made no protest when he dragged her roughly to her feet. She would go crazy with terror before long, then her brain would switch off. It didn't matter what he did to her after that. If only the children weren't here, they were her only concern.

A movement beyond Koot caught her eye as he dragged her across the room. The window was barred with criss-crossed wooden slats, the shutter was still open. Just a fleeting glimpse, it might have been a trick of her tortured mind. A face, she couldn't be sure, it might have been a shadow caused by the glow from the fires outside. It was gone as quickly as it had come.

She shuddered but it didn't matter whether it was somebody or nobody. A voyeuristic Kiote or mountain man guessing what was taking place inside had crept up to satisfy a sadistic lust.

Oh, merciful God, Koot was going to take his clothes off! She shut her eyes tightly.

'I bet there's a few bin atop you.' He tore at her jeans, yanked them down below her knees. She almost felt his gaze burning her thighs as his calloused hands prised them apart.

'Just my husband, no other man has ever touched me!' Even at the peak of her terror she made her protest. It was something that had always been a great source of pride. She had been a virgin until her wedding night.

'Liar!' he jested coarsely. 'Wal, you'll know it when Koot's finished with yuh. Yuh'll plead for more!'

Suddenly his lips found hers, cold and dead, stinking breath that could only have come from something that rotted and gave off odours of putrescence. His tongue forced its way into her mouth, like a dead and decomposing fish. His hands pawed at her, she felt an arousal pulsing against the inside of her thighs.

Please, God, don't let it go all the way. Let me die first!

The wind was tearing at the cabin; something clicked, like the latch had been lifted. Maybe that peeping tom had come inside to watch. He wouldn't save her, though. He would not dare to enter. Surely even Koot, in the depths of his depravity, would not allow others to be spectators to his debauchery.

All the same, Adele got the feeling that they were not alone. Her eyes flickered open, she stared into Koot's eyes, saw his expression and screamed into the lips that crushed her own.

No, please, don't go inside me! If that happened, then she wanted to die. She prayed that her heart might give out.

'Koot!'

The shout vibrated in her crazed mind, bounced around her brain like a bagatelle ball. It was a reaction to the ultimate in degradation, her sanity was preparing to snap.

She felt Koot tense, his lips came off hers, she heard him grunt. For a moment his filthy fingers checked their painful squeezing of her breasts.

She sensed his head turn, a guttural, 'Whossat?' His body lifted up from hers as he turned to look behind him.

She opened her eyes again, shied from what she might see. Some ragbag of a trapper watching from the shadows, a half-naked brave crouched inside the door? But the man kneeling astride her blocked her view. 'You better get off'n that lady, Koot, 'cause I don't want your filthy bullet-holed body sprawlin' all over her!'

Adele sensed the fear in Koot, the way he jerked up, cursed incoherently. The voice of the man who spoke from beyond his obstructing body was vaguely familiar but Adele could not place it. It wasn't Blair, it didn't sound like the one who had acted as their jailer. It didn't matter who it was. The interruption, the brief respite, would only prolong her ordeal.

'Crawl off her, you bastard!'

Koot eased himself off her, she felt how he shook, it was probably with anger. She could not imagine the outlaw leader being afraid of anybody who walked this earth and not many who came from beyond it, either. The light from the kerosene lamp on the table was dim, the wick had been turned right down, she could just make out a silhouette standing inside the doorway. And there was something very familiar about that, too.

'*Sage!*'

Koot's cry had a ring of fear in it, the name he uttered numbed her mind to all comprehension. Sage, mountain man and army scout, their only brief hope in this valley of evil, had been hacked down by the Kiotes. It was some kind of cruel trick that her brain was playing on her, adding to her ordeal. An hallucination.

'Gawd, Koot, you look wuss without your clothes'n ever you did wearin' 'em.' The figure moved into the circle of wan light, he held a pistol in either hand. His heavily-bearded features were in shadow, his fringed buckskins were torn and filthy. A long rifle was leaned up against the table. 'Now, you jest stand there 'n' don't so much as try to cover yourself, 'cause I'm tryin' not to look below your fat belly, case I throw up. One move an' that'll be the fust thing I'll blast.'

Adele sat up, even in her confusion she instinctively tugged her jeans back up. She was shaking uncontrollably, her lips moved but no words came. It was all so unbelievable.

Because it was none other than Sage who stood there, his pistols trained on Koot.

'You all right, Adele?' The mountain man's eyes never left Koot for a second.

She nodded, she didn't try to speak. Even had speech been possible, words would have failed her. She did not know how Sage came to be here, she made no attempt to reason it out. Suffice that he was.

'I bin huntin' you fer ten years, mebbe longer, Sage.' Koot spoke in guttural tones, there was no sign of his initial fear and surprise. 'The Kiotes boasted they'd gotten you, but like they allus do, they lied. I got things I want to do to you an' when I've finished I'll mebbe let the Injuns have what's left. *But this time there won't be nothin' left fer 'em to raise up!*'

'You talk big, Koot.' Sage never moved. 'Talk is all you got, all you ever did hev. From what I seed out there, them Injun friends o' yours ain't friends no longer. They're doing one or two things to your gang that even I never thought o' doin'. Seems Black Bear don't have a need for renegades no more.'

A flicker of fear came and went in Koot's deep-sunken

eyes. 'The wagons won't come west no more without my boys to guide 'em. There ain't a wagon master who'll come this far, the army cain't hold back the Injuns.'

'Try tellin' Black Bear that.' Sage mocked the other. ''Ceptin' you won't get the chance.'

'You can't harm me none, Sage, yuh should know that. Shoot me and Black Bear'll—'

'He won't raise you up agin, Koot, not if he don't have no further need o' yuh.'

This time it was definitely a flicker of fear in Koot's expression.

'Adele,' Sage spoke to her but still his eyes never left the one he held at gun-point, 'he never . . . uh, that is, he didn't do nothin' awful bad to yuh, did he?'

'Bad enough, but it would have been terrible if you hadn't come just when you did, Sage.' She found she could speak again in a quavering voice. Her relief and gratitude had her fighting back tears.

'Then just yuh put yer hands over your ears, real tight, 'cause it's goin' to be mighty deafenin' in here.'

Adele clasped her hands over her ears. Koot's body tensed, every muscle prepared to launch him at the one who threatened him. He swayed forward on the balls of his feet, his arms came up, reached out.

Sage shot him twice, the reports sounded as one, heavy flintlock pistols bucking in his fists, belching flame, black smoke sparing Adele the sight of .50-calibre balls mutilating flesh and bone at a range of no more than a yard.

Koot's body was thrown back by the dual impact. His snarl of rage was obliterated along with the rest of his features, his throat torn out as though by a slavering timber wolf.

Somehow he remained upright. He swayed back on his heels, tottered forward as if some invisible hand had pushed him from behind. A barefoot stagger kept him vertical. His arms were upraised, broken fingernails clawed at his wounds in an instinctive, futile attempt to staunch the flow of blood. A long-drawn-out cry came from the ripped cavity that had once been his mouth, a shriek of rage and hopelessness that was drowned in a gush of scarlet fluid.

Those arms were upraised, it might have been a gesture of final surrender. Then, slowly, he sank down to the floor.

166

Outside, the storm threw all its might at the cabin as though venting its fury upon the one who had dared to defy the powers that were unleashed in this dark and terrible night that was only just beginning.

And borne on that same howling gale were the cries of the demented, rampaging Kiotes.

'I guess Black Bear don't need Koot and his crowd no longer.' Sage busied himself reloading his pistols. 'He's received a sign from the Evil One that he's a-comin' tonight and that'll spell the end o' all the whites. Injuns'll rule agin like they once did. Wal,' he checked his weapons, thrust them back into his belt. 'I guess we can't hang around here too long. My guess is that once the Kiotes've finished with the outlaws, they'll come lookin' for Koot.'

'We'll have to get the children out of the jailhouse.' Adele wrung her hands together. 'If Koot was telling the truth, Blair's in there with them.'

'I had me a listen on the way.' The mountain man winked reassuringly. 'They're all in there, safe and well. But I couldn't bring them along until I'd done what I had to do.' He grimaced, 'Judgin' by what I saw, it was just as well.'

'We'd better go and get them right away.' Adele kept her head turned away from the body on the floor.

'Got a job to do fust.' Sage was suddenly tense. 'Daren't leave here without I make it so's Koot ain't no good to the Kiotes. If they did decide to keep him on, then by mornin' we could find him back on our trail, an' after what I done he's gonna be meaner and more dangerous than a wounded grizzly. Won't take me more'n a few minutes.'

'What . . . what are you going to do to him?' Adele was apprehensive, every hour seemed to bring a new and more terrible horror.

'You'd best not look.' Sage had drawn a huge skinning-knife from a sheath on his belt. 'Go stand over by the door. Any other time I'd say go wait outside but right now outside ain't no safe place to be.'

Adele walked unsteadily towards the door. Already she had a rough idea of what the trapper was going to do to his sworn foe: it had an element of revenge as well as necessity about it. She experienced a wave of dizziness; it passed as quickly as it came.

A sudden thud, followed by a tearing, squelching sound had bile burning the back of her throat. The other was cursing beneath his breath, there was no mistaking his sadistic delight.

'How did you escape from the Kiotes, Sage?' She felt the need to talk, it might detract from the hacking and cutting that was going on behind her.

'Same as I escaped from the Alamo that time.' He grunted with exertion. 'Let 'em have their fun then I upped and run. Whole damned lot of 'em were howlin' after me but even the Kiotes don't know the woods like ol' Sage. I lost 'em, but none too quickly else they'd've caught you lot for sure. Ran 'em round in circles a few times then left 'em there lookin' under every bush fer me!' He laughed. 'At least I still got ma rifle and pistols, even if I did have to part with ma scalp!'

'Oh!' She clung on to the door, thought she might faint.

'Won't do me no harm.' He chopped, sawed with the knife blade. 'Jest keep ma hat on and nobody'll know any different!'

'The Alamo?' She was puzzled, tried to change the conversation. 'I learned about it at school, I didn't think there were any survivors. Ben has a video of the film, I watched it once, they let a woman go, one of the defenders' wives, I think.'

'Don't remember that, don't remember anybody gettin' away. All slaughtered, Crockett, Bowie,' he fingered the blade of his knife almost reverently, 'whole damned lot of us. But a bullet don't make that much difference to ol' Sage, knocks him about a bit. Black Bear'd made sure he wasn't gonna lose me way before the Alamo. So after the Mexes were gone, I just upped and headed north.'

Adele shuddered. 'You said you'd *heard* of the Alamo that time we mentioned it?'

'No point in goin' into too much detail. Less you knew, the better, then. Now it don't make no difference, p'raps better that you do know. Yep, I'm same as Koot an' his lot, an' all them Injuns out there. Jest one difference, an' even I don't understand it. We're all dead an' walking but somehow I'm . . . *different*. Cain't explain it, don't know myself, but I ain't *evil*. Not like them out there, anyhow. Not like *him*!' He gave the morass on the floor a kick, it reminded Adele of a piece of wet fish smacking. 'But if'n they get their hands on me agin, they'll make sure that Sage don't cause them no more bother. Jest like I'm doin' to Koot!'

He returned to his task, he was hurrying now, slashing and cutting, muttering to himself. 'Skinned me many a buffalo in the time when I was supplying the fort with meat. Them soldier boys would've starved if they'd had to wait for any o' them to do it!' He chuckled. 'Once you got the know-how, yuh never ferget it. Human ain't much different, looks much the same, time you've finished!'

'Are you . . . finished?' She held her breath, the stench in here was vile, like a beast that had lain in the hot sun for days before it was flayed and jointed.

'Yep, just about!' There was no mistaking the grim satisfaction in his tone. 'There ain't no Kiote that'll make much outa tryin' to put *him* together agin. I guess we'd better make tracks.'

As he pushed past her to pull the door open, Adele noticed something hanging from his waist; a piece of hairless skin that dripped blood, was clustered with black pimples.

'Ugh!' She was unable to contain her revulsion. 'Sage, how could you? It's vile, there wasn't any need to . . .'

'Ma'am,' he was apologetic, 'I'm sorry if I've offended yuh. T'ain't jest Injuns that takes scalps out here, mountain men do it as well. Not just fer show. If I carried all the Injun scalps I've lifted in ma time, I'd have ma pack horse down on its knees. Way o' life, way I wuz brought up. Some put notches in their pistols but that spoils a good pistol. Me, I'd have nothin' left to hold the barrel with! But with Koot it's kinda special. The way things've turned out, I reckon Black Bear will be a-hankerin' after his skelp to offer up to his Master. And if'n I've deprived him o' that, then it's bin worthwhile. I'd like to have Black Bear's hair danglin' from ma belt but I guess we'd better not hang around lookin' fer that. Let's go.'

They stepped outside into the night, sheltered for a moment against the side of the cabin from the full force of the wind. The night sky was lit up by the flames of burning buildings, it looked as if the whole of Dark Pines was on fire. Shadowy shapes danced around the flames, a trapper was screaming insanely as he fled one way, then another, his clothing ablaze. He fell, rolled, tried to put out the flames. A Kiote ran forward, prodded him back up to his feet with a lance. The fiery victim staggered, was lost from view. The watchers could still hear his shrieking even against the gale.

169

'No sign o' Black Bear.' Sage spoke against Adele's ear. 'Wonder what the devil's up to. Maybe he's talkin' with his Master, tryin' to persuade him to show hisself. This place ain't much different from hell, the way I was told.'

Adele clung to her companion. Sage was deathly cold, he stank of everything that was repulsive and terrifying to her, but right now he was the most marvellous person on earth.

'The Kiotes've raided the bar,' Sage surmised, 'drunk whisky till they're outa their evil minds. Mebbe Black Bear wants 'em that way when the Evil One appears.'

'It's awful,' she whispered.

'Too damn right it is.' He pulled her alongside the cabin wall with him. 'They ain't got as fur as the jail yet. We'll go and get that husband o' yours and the kids, then we'll . . .'

They rounded a corner, found themselves suddenly confronted by a terrifying horned figure. The Kiote brave's howl of anger had barely escaped his lips before Sage struck. In one flowing movement the mountain man drew the bloody bladed knife with which he had skinned and jointed Koot: its upwards thrust buried it up to the hilt in the brave's groin.

Sage pushed up as the Kiote fell forward, the warrior's weight aiding the impetus of the knife. Like a shot jackrabbit, the brave was slit right up to his throat. Sage eased the brave free, allowed him to fall on to his spilled intestines.

'That's one that won't be chasin' after us.' He wiped the blade clean on the twitching body, then stared upwards. 'Jest look at that sky!'

Adele looked. The dark clouds radiated the glow of the burning settlement but their hue was of a frightening density. They spat jagged fire to the accompaniment of rolling thunder, were split asunder as if their burden was hell itself, borne aloft to this valley of escalating evil. A cavalcade of fiery chariots hastening to announce to arrival of Satan himself.

Below, the warriors were screeching their terror. Many had thrown themselves prostrate. The fire leaped across the street, secured a hold on buildings opposite, an unstoppable force fanned and driven by the gale. Rain spots heralded the advent of another downpour. Within seconds Adele's clothes were clinging damply to her body, her hair was plastered on her head. Lightning struck in every direction; a majestic oak behind the jail was shrivelled, blackened into a deformed caricature of its former self. It smouldered, smoked. Then its twisted boughs sprouted flames that hissed defiantly at the torrential rain.

'T'ain't no normal storm.' Adele thought that maybe even Sage shuddered. 'Whatever Black Bear's been doin', I'd say that this time he's got the devil hisself t' come to Dark Pines!'

Twenty-Two

Blair crouched in a corner of the filthy prison room, shielded Nicola and Ben with his body as the door creaked open. If danger threatened them, he would fight to his last breath.

'Take it easy, it's only me, and I've got your woman with me.' Sage hustled Adele inside, held the door wide enough for the constant lightning and the glow from the blazing buildings to illuminate the interior like a fluorescent tube that had gone on the blink. 'And afore you ask, to save me wastin' valuable time explainin', I got away from them Kiotes and Koot's all jointed up like a buffalo ready for roastin'.'

Adele embraced Ben and Nicola, hugged Blair, too. Crying prevented them from talking coherently.

'When you lot done with sheddin' tears, we better be movin'.' It was all that Sage could do to prevent the door from slamming shut. 'Wind and lightnin've gone crazy. Dark Pines'll be glowin' in its own embers 'fore long, and then them Injuns'll come here next. Only reason the jail's not burned down is 'cause it's set apart from the rest.'

They could feel the heat, the gusts seared them as if the wind blew straight off the desert.

'Where are we headed?' Blair lifted Nicola, her thumb was in her mouth and her head lolled against her chest. Mercifully, exhaustion had spared her the trauma of the last few hours.

'Up to the forest.' Sage pushed them outside.

'No!' Adele breathed. 'Not *there*!'

'Only place left to go.' Sage let the door bang behind them. He turned, led the way; the wind tore at them as if even the elements were intent on holding them back. A jagged fork of lightning lit up the entire landscape.

Trees on the mountainside bent double as the forest yielded to a mightier force than it had known in centuries.

'*Look!*' Blair had glanced behind him, an expression of terror on his face.

They turned, bunched at what they saw. Even Sage appeared to cower from it.

Black Bear had appeared, stood amidst the burning debris, terrible to behold in his dark robes. His features were scarcely recognizable, his former evil had transcended to something that could only have come from hell itself. He seemed impervious to the heat and the flames. His arms were uplifted as if he called upon the fury of the heavens to give him power over all the earth.

'Gawd help us all,' Sage muttered. 'Them Kiotes've waited several lifetimes for their Evil One to come and drive out the white invaders. Now he's arrived. *Their Master's come in the form o' Black Bear, taken the Kiote's body for his own!*'

The braves had flung themselves prostrate in a trembling circle of obedience around their Master. They, too, seemed impervious to the fire.

Black Bear turned, seemed to pivot slowly until he was facing towards the jailhouse building, his eyes burning with the light from the inferno. Searching. Finding what he was looking for. *Seeing the fugitives.*

A roar of wrath, the slitted mouth became a cavity of festering evil. Words that vibrated with the storm in a tongue so old that even Sage was unable to translate even though he spoke the lingo of all the tribes with the fluency of their own braves. The listeners did not require an interpreter, the order was only too clear.

Catch the whites, bring them here so that their tortures will be as none that have ever gone before, and they will writhe and scream in everlasting torment. Bring them to me!

'Start runnin',' Sage ordered even though he knew it would be futile. A token attempt to escape was all that he could offer these strangers in a land where they had no right to be.

The warriors who only minutes ago had been staggering in a drunken stupor were instantly sobered; their initial terror of the Evil One was transformed into a raging fury as the living dead obeyed the orders of him whose coming they had awaited.

Piercing death-cries came from their painted lips, lances were grabbed up, knives brandished. It was like the start of some bizarre marathon where the only prizes were torture and, eventually, death. And the agony would live on even beyond that.

Blair knew that they would never outdistance their pursuers, they had no hope of even making it as far as the forest. Long before that they would be pulled down, beasts of the chase, mauled and savaged. In his own mind he had already given up. Had he still had the Browning five-shot then, he knew, without any doubt this time, that he would have given them all death, and spared them a fate far worse. But he did not have the automatic shotgun. Sage had a brace of pistols and the Hawken; three shots, enough for Adele and the children.

'Sage!' He shouted a hoarse whisper, knew how a judge felt when proclaiming a capital sentence. 'Your guns . . . Adele and the kids . . .'

The scout appeared not to have heard him. He looked like he was attempting to lead the flight but his limbs would not respond. Nicola hung heavy in Blair's arms, Adele was bent double with Ben.

Oh, Jesus, we can't do a thing except wait for them to come and get us!

Somehow Sage managed to move, hands which in the past had drawn those pistols and fired them with incredible speed and accuracy dragged them clear of the belt; their cocking seemed to take an eternity.

'*Don't look at his face!*' Sage shouted to the wind.

Blair felt himself wilting beneath the Kiote's stare. Even at a distance of two hundred yards, perhaps more, it was clearly visible, like a fixed bronze statue reflecting the firelight. You wilted before it but you could not drag your eyes away. You felt the sheer malevolence of those orbs scorching you. You want to flee but they command you to stay. So you obeyed.

Everything seemed to be in slow motion. The warriors hesitated over long strides, at times floated on air between them, horned demons who would run their prey to the end of the earth if necessary. Into hell itself, if the Evil One commanded.

Blair wanted to check on Adele but he could not turn his head. Nicola was slumped motionless in his arms, he did not even notice her weight. He wondered why Sage did not use the Hawken, probably because he did not have enough willpower to defy that demon from hell and unsling it. Only the scout's own strength of mind had enabled him to draw his handguns.

The Kiotes did not seem any closer, it was like they were caught in a freeze, their Master toying with both hunters and prey, savouring every moment. He would unleash his minions when he had tired of his game.

Thunder crashed and rolled, Black Bear's uplifted arms seemed to be drawing power from the dark clouds. His lips moved, he communed with the forces which had bestowed upon him power absolute. Sage was his for the taking, it was a time for gloating. The intruders were but fodder for the torture celebrations that would follow the total destruction of his foe.

Suddenly the entire dark heavens opened. Storm clouds which had gathered were split asunder, parted by a fiery explosion that shredded them; lightning was but sparks from the fiery bolt that hurtled from their midst.

The ball of fire came earthwards, straight and true as if some vengeful dark god had fired it with precision. One moment Black Bear was extolling his supremacy over all who walked the earth, the next he was enveloped in molten fire, a missile that struck him down, rolled him, burst him into flames.

Even then he struggled up, stood precariously, deformed and unrecognizable in charred form, shook his fists, cursed the power that had smitten him where seconds previously he had given praise and thanks.

Cursing with a mouth that glowed and a tongue that was a shooting flame; seeing with eyes that burned and blackened their sockets. His robes were ablaze, his horns burned like kerosene had been splashed on them.

His flesh melted with the heat, revealed a warped skeleton whose bones were starting to splinter and crack. Fragments flew in all directions. Still living, still mouthing obscenities which the thunder drowned lest it offend ears that heard it.

Sightless, featureless, a charred cadaver clinging to a life that went against all the laws of God and Nature. Until, finally, it collapsed into a heap of smouldering rubble. And was nothing.

'*Run!*' Sage was fully mobile, pushing the others into action. 'Run like a grizzly and a puma and a pack o' wolves were after yuh!'

Because the Kiotes were coming again and this time there was nothing sluggish about their movements. Death-cries rent the air, lances and knives glinted in the fiery night. The demise of their Master demanded vengeance.

Blair was carrying Nicola and attempting to help Adele and Ben, too. The terrain was uphill and becoming steeper by the second, for every three paces forward they slipped back one. Behind them the Kiotes were closing the gap; barefoot and sure of step, muddy ground presented few obstacles to them.

The fugitives topped a rise. Beyond them, silhouetted against the skyline, they saw another. The forest seemed unattainable, slipping further from them at each brow. Blair yelled to himself that they would never make it, the warriors were no more than forty or fifty yards behind them. As if to confirm his worst fears, a hurled lance clattered harmlessly at his heels. The next one might be more accurate.

'Why the fuck don't you shoot?' he shouted at Sage, who was bringing up the rear. The Hawken would have dropped one, the body might have rolled half a dozen more on the incline. Then the pistols, and they could have hurled rocks if they could have found the strength.

Sage appeared to be moving with renewed strength, caught up with Blair. 'Keep goin'. I'm gonna duck down behind that rock up there. Don't stop, even when you reach the forest.'

Which made sense even if it made you feel guilty. Blair nodded to show that he had heard. His outstretched free hand gave Adele the pull she needed. Then Sage was gone as if the ground had opened up and swallowed him.

The forest disappeared until they topped the next rise and saw it again. Blair paused to look back. There was no sign of Sage, only the Kiotes, who seemed to have floundered on this last stretch just when their prey was in reach. Maybe they, too, were savouring the final stages of the chase.

Two pistol shots split the storm-lashed night, vied with a clap of thunder that followed. The watchers saw two warriors straighten up, arms flung outwards, topple into the shadows. The renewed cries from their companions were terrible to hear.

The lightning came, forked and angry tongues, but there were only warriors to be seen, scattering on the slope, diving for any scant cover that was available. They had closed in for the death and two of them had died. But they would not give up until their nemesis was destroyed forever.

'We can't just . . . leave him.' Adele leaned up against Blair.

'That's what he wanted,' he replied. 'He wouldn't have it any other way. It's them or him, just like it's always been, since eighteen forty, maybe a lot longer. We don't figure in it, it's none of our business. We just have to do like he says, make the forest and keep going.' To where?

'They'll kill him.'

'No, not in the way you mean. He's already dead, has been for a very long time. We don't have any part in it. All we have to do is try to stay alive.'

They pushed on, a weary uphill step at a time. Up above they could see the outline of the forest. It did not look quite so far away now.

They struggled up on to yet another rise. Far down below they could see a glowing mass of embers; Dark Pines was just about burned out. In between there were only black shadows.

Suddenly those shadows were split apart by a stab of flame, a second or so later they heard the roar of the Hawken. Then an anguished cry. Shouts, screams. Another yell.

The wind stilled momentarily as though to let them hear. Stones were sliding, gathering force in a miniature avalanche. Kiote-cries of rage and fear. One was cut off abruptly, a heavy body rolled. Blows, a clashing of steel.

But the darkness was unyielding, ruled that they should not become spectators to Sage's last stand.

Twenty-Three

'We've got to rest, I can't go a step further.' Adele lowered Ben to the ground. He leaned up against her, his eyes still closed.

'We can't, we daren't.' Blair, too, was struggling to stand. Nicola had slipped into a position that was pulling on his arm sockets; if he put her down, he might not be able to lift her again. 'Sage said to keep going.'

'Sage is de . . . *destroyed.*'

'Then we owe it to him. He sacrificed himself for us.'

'No, he didn't.' She experienced a rush of guilt. 'He got what he wanted, those Kiotes. It's a feud that's been going on for a century and a half, perhaps longer. Scout versus Injuns and renegades, as he calls them. He lured them right where he wanted them. We were the bait.'

Blair sighed with resignation. They were standing on the edge of the forest, it had not changed any since the last time they were here, you didn't need to see it in daylight to know that. The huge trees offered only one small consolation, shelter from the worst of the wind and the rain. Apart from that it was pitch dark and stank of decay and evil. And it had innumerable, unthinkable terrors lurking in it. It was akin to sitting in some dingy downtown cinema watching a second-rate horror film go round and round. The set was the same each time, only the shocks had been varied. They became worse with each subsequent viewing.

'All right, we'll rest up for a short while.' And as his watch wasn't working there was no means of gauging the passing of time. 'Maybe a quarter of an hour.'

He felt vulnerable without a gun. Even if the Browning was incapable of *killing* anything, it had proved its worth. He shuddered to think where that wolf might have landed if he had not blasted it, caused it to vanish in midair.

If he had been responsible for its disappearance. *Because it was undoubtedly an astral projection.* It couldn't have hurt them, neither could the grizzly. Could they?

They sat with their backs to a huge redwood, its branches dripped like a Chinese torture and the trunk trickled rainwater, but, as they were saturated already, it didn't make much difference.

Blair wouldn't sleep, he'd see to it that Adele didn't either. Because if they did they would probably catch pneumonia. The warmth of their combined bodies would protect Nicola and Ben.

Adele was cold and uncomfortable. Being naked didn't help, and having her wrists and ankles strapped, arms and legs spread wide, made it worse. A sense of helplessness added to her rising terror.

The children weren't here or else she would not be in this predicament. They'd gone to stay overnight at her parents' in Midtown, a special treat. A special treat for Blair, too. She had agreed to 'play' because he was a good husband and it turned him on. It would relax him from the pressures of work. After the game-playing was over, he always made it good for her. So, on balance, it was worth it. At least, she *almost* convinced herself of that.

She didn't like it when he left her tied and went downtown; exciting for him, scary, cold and uncomfortable for her. He might be gone an hour, it could be three. He'd told her that he'd leave the front door unlocked so that anybody could walk right in off the street. And fuck her.

That was Blair's big turn-on, a stranger screwing his wife. But he wouldn't leave the door unlocked, really. Would he? Probably not, but it was the fact of not knowing that scared her most of all. There were other dangers, too. Like fire. There was no way she would be able to get free of these restrainers unaided. Blair wouldn't really leave her at risk.

He just might.

Her skin goose-bumped all over, her nipples were erect but that wasn't anything to do with being switched on. Right now, she had never felt more sexless. She would willingly have settled for a good screw seven nights a week. With Blair, of course.

The shadows on the wall told her it was late evening. She wasn't wearing a watch and the digital alarm was out of her restricted radius of vision. But it was late evening and Blair must have been gone well over an hour. It was going to be one of those long sessions when he left it until after dark before returning. She hated being left in the dark worst of all.

There weren't shadows on the wall any longer because the sun had gone down. Dusk; then darkness. She found herself listening to sounds. Any sound. Every sound.

The traffic in the street down below was sporadic, the late evening rush began around eleven after the cinemas and theatres turned out. Then a lull before it started again; restaurants and takeaways mostly closed at midnight.

People walking quickly, loitering. Conversing in low voices. A man's guttural tones, but she could not make out what he was saying.

There's a woman up there waiting to be fucked.

Adele tensed. She heard a door click softly. It might have belonged to the apartment directly below. Or the one above. Not here.

Now it was dark, as dark as it gets in any city. There were patterns on the walls, orange ones from the street lighting and an alternating red, amber and green from the traffic lights at the junction of Third and East 96th. The noises faded, died away; there wasn't any traffic going up and down the street because everybody was in the cinemas and theatres and it was too early to eat out yet.

Music was playing somewhere, heavy rock that grated on anybody over twenty-five. It probably came from three apartments down and was deafening the occupants of two down. One acted as a buffer for this place; it was probably empty as the Schumachers complained about almost anything. They weren't nice people but it would have been reassuring to have them home.

Just the beat and the flashing lights for company, they got on your nerves after a while, made you edgy. There weren't any other sounds, she wished there were. Identifiable ones.

She picked out smells. Her own perfumes, musk because it was Blair's favourite, he claimed it turned him on. Elderflower toner because she liked it. The two blended. In any other situation she could have savoured them. Right now she was too tense to do more than notice them.

Blair's Brut 33, she'd once lied and said it turned her on, in a way it was an oblique preference for shaven men. She hadn't the heart to ask him to shave his beard off, particularly when he was going through a bad patch. One day, perhaps. But he always splashed Brut 33 on it. He'd used a different kind of deodorant this evening, she wasn't sure what but it certainly wasn't his usual Lynx Oriental. The aroma wafted through from the bathroom, he had an annoying habit of leaving doors open wherever he went. She was glad he'd left the bathroom door ajar.

She hoped fervently that he'd locked the outer door. He wouldn't leave it open intentionally.

But he might just have forgotten to lock it.

But the nice smells didn't mask the bad one.

Ugh! She pulled a face, had an urge to spit. It was the garbage-disposal unit, without a doubt. Maybe it hadn't been cleared or, more likely, Blair had forgotten to empty the pedal bin in the kitchen, the remains of the weekend's chicken had gone bad. Today had been exceedingly warm for spring.

It stank real bad.

No, it wasn't quite right for chicken, no matter how far it had gone. There was a putrescence about it, a hint of urine and excrement. Maybe Blair hadn't flushed the john.

Smells, like sounds, could be reminiscent, you remembered events, places by them. People. Like *Sage*. She stiffened, her panic had her tensing so that her bonds tightened, pinched her skin.

No, not again. Not here. Please, God.

They were back in the city. Safe. She didn't know how they had got here but they had to be home because she was lying in the apartment and Blair would be back soon.

He's back now, I can hear him in the hallway.

A slight, almost imperceptible noise, as if somebody moved stealthily but didn't so much as creak a board or rustle a thick-pile carpet. Sensing that they were there rather than hearing them.

Smelling them.

She heard a car in the street. It turned out of 196th, slowed. She prayed that it would stop. It didn't, it picked up speed and she followed its progress until she could not hear it any longer. Blair wouldn't have taken the station wagon, the new one, he would have walked like he always did on these occasions. It was the wrong engine-sound, anyway; too high-powered.

She was all alone again with that stench.

It was stronger now, she tasted its vileness, turned her head to one side in case she threw up. She didn't want to risk drowning in her own vomit.

She thought she heard someone breathe, phlegm rattle in wasted lungs. Whoever it was, they were standing in the half-open doorway, maybe squinting through the crack at her and getting a thrill out of it.

A shadow fell on the wall, was bathed eerily in red. Then amber. Then green. It was the close-fitting animal-skin cap that brought a scream right up to her throat, but she was afraid to release it. She lay and watched, and trembled.

You're a real looker.

Blair, where are you? He wouldn't be coming, because they'd got him locked up somewhere.

The intruder stepped just inside the bedroom, she couldn't see any more than a silhouette, she didn't want to. Sage had saved her last time but he wouldn't come to her rescue again because the Kiotes had got him at the finish. Nobody could save her.

A pair of eyes gleamed in the half-darkness, mentally groping her, feeling her with coarse calloused fingers, rubbing her so that it hurt. Koot had returned, followed her all the way back to the city to continue where he'd left off last time. Because there were no boundaries to restrain him.

Adele was restrained by her bonds; she couldn't go anywhere.

He moved forward another half-pace, removed his hat. A beam of orange street lighting fell on a hairless head, gleamed on crusted blackheads and raw flesh that sprouted ulcers. The scar of the scalping knife formed a complete circle around the skull.

Koot advanced on her and Adele let her scream go.

'What is it?' Blair came out of his uneasy doze fast, grabbed Adele.

She was shaking violently, Nicola was crying before she

was properly awake and Ben was staring wide-eyed. Here, in the dark forest, you didn't have to see anything to be afraid.

'For God's sake, what's the matter?'

Adele was confused. The restrainers should have prevented her from sitting up; there was no street lighting or traffic lights playing on the wall. Because there wasn't any wall. The apartment was several states away. It was all a bad, bad dream.

Except that she could still smell that stench and it was as strong now as it had been then. The odour of putrescence and evil had given her the nightmare, awoken her from it into awful reality.

'Blair . . . *there's somebody stalking us and they're very close!'*

He wanted to reassure her but he knew better. Because he smelled it, too. It wasn't just the odour of the forest, it was that of somebody. *Or something.*

'All right, don't panic. Leave it to me.' He had to take charge now that Sage was no longer with them.

'What is it, Daddy?'

'Nothing, probably, but we can't take any chances.'

Play it down. He wished he had a gun. 'Quietly, now. Up on your feet, we're moving on.'

The storm was still raging, torrential rain cascading down the trees like a hundred miniature waterfalls, and every few seconds the night sky was illuminated by flashes of lightning. It enabled them to see the track ahead of them. The stench appeared to be coming from behind, it had to be because there was no way it could have travelled upwind in a gale of this strength.

Blair lifted Nicola; at least the brief rest had eased his aching joints. Ben opted to hold on to Adele's arm. 'Right, let's go. Walk fast but don't run.' And if the electric storm passes on we'll be left in total darkness.

It wasn't the grizzly, they would surely have heard its maddened rampaging. The wolf would have sneaked downwind of them, they wouldn't have smelled it. Which ruled out wild creatures of the forest. Which meant that whatever followed them was . . . *sort of human.*

'It's probably Sage trying to find us.' A lie designed to reassure the others.

'The Kiotes got him.'

183

'Like they didn't the last time.'

'If it was him, he'd've caught up with us by now.'

Which was true. That only left the Kiotes and that was a more frightening prospect than either grizzlies or wolves.

They stumbled along the winding track, took forks without even a flippant toss of a coin because direction was meaningless. So long as they kept the wind on their backs, that was fine; so long as they smelled that vile stench there was little chance of their pursuer lying in ambush somewhere up ahead. U-turns, animal backtracks, were the most worrying aspects in case they came face to face with the fearsome thing that dogged them.

Whether they hurried or slowed, whoever or whatever was behind them neither gained on them nor fell behind. Frequently they looked back, but there were too many shadows in the deep woods for them to be able to discern a lurking shape.

On and on, maybe going somewhere, probably going nowhere. And, throughout, the storm showed no signs of abating.

'I can't go much further.' Adele was dragging her feet, soon she would be forced to carry Ben again and she knew that that was beyond her drained physical capabilities.

Blair had known for the past hour that fatigue was inevitable. Their pursuer knew it, too. He had not gained upon them because he had no need to, he was simply wearing them down in the same way that hounds chase a fox until it can run no more. Then it lies down, resigns itself to its fate.

'We'll wait here,' Ben said, choosing a wide clearing where it was impossible for anybody or anything to creep unseen upon them. He bent, picked up a seemingly stout stick; it snapped even as he lifted it. Everything in this place was rotten.

The sky flashed continuously; it was sheet lightning now, a sure sign that the electric storm was running out of power. Even the rain had slackened to a fast drizzle. Only the wind showed no signs of dropping.

They waited, Adele and the children behind Blair as he stood on open ground, prayed for the lightning to continue. If it stopped, they were vulnerable.

An overhead branch snapped off, hit the ground and broke into three lengths. Somewhere, not too far away, a giant tree came crashing down. It was a wild night and likely to get wilder before dawn.

'I saw something!' Adele pointed over her husband's shoulder.

He stared, narrowed his tired eyes. A flitting shape, it might have been a shadow from the last flash. He watched carefully; the sky illuminated another three times before something detached itself from a tree trunk, moved back on to the path.

It was a man: he walked with bowed head and stooped shoulders, his step was unsteady. It wasn't a Kiote, unless a brave had dressed in a victim's fringed buckskins and hide cap. He stumbled, almost fell; came on.

'Hold it right there!' Blair shouted against the storm. He found himself inwardly cringing from this unknown night-walker. The hairs on the back of his head stiffened and Adele was gripping his arm until it hurt.

The other halted on the opposite side of the clearing, raised his head, but his features were in deep shadow.

The gale blew ever more strongly, a tall poplar creaked. Blair felt the ground around them quiver as if with a small earthquake.

'Who are you? *Show us who you are!*'

Slowly the head was lifted up, seemingly with a great effort as if the neck muscles had wasted away. The other stood there, a scrawny hand came up, clawed the hat away and the next flash of lightning revealed a disfigured and weeping skull that was only too familiar.

'*Brock!*' Adele screamed a continuation of the terror-stricken shriek that had brought her out of her nightmare. 'Oh, my God, I should have known!' Her subconscious, an inbuilt alarm system that defied the theories of biologists had, by some telepathic means, warned her of the coming of Brock. Now he was here, and even the night could not hide the crazed hatred in his rictus.

'You hanged me.' The cracked voice carried on the wind. 'But the Injuns raised me up. Look at me now, *look what you've done to me!*'

'I had no choice, Brock.' An explanation that had a whine to it, a trace of fear. 'And you yourself begged me to hang you.'

185

At a distance he looked a pathetic wretch but his stamina had kept him on their trail. He was holding something in his hand, the shadows concealed it.

The ground shook, much more strongly this time.

Brock's arm came up in shaking stages, levelled. And that was when Blair found himself staring into the barrel of a .50-calibre pistol. It was cocked and a trembling, skeletal finger was curled around the trigger.

'I'm the only one that's left out of Dark Pines, Doctor. I had the gift of rebirth before they turned on the others. They wanted to destroy me. Now look what I'm cursed with, for ever!'

The ground heaved up as if some monstrous mole was digging its way out of a subterranean tunnel. The pistol flash was vertical instead of horizontal, its report muffled by an overhead thunderclap. The tree tilted crazily, resisted for a second or two, then crashed down.

Blair flung himself to cover Adele and the children, a branch struck them but it was too rotten to have any impact. They felt the ground shudder, lay still and dazed, afraid to believe that they were unscathed.

Then they stood, shakily surveying in the flashing lights from the heavens the uprooted tree, a dead monster. They thought they heard a faint cry from beneath it but it might have been a gale creaking the branches.

Certainly, from now on, Brock would not be stalking them. The forces that were unleashed on this terrible night had destroyed him just as they had destroyed Black Bear whose earthly form Satan had taken for his own.

They stumbled on, not daring to rest again, fearful of what further evil was abroad on this night that the Master had chosen for his promised return to earth from whence he had been cast down.

There was no hint of dawn breaking when the Lunds staggered from the forest. The overhead blackness was only broken by the incessant lightning; even the stars hid on this night when the powers of Good and Evil threatened an Armageddon, for surely this place was to become the Apocalypse.

Blair, like the others, was physically and mentally drained. The faint spark of hope that had lingered within him had died.

He only kept going for their sakes. A few months ago he would have welcomed death, now he was fighting it all the way even though there was nothing left to live for.

'Well, at least we're out of the forest,' Adele announced because nobody had spoken this past hour. 'Not that I suppose it will make any appreciable difference to our plight.'

A vivid flash gave them a glimpse of open land, then it was total blackness again. The drizzle turned back to torrential rain as if the skies had seen that the humans no longer had shelter.

'We've got to find cover of some kind.' Adele kept walking. If they stopped now they would never start again. Exhaustion would turn to pneumonia. Then death. If death existed here in the form that they knew.

Another flash illuminated the whole scene, there was a stark familiarity about the landscape. One that had their stomachs balling and was all the more frightening because it was like something was being kept back from them. The good news is you're out of the forest; wait for the bad news.

Their worst fears were confirmed by the next flash, and it kept them waiting for several minutes. At one stage they thought that maybe the electric storm was finished, they were just left with the rain.

Every tree, every tuft of grass across the open stretch was lit up, there was no hiding place, no detail, however cruel, was spared them.

Adele's cry of despair died in her throat, she felt herself wilt, a surrender to fate that had her slumping against Blair. Together they huddled, were afraid to return to the scant shelter of the forest, even more fearful of going forward.

'What's the matter, Mommy?' Nicola stirred against Adele, clutched at her.

'Nothing, darling. Nothing's any different from what it's been all along.'

Which was the brutal truth as a further, even more dazzling, illumination revealed.

To their right was a gaunt and wind-blown willow grove. Beyond it, a heap of broken timbers that had once been a holiday cabin. An inexplicable return to a former era and a fire had reduced it to what it now was. Outside it was a rusted wreck that was the remains of the vehicle that had brought them here. Their latest attempt to find a way out of this valley had, once again, resulted in their return.

Victoria's prediction echoed in their distraught minds with an undeniable chilling ring of truth.

Nobody would ever leave this place alive.

Twenty-Four

Shelter was a priority and there was no place other than the burned-out cabin. It was a cruel and demoralizing fact. Standing out there in the darkness and the pouring rain, they made their choice.

The walk across the stretch of open ground from the willow grove to the charred shambles of their former temporary home seemed never ending. Each time the sky lit up, the shack seemed just as far away as ever. Sometimes further.

Finally, they hauled themselves up on to the broken veranda, retched at the acrid stench of charred wood, hung back from the partly collapsed doorway.

'Is . . . is it safe to go inside?' Adele whispered the question that they were both asking themselves. Nicola cowered in her arms, Ben stood close behind his father.

'Is anywhere around here safe?' Blair stepped forward, they would have to squeeze through the gap.

'I mean . . . the whole place might collapse and bury us.'

Surprisingly, as the lightning revealed, more of the building had survived than they had originally supposed. The partial collapse of the roof had resulted in an avalanche of soil which had contained the blaze and saved the interior from being totally gutted. It had transformed it into a somewhat precarious lean-to shelter such as homesteaders often erect on the side of a dwelling for the purpose of storing logs.

It was open at the front, leading through to the hallway, but it was possible to close the kitchen door by forcing it. Apart from the filth and the stench, the area afforded a dry shelter.

An arrow was still embedded in the floor, an unmistakable odour of powder smoke lingered, impregnated in the frail timbers.

Little had changed otherwise.

A pile of blankets in the corner was scorched but dry. Adele's

189

first task was to strip Ben and Nicola of their saturated garments and roll them up in this makeshift bedding.

'Will it ever stop raining?' The downpour beat incessantly on the sloping roof that sheltered them. In places it leaked, but by a process of trial and error they found a dry area in which to stretch out. By comparison with the forest floor, it was luxurious.

'Will it ever get light again?' Blair watched the window, but there was no hint of the blackness paling. Even the lightning had become infrequent now, the rumbles of thunder were distant, barely audible unless they listened hard. Only the rain was incessant; if anything, it was heavier now than ever.

'It has to, eventually.'

'Does it?'

She tensed at his reply. Nothing was a certainty here. Not even death; at least, not as they knew it, that grim finality from which there was no return.

'We don't have any food now, Blair.'

He nearly said, 'I'll shoot us some meat'. He wouldn't because he didn't have a gun any longer and, even if he had, there did not appear to be any wildlife in the vicinity. Instead, he said, 'We can't do anything about anything until it gets light.' And even without a timepiece, he knew that dawn was long overdue.

It was as though this valley had been ostracized from everything that made for normality. Life had been destroyed, day had been taken away; all that was left to them was eternal night.

Armageddon had been and gone. They were the unfortunate survivors.

Adele stirred restlessly in her sleep. Something disturbed her but she was too exhausted to waken. She groaned, she didn't care any longer about anything. Except the kids. Whatever it was, she would offer no resistance. Her mind and body were anaesthetized to anything that might happen to her from now on.

There came a time when you finally gave up. She had reached that point. There was nothing left to go on for.

Music played. It wasn't the heavy rock that came from that punk two floors down. Or was it three? It was country music from her youth; it was delirium caused by exposure to the elements. Pneumonia was only a step away.

Mississippi, that was it. 1976. It was funny how you remembered trivialities; smells and sounds revived memories that had lain dormant for years. They'd played it on the radio about a dozen times a day when it was in the charts. It had received a kind of immortality. Like Sage and the rest of them.

That tune had lodged itself in her brain, got under her skin after a time, nearly driven her crazy because she couldn't get rid of it. It's stuck with you for twenty-four hours a day and, years later, when you thought you'd forgotten it, it came right back.

The fever had stirred it up. Funny, though, she didn't feel hot, she didn't ache. Maybe that would come later.

For Christ's sake, shaddup!

It must have heard her, it was fading. Now somebody was talking, a man's voice. Blair occasionally talked in his sleep, when that happened she used to shake him and it usually stopped. Right now, she couldn't be bothered.

Christ, he was going on! He'd put on a posh accent, the one she called his 'telephone voice' on those times when she phoned him at the surgery. All the same, it didn't really sound like Blair.

She rolled over, tried to shut him out. It didn't work; she pulled the blanket up over her head. She could still hear him. And what the hell was he on about? She sighed, listened.

'The area of low pressure that has affected western states over the past three days has now moved away into the Rockies, where it is reported to be petering out. The hurricane is the worst ever recorded and has left a trail of damage through Utah, Wyoming and Montana. The cost of the damage runs into billions of dollars and twenty-seven lives have been lost. Although the worst of the storm is over, widespread flooding is expected . . .'

Blair must have lost his marbles or else he'd got the fever, too. Shaddup!

Oh, Jesus Christ Alive!

Adele sat upright in her rumple of blankets, twisted her head around, stared with widening eyes.

'Whassa matter?' Blair growled from beneath his own bedding.

191

'Blair. . .' She was staring fixedly as she had been when Black Bear had held her with his hypnotic gaze.

'What?'

'Blair . . . *the radio alarm's working!*'

Now it was Blair's turn to surface fast, pawing the sleep out of his eyes. 'Jesus Almighty!'

'And . . . and *look!*'

They gazed around the room together. Sure enough there had been some storm damage, a couple of bad leaks in the roof, but it had not collapsed. Or, if it had, somebody had mysteriously and silently restored it to its former state under the cover of darkness. Neither was there any sign of charring, there were new uprights where the old ones had rotted, replacements that smelled sweetly of resin. No slits in the wall through which to shoot at marauding Kiotes.

'Well!' Blair rubbed his eyes again, checked. 'Hey, Adele, do you notice anything else?'

'The floor's clean, the way I swept it on the day . . .'

'The radio alarm!' His pointing hand shook visibly. 'Oh, my Christ, just look at that time!'

She followed where he indicated. The green digits flicked on another minute. '*Two seventeen, your watch stopped at two fifteen!*'

'And it's started again!' He shook his head in bewilderment. 'Digital clocks and watches that work off batteries aren't governed by electricity.' He stretched out his hand, flicked a light switch. 'See, the generator's working again, too! *Everything's back to normal!*'

'So it was the storm that was responsible.'

'Yes, but not in the way we might think. The storm came in, brought the evil with it, and dropped us into a time-warp. Then, along comes another storm, destroys all it created, and whisks us back into the present. There isn't any answer, Adele.'

'It's crazy but I have to believe you, Blair. I also have to believe everything I see around me. It's enough to drive you crazy just trying to figure it out.'

'Mommy, what's happened?' Nicola was sitting up in her makeshift bed. 'Have you and Daddy mended everything?'

'We haven't, but somebody has.' Adele closed her eyes, opened them again, just to make sure that this wasn't all another dream, a cruel one where you woke up thinking everything was fine and it wasn't.

Everything was fine.

'I'm going outside to check a few things.' Blair moved towards the door. Adele was right behind him, Nicola and Ben on her heels.

'*Oh, no, Blair, that spoils everything!*' Her tone was one of total disillusionment. 'I thought it was too good to be true.'

They all stood looking across at the station wagon. It wasn't how they expected to find it, pristine except for a few mud splashes and a coating of dust. Instead it was a heap of crumpled metal, the way the Great Storm had reduced it to scrapyard material.

'So . . .' Adele's voice quavered, she was close to tears, maybe hysteria. 'Everything hasn't really come right, after all. I thought it was just too marvellous to be true.'

'Hang on a minute.' Blair ran forward, cleared the veranda steps at a jump. He walked round the vehicle, bent and peered closely, and when he stood up he was smiling. 'The hurricane overturned it, smashed it up. It's a write-off, the insurance will have to pay out on it, *but there's not a trace of rust on the bodywork and neither are the tyres perished!*'

'Thank God!' Adele clutched at the veranda rail. The last time she had stood here the whole structure had been reduced to matchwood.

'Dad, can we finish our vacation? Why don't we go hunting?' Ben's keen eyes had spotted a rabbit grazing the grass on the edge of the willow grove. Overhead, a pigeon clapped its wings, glided in to its daytime roost.

'I . . .'

'No way,' Adele snapped. 'We're getting out of here whilst the going's good. There might be another storm and then we'd be back . . . I don't even want to think about it.'

'We don't have any guns, Ben.' Blair pulled a wry face.

'But, Dad, if everything's come right, the cabin's mended, and it was just the wind that wrecked the station wagon, then . . .'

'Not everything's come right, Ben.' The doctor's face was suddenly grim. 'I guess somewhere, a century and a half back, some of your mountain men heroes are right now picking up a couple of shotguns and wondering how the hell guns came to look like that. That feller rammed a muzzle-loading charge down the twenty's barrels, right on top of a couple of breech-loading shells. As a result he blew his head off. The Browning's still lying there, maybe somebody else will do exactly the same with that. I guess, even in a time-warp, there's some things you can lose.' And we damned near lost our lives on more than one occasion.

'I'll start packing.' Adele turned back towards the cabin. 'Fortunately, most of our possessions are still intact. I—' She broke off, gave a strangled cry and pointed above the window.

An arrow was firmly embedded in the wall.

'Well, I guess we're going to have to walk to the highway, after all.' Blair checked the baggage over, there was one helluva lot more than the last time they'd set out on foot. 'We'd better distribute it amongst us. Now, Nick, you take these carrier bags, they're light. I'll carry the heavy suitcase.'

Adele was scared, she hoped that the others did not notice that her hands shook, and it wasn't just because of the weight of the two small suitcases. That arrow, for a start, it hadn't been there on the day when they first arrived. OK, so maybe the odd thing did get overlooked when a time-warp reverted. She would not relax until they were well clear of this valley and reached the highway. And actually saw modern traffic travelling it.

'See,' Blair was clearly euphoric, Adele wished that she shared it, 'the track's been returned. A lot muddier than when we came here but that's due to all the heavy rain. And there's no massive forest blocking the skyline so that we can't find our way out of here.' He gave a nervous laugh.

Adele wished that they could walk faster. Even run.

'Dad, what's that?'

'What, Ben?' Damn it, the boy had lagged behind, he had to put down the bags he was carrying and was stooping to examine something in the track. 'Hurry up, Ben, we've got to rely on picking up a lift to get us somewhere where we can hire a car.'

'Come and look at this, Dad?'

Blair clucked his annoyance, Adele gave a sigh of frustration. Ben's interest in fieldcraft knew no bounds, he had a *Spot the Tracks and Identify Them* picture-book for young backwoodsmen at home. Every time he saw an imprint, he investigated it. You couldn't fault his enthusiasm. Except when you were in a hurry.

'Probably a buck.' Blair gave it a cursory glance and felt his spine begin to tingle. He didn't want to look any closer; he wished fervently that he had not turned back.

'Deer have *slots*, Dad. Like sheep. This isn't a slot and, anyway, there aren't any sheep in this valley. It looks like a pony to me.'

'All right, it's a pony's hoof-print. Lots of people come out here for riding holidays like we come hunting and fishing.'

'*But it isn't shod, Dad!*'

Oh, shitfire! The tingling was travelling right up Blair's spine now, icy cold. 'Maybe they haven't shod the pony.'

'Most folks do who go riding else a pony can get bad feet, go crippled. I read it in a book, Dad.'

'Well, it looks as if whoever rode this one didn't and there's nothing we can do about it.' You read too many books for your own fucking good, boy! 'Come on, we can't hang around any longer.'

'OK, I only wanted to know.'

Blair glanced towards Adele, she had gone deathly white. He made as if to say something, changed his mind. Once Adele had her mind made up about something then nobody changed it, and the more you said, the worse it became.

'It seems an awful long way to the highway.' Adele stared at the skyline.

'It's just over the horizon,' Blair answered. He knew she wouldn't be satisfied until she saw lines of speeding traffic. He tried to listen for the sound of cars and heavy lorries; he could not hear any, the hill between the road and the valley probably deadened the sound.

'Dad, I can hear a car.'

'Good, I told you we're not far away.' Ben had acute hearing; Blair still had not forgiven him for eavesdropping at their bedroom door last Christmas. It had caused an awful lot of problems. The children would never forget that their father had threatened to shoot himself.

'I think it's coming this way, Dad.' Ben had his head cocked on one side.

'Well, there's nothing wrong with that. It's maybe some folks who are renting it after we've left.'

'They wouldn't know we'd gone.' Adele's suspicions, her concern was only too obvious. 'We've chosen to leave early. We didn't tell anybody, they couldn't possibly know.'

'Maybe it's an engineer on his way to repair . . . to *overhaul* the generator.' Christ, stop surmising, you're getting her in a right fucking state.

'Here it comes now, Dad.'

A vehicle came into view over the horizon, beyond which lay the main highway. Even from this distance Blair could see that it was a long-wheelbase Land Rover, trundling like a small coach, splashing through puddles, showing contempt for ruts and potholes.

'Get on the side of the road, all of you,' Blair called back, 'or you'll get sprayed with mud.'

The Land Rover was slowing. As it approached, Blair could see that the driver wore a dark wide-brimmed hat that was pulled hard down over his forehead, doubtless to shield his eyes from the morning sunlight. Two women were seated in the front alongside him; they also wore large hats.

'Good morning.' The driver braked, sat with the engine ticking over. 'Might you be the Lunds?' His features were sallow, his thin lips stretched in a weak smile.

'That's right. I'm Dr Lund, this is my wife and family.' Blair was unable to disguise his surprise, he had a feeling that the other's face was familiar but he couldn't place him.

'Leaving already?' The man behind the wheel raised an eyebrow. 'You've booked for next week as well, and paid for it! The name's Becker, by the way, I own the cabin. I hope that you're not dissatisfied with the accommodation.' His half-smile changed to an expression of concern.

'Oh, not at all.' Blair swallowed, he wasn't accomplished in the art of off-the-cuff lies. 'It's just that we . . . well, my wife misses the city, and after that awful storm she can't settle. And our station wagon was wrecked in the gales. We're walking to the highway, doubtless we'll be able to hitch a lift to somewhere where we can hire a vehicle.'

'Look, I can give you a lift back to the highway.' Becker was smiling again now, doubtless relieved that he had not got a complaining tenant to contend with. 'I'm on my way down to the cabin to pick up something I inadvertently left there. It won't take many minutes. In fact, you'll be at the highway

196

a lot quicker if you let me take you. Climb in the back, it's an eight-seater, there's room for all of you and your luggage as well.'

'That's most kind of you, Mr Becker.' Blair felt a surge of relief, indicated to the others to go round to the rear of the Land Rover. 'It is rather a long walk and we'd like to be on our journey as soon as possible.'

'Of course.' Becker let in the clutch and the vehicle eased forward, negotiated a deep rut. 'I'm so glad that you aren't leaving because you're dissatisfied over something. If you are, please tell me and I'll sort it out at once.'

Blair was studying the other's face in the rear-view mirror. It was uncannily familiar . . . and yet he'd never met the cabin owner. He'd hired it by mail, sent a cheque.

The doctor's glance flicked on to the other two front-seat passengers. Those hats were years out of fashion and he was no connoisseur of female attire. He might have expected to find middle-aged or elderly women wearing them but, from the rear, they seemed comparatively young. Their necks were smooth and slender. He wondered why they wore veils. Perhaps they were eccentrics. It was none of his business but those icy goose-pimples refused to go away.

He glanced at Adele. She was sitting stiff and straight, her tension was only too evident in her expression. It went deeper than unease, he had become familiar with it these past few days.

Adele was scared to hell.

Nicola was sitting close to her mother, clutching nervously at her hand. Ben wasn't relaxed, either. Blair consoled himself that neither of them was happy in the presence of strangers.

'Excuse me, Mr Becker,' Blair cleared his throat nervously, 'but I . . . I don't think we've met, yet your face does somehow seem familiar to me. Perhaps we've been introduced somewhere?'

'Possibly,' the driver spoke slowly, carefully. 'Come to think of it, I feel that I might have met you too, at sometime. Your wife and children, also. But, let's dispense with the formalities, I do hate formalities, so unfriendly, almost to the point of hostility, don't you think?'

'I agree entirely. I'm Blair, my wife's Adele, and my children are Ben and Nicola.'

'Lovely names.' They were at the cabin now, the driver eased the Land Rover close up to the veranda. The arrow sticking out of the wall seemed a prominent feature, everybody was staring fixedly at it. 'Oh, yes, allow me to introduce my companions.' He waved a hand in the direction of those sitting by his side. 'The one on the far side is Prudence, she's my cousin. This is Victoria, my sister . . . oh, and my name is James . . .'